Pick Your Genre Collections

Who Steals a Dragon

Who Steals a Dragon

A Pick Your Genre Collection

Kat Simons

T&D PUBLISHING

WHO STEALS A DRAGON
Copyright © 2023 by Katrina Tipton
All rights reserved.

Published 2023 by T&D Publishing
Cover design: © 2023 T&D Publishing
Interior book design © 2023 T&D Publishing
Cover Art: © Tudorpopaart | Dreamstime.com
Interior Art: © Christos Georghiou, © Quicksilver77, ©
Miceking,
© Akv2006, © Lion98, ©Pixxart, © Mikesilent|Dreamstime.com

ISBN-13: 978-1-944600-70-9 (Trade Paperback Edition)
ISBN-13: 978-1-944600-71-6 (Large Print Edition)

This is a work of fiction. All of the characters, places, organizations, and events portrayed are either products of the author's imagination or are used fictitiously. Any resemblance to actual persons, living or dead, business establishments, events, or locales is entirely coincidental.

First printing T&D Publishing edition: July 2023
For information, contact T&D Publishing:
https://www.tanddpublishing.com

WHO STEALS A DRAGON

Contents

To my boys. My sons and my husband. Always and forever because I love you.

And a special shout out to my youngest, who thought this was such a fun idea, he was my consultant for cover art and design.

Introduction

INTRODUCTION

Welcome to this strange and fun collection, where I play with the question, *Who Steals a Dragon?*

Readers can start here for a little more about the collection and some background on where the idea came from, or you can feel free to jump right into the stories.

There's something here for every mood. Want a space adventure, jump to the Science Fiction story. You're more in the mood for something a little romantic? There's both a Contemporary Romance and a Paranormal Romance to dive into. The two stories I hope will satisfy your longing for some crime fiction fall into the Heist Mystery genre and the Romantic Suspense genre. And, because we're talking about dragons, we have to have a High Fantasy version.

Each of these stories stands alone. There are no overlapping characters or situations. Not even the dragons are the same. None of them come from any of my pre-existing series, so you won't need to have read anything prior to this to enjoy these tales. Although the Paranormal Romance story already spawned a second short story, so, yeah, that'll be a series eventually.

They can be read in any order, to suit any mood. You can read the collection from start to finish, or dive in and pick and choose as you like. The collection hasn't been arranged in any particular order, so it really doesn't have to be read from beginning to end. It truly is a Pick Your Genre book, for readers who just never know what they might be in the mood for but who would still like to know...

Who steals a dragon?

This concept has been percolating in my head for a few years now, the idea sparking from a few different places. The first, where the initial idea to do a Pick Your Genre collection started, happened during a writing workshop. One of the assignments included writing an opening scene. And when I got to the end of the eight hundred words I needed for the class, I realized I could take that story off into a bunch of different directions, depending on which genre I wanted to write in. And then I thought, hey, that'd be fun doing this same start and then writing all those different stories in different genres.

I mulled the idea for a while, and I even wrote one of the stories. But it turned into a long novella, short novel length book, instead of the shorter novella I thought would work for this idea. So I set it aside and wrote other things. The idea was still there. Something I'd get to eventually. But for a time, I just had other books calling.

Then I wrote a short story for a submission call. While coming up with an idea for that call, I ended up with two stories I really liked. One fit the anthology better, so I wrote that one. The second stayed in my head for a few months. After finishing a really big novel, as a sort of palate cleanser, I decided to write that second idea.

That story started with the line... Who steals a dragon?

As I wrote the original idea, though, I realized that opening line could do the same thing as that opening scene from a couple of years earlier—it could lead into any genre and to some very different stories. So when I finished the first novella, I decided to start with that line and try another genre. And then another.

Six genres all together before I felt satisfied. And because I'm the author I am, half the stories fit under the Romance genre umbrella, though the Science Fiction and Heist stories don't have even a hint of romance if you're just not in the mood.

I had such a great time with this collection, I do

intend on getting back to that first spark, that opening scene that could go off in multiple directions. It will be a different way of doing a Pick Your Genre collection but will still give readers the chance to choose something that suits their reading mood.

For those of you who like different stories for different days in different genres, I hope this collection is a fun way to satisfy those cravings all in one place. And I really hope you enjoy finding out...

Who steals a dragon.

Kat Simons
July 2023

Pick Your Genre

Paranormal Romance

Romantic Suspense

Contemporary Romance

Mystery Heist

Science Fiction

Fantasy

Paranormal
Romance

Chapter One

Who steals a dragon?

Myra had stolen a lot of things in her life. Jewels. Magic objects. Money. But a dragon?

Even she wasn't that brazen.

Yet, here she was, breaking into a high security building the middle of downtown Manhattan because someone else had the stupid idea to *steal* a dragon shifter. Just... Myra wasn't even sure what to call it. Hutzpah. But that felt too complimentary. Gall felt too weak. Idiocy maybe? Idiocy seemed like a good word.

She felt like a bit of an idiot, too, for allowing herself to get roped into this.

But she supposed this was what you got when you messed with a dragon king.

She crept silently from the closet where she'd used an untraceable, and disposable, laptop to hack into the building's security system and disable the motion sensors along the routes she needed. She'd also set the security cameras on a loop so they wouldn't record her activity. The guards outside her destination were going to be a little trickier, but according to the schedule she'd found in the security records, they'd be changing in less than ten minutes which gave her a little window of opportunity.

She just had to get into the locked room. She'd be getting back out again through a route that bypassed those guards.

If all went to plan, she'd get in, get the dragon king's son, and get out again without anyone being the wiser. His kidnappers would walk in to discover an empty room, and it would take them a week to figure out how it had all happened.

But that was if all went to plan.

Unfortunately, in Myra's experience, things rarely went to plan.

She waited in a corridor where she could see the guards outside her destination, but hear the changing guard coming in. There would be a moment, when they stood outside the antechamber exchanging codes and information. Not long. Forty-five seconds maybe. But that should give her enough time to pick the lock and get inside.

The sounds of the approaching guards had her

gut tightening and a small smile played across her mouth. She did love her job. Even the anxiety was a rush.

Using a little touch of magic to disguise herself—hiding her scent and any visual cues that might give her away to people used to working with shapeshifters—she waited for the guards inside the antechamber to step out and speak with the incoming guards. All of them were large, three men, one woman, every single one dressed in a pants suit, except one of the men who wore a kilt. She admired the fashion sense in what would otherwise be a pretty matched set of individuals.

She snuck across the hall behind them, relying on her magical screening spell to keep herself hidden, then paused just inside the antechamber and listened. No alerts. No one had heard her.

So far so good.

Hurrying to the locked door, she pulled her lockpicks out from inside her multi-pocket vest and knelt down. It wasn't a complicated lock. The lock on the door was mostly for show. What they had inside couldn't be contained with an ordinary door lock.

She finessed the lock in fourteen seconds, without even having to use a magical push, and slid inside, quietly closing the door behind her. She relocked the door from inside, just in case someone thought to test it. Then she held perfectly still, her ear to the door, listening as the new guard settled into place with a minimum of conversation.

When no one sounded an alarm, she took a deep breath and turned to face the room. Smiling. One step down. Now the important part.

The room was a large, bare, concrete box. The floor, the walls, even the ceiling just bare concrete. No paint or decoration. No rugs or carpets. No wood. Nothing that would easily burn. There were no windows either, even though the room was located on an outside corner of the high-rise.

The door she'd come through was "wood" on the outside, but inside it was obviously solid steel. From this side, it looked like a vault door. A vault door with a shitty and useless lock, but still a pretty solid door.

It wasn't the lock that was keeping the occupant inside the bare concrete room, though.

No. That was the chains.

Because the lights in the room were very low, barely above nightlight for visibility purposes, she heard the chains before she saw them. The dragon king had warned her those would be there. She came prepared. Still, hearing the chink chink against the concrete floor gave her a little shiver. Poor kid.

She didn't dare speak until she got closer, because while the guards looked like ordinary humans who relied on more mundane forms of security, they were guards used to working with shifters and might well be shifters themselves. She didn't dare tempt their hearing. She was only confident they wouldn't pick up her scent because she'd disguised that to open the door.

They weren't the only ones used to working around shifters.

She wasn't one herself. Just a garden variety thief. With the right kind of magic to make that job infinitely more fun. But when you went in to steal a certain grade of collectibles, it did put you in the way of shifters as well as other members of the magical community.

Myra didn't mind. She liked the challenge.

Though, as she crept closer to the hunched form opposite the door, huddled under what looked like a thick blanket, she decided dealing with dragons who could breathe fire and crisp her in under a second was not the kind of challenge she wanted to repeat in the future if she could at all help it.

She stared at that hunched form under the blanket as she approached carefully, wondering if the kid was okay since he wasn't moving. She had no idea what to expect from the dragon king's son. She hadn't even been shown a picture. Something something, no pictures of royal family taken, something something. Hadn't made sense to her, but whatever. The dragons could do as they liked. She was just told the stolen shifter was the king's son. And he wasn't being held for ransom or anything normal like that. Apparently, there was some other nefarious plot afoot. Which the king had also not seen fit to explain to her.

And that was fine, too. She didn't need to know what the kidnappers had in mind for the king's son. She just needed to know where he was so she could get him out. Steal him back, so to speak. Then she got the dragon king off her back for their little misunderstanding, and all would be right in Myra's world. She could go back to stealing what she wanted to steal.

The hunched form remained motionless as she neared. She was pretty sure the little guy would know she was here by now, because even though her spell to confuse shifter senses was still in place, she suspected a dragon shifter, even a young one, would just *feel* someone in the room with them.

Not taking that into account was what had gotten her into trouble with the dragon king.

But the closer she got to the king's son, the more she worried. Was he okay? The king said he was young, but hadn't said how young, and her imagination conjured images of a shivering, shaking, terrified child trying not to show just how scared he was as he huddled underneath the blanket.

When she was close enough to whisper without being easily overheard by the guards, she murmured, "Hey, it's okay. I'm here to get you out. You don't have to be scared of me. I'm a friend of your dad's. I'll have you out of here and back to him soon."

The hunched form finally moved a little, so Myra stilled, giving the boy time to adjust to her. She didn't want him to accidentally fry her with a blast of fire he couldn't control because of fear.

But as she watched, the hunched form got larger and larger. And now she worried he was trying to shift inside this concrete room on the fortieth floor of a high-rise building.

That would be really really bad.

"Listen, don't shift. Okay. There's not enough room." There were innocent people in this building as well as the thieves. She did not want the place brought down by a youngling dragon shifting and destroying half the building in the process.

The form unhunched completely as a very deep voice said, "I'm not an idiot and neither are they. I can't shift, even if I was stupid enough to do it."

Myra blinked a few times. That voice sounded very...adult for a kid.

She blinked a few more times as the hunched form tossed off the blanket that had been covering him.

Uh.

That was no youngling kid.

Chapter Two

The fully grown adult man sitting on the concrete floor was a revelation to Myra who'd been under the impression she was here to rescue a child. And wasn't that the last time she took a dragon king's phrasing at face value.

"Youngling my ass," she muttered as she approached the man. "Do not fry me. Your father did send me."

"Why you?"

"Because I'm an excellent thief," she murmured as she got close enough to inspect the chains.

And close enough to get a good look at the king's son.

He wasn't what she might call ordinarily handsome. The messy dark hair and blue eyes were pretty conventionally attractive, she supposed. But his features were too broad, and heavy, and maybe a little too sharp. There was a scar across his jaw, under beard scruff. And another across his forehead.

He looked a little worse for wear, and not just because his button-down shirt and dress pants were rumpled. He looked like he'd been going a few rounds in the shifter fight club.

No, not conventionally handsome, like his kingly father. Definitely not pretty.

But all of it together—his broad face and messy hair and scars—really...worked for him. He didn't need ordinary handsome. He had something more, something compelling that was...

Frankly, a little distracting.

She couldn't afford to be distracted right now. Breaking magic binding chains took a very special sort of concentration. And they only had a small window of time to make this work.

"I've had my fill of thieves over the last few days," the dragon muttered. There was a rawness to his voice, like he hadn't had anything to drink recently.

"You'll be rid of me soon enough," she said. She pulled a bottle of water from one of the myriad pockets in her vest and handed it to him.

He stared at the bottle for a long moment.

She waved it at him and held his gaze. "Just water. No spells. I'm a thief, not an ordinary witch. My magic doesn't do poison or anything like that."

"What does your magic do?" he asked as he took the bottle.

She smiled a little as she looked down at the cuffs on his ankles and the one on his wrist. "Makes locks into puzzle toys," she murmured.

The cuffs keeping a fully grown dragon shifter captive weren't things to be taken lightly, of course. These were some of the best quality steel she'd ever seen, infused with a copper alloy that held the magic, which raced over the surface of the cuffs in a swirl of purplish-blue light. The cuffs were attached to chains with links as thick as her forearms, and those were bolted to the floor by more thick, fused metal with lines of magic swirling through it.

So, not easy. But also, not outside her skill set.

A little rush of adrenaline-fueled excitement moved through her as she pulled out her lockpick case again.

"Why can't I smell you?" the man asked.

"Spell. Lot of shifters around." She had most of her attention on the cuffs, but his voice sounded less raw so she assumed he was drinking the water she'd given him.

"But you're not a witch?"

"No witch magic. Just thief magic." She grinned at him. "Don't worry. I'm a good thief."

"Is that why my father sent you?"

She winced inwardly. "Mostly."

"What does mostly mean?"

"Shh. I have to concentrate." She returned her attention to the cuffs, and her leather lockpick satchel as she selected her tools.

"No one shushes me."

"Maybe they should. You're not very good at it." She pulled out two long, thin picks, then set her fingers against the ankle cuff. Shook her head. Replaced the two picks and pulled out another two. Yes, those would do.

"I'm a king's son and a dragon shifter. No one shushes me."

She let out a deep, impatient breath and met his gaze again. "Listen, do you want out of here or not?"

"I want out of here."

"Then hush. I have to focus. And we only have so much time."

His eyes narrowed, but he didn't speak again.

"Finally," she muttered. Then she set to work on the locks.

Not her best time. The ankle cuffs took a little more finessing than she'd hoped and there was a moment there when she actually worried a little. But still, in under ten minutes she had him completely free and was setting the magic infused cuffs gently aside.

"Don't burn anything, and don't shift," she said as the man stretched his legs out and gave his body a big shake.

"I'm not an idiot," he said, glaring at her.

"Just have to make sure. Dragons..." She waved her hand in the air and hoped that explained everything.

From the way his gaze narrowed further, she assumed it hadn't. Or he was just unhappy with the explanation.

Either way, they didn't have time for her to sort through his grumpy facial expression. "Can you stand? Do you need help?"

She had no idea how long he'd been chained in place, and the chains weren't long enough to have allowed for a wide range of movement. He'd been taken a week ago. If he'd been chained in this spot for all that time, he would probably be pretty sore and stiff.

"I can stand," he said, giving her a condescending look.

She snorted and shook her head. "Lot of smugness for someone who went and got themselves stolen."

She stood back while he climbed to his feet, using the wall behind him to push upward. She collected his empty water bottle from the floor so he wouldn't have to bend down again, and slid the crumpled plastic into one of her inner pockets for later recycling.

His full height was something to behold. She wasn't what one might call tall. In fact, she had to stretch to reach medium. He, on the other hand, was... Well, tall was an understatement.

And that was going to complicate things.

She scowled. Glanced back at the door. No one seemed to have noticed them yet, which was good. But her escape plan had just taken a hit.

"Your dad should have warned me you weren't a kid," she muttered under her breath.

"He implied I was a child?"

"He called you a youngling." She faced him again, moving close enough to make sure they could speak quietly. He wasn't as stinky as she'd have expected after being held captive for a week in a concrete room. Little ripe, but not the sort of pungent sweat and fear stench she'd have expected. "Failed to give me your name, too. Lot of 'my son' but not a lot of name usage. What's your name?"

His expression was hard to read when he stood so much taller than her. How had he hunched in on himself enough to look like a kid when she'd walked in? Must be a lighting thing. And no that wasn't a flutter in her stomach because she adored tall men. That was...nerves. Just nerves.

"Christopher," he said, his voice deep.

Did he sound irritated? She thought he sounded irritated. But she didn't have time to deal with his irritation. "Listen, Chris—"

"Christopher. I don't like Chris."

"Fine. Christopher. My plan for getting out of here was predicated on the fact that you were...well, small. And since you are not small, things are going to get a little cramped. Are you claustrophobic?"

He shook his head. "But if you're thinking we can exit through the air ducts, they have motion sensors and alarms in those. It's not a viable option."

"Are you the thief here? No. I'm the thief. Trust me. I have that part covered." Questioning her bona fides. How rude. "And we only need the air ducts for a short section. Can you squish yourself up enough to do this? I don't have a plan for going back through that door without it bringing all the security in the building down on us. And that would be bad."

More than bad. It would be suicidal. The kidnappers knew how to contain a dragon or they wouldn't have gotten Christopher here. They'd know how to stop him trying to escape in an obvious way. The whole reason *she* was here was to sneak him out without anyone knowing until it was too late. So front door with the handy guards who would raise an alarm was not an option.

"I can manage." He didn't sound particularly confident, but he wasn't arguing with her either.

Good. She hated when the loot argued with her.

"You good to go now?" she asked. "All the blood returned to all the various body parts?" For reasons she refused to acknowledge, mentioning his body parts and blood flow made her stomach flutter again. Weird.

"I'm fine. I can manage."

"Groovy. Let's go."

If he'd been the child she was expecting, she'd have taken his hand. But since he wasn't a child and there was all this stomach fluttering stuff going on—nerves, just nerves about the plan getting complicated—she motioned him to follow her instead.

And tried to ignore the feel of all that muscle and heat just at her back.

Chapter Three

The air duct was located high on the wall, near the ceiling. And of course, the screen wasn't just a simple, easily removeable screen. It was thicker metal than the usual vents, and it was locked into place. But it hadn't been massively reinforced with complicated locks and stuff either. After all, there were supposed to be motion sensors in the ducts. Why waste too much energy on an impenetrable screen?

The duct's location was a little tricky since Myra couldn't bring a regular ladder with her. The room had high ceilings, not outrageously high, but high enough she couldn't just jump up and touch the screen.

Because she'd assumed she was stealing back someone child-sized who wouldn't be able to just reach up and boost themselves into the vent, she had brought a foldable ladder she could hook into the duct once she had the screen off. She glanced at Christopher. Her ladder would not take his weight. But since he was tall enough—and she presumed strong enough by the looks of him—to boost himself up to the air duct, she figured they were still okay.

For her part, she just needed some wall climbing sticky pods. Like the kinds of thing used at rock climbing centers to simulate hand and foot holds along climbing walls, her pods did a similar thing, giving her hand and foot holds for scaling sheer surfaces. Her pods weren't bolted into anything of course, she just slapped them onto the wall. But since they were reinforced with a little magic, she didn't need the bolts.

The first pods went onto the wall just above her head level with one for a toe hold at her waist. She set an additional three pods as she needed them while she climbed, pulling them from another convenient vest pocket. She loved her vest pockets. There were so many of them. And they held so much. She wasn't sure how she'd managed to do stealing before she'd gotten this vest.

Once she reached the screen, she had it removed in short order, a few handy twists of her lock picks to deal with the basic lock. With one hand holding a sticky pod, she hefted the heavy screen down the wall with her other hand.

"Take this," she grunted. "Gentle on the floor."

Christopher didn't argue with her or comment, just took the screen like it was a piece of paper and set it against the wall a foot away. She supposed that was better than if he'd been a kid. If he'd been a kid, she'd have had to climb back down the wall one handed to set the screen aside. It wasn't a long climb of course—the room wasn't that tall—but this did save a step.

"Can you climb using the hand and toe holds?" she asked. "Or can you just boost yourself up?" He didn't really have to stretch much to reach the air duct. His height really was pretty impressive.

"I'll follow," he said.

From this angle, looking more down at him than up, she could sort of see him better but that didn't help her read his expression any easier. Heavy eyebrows pulled down over his blue eyes, which were pretty arresting when she got a good look at them. His mouth was set in a line. His muscles were tight. And he kept glancing at the door.

But whether he was scared, irritated, bored, or angry, she couldn't tell.

And she supposed it didn't matter so long as he followed her instructions so they could get out of here.

"Follow as quietly as you can," she said. "You'll have to lay flat on your stomach and push using your feet and hands, but try to be as gentle on the duct as possible so we don't make much noise."

He grunted. She assumed that was a yes and shimmied into the duct. She had some wiggle room, enough she could turn back to make sure he was behind her. But he filled out the entire rectangular space, his shoulders brushing the metal walls.

Good thing he wasn't claustrophobic. She had a twinge of it just looking at how little space he had in here.

She led the way, slowly and carefully to keep from drawing attention to movement in the duct should anyone happen to be paying attention. She doubted anyone would be since they assumed their motion sensors were still working. But she was a careful thief, if not an entirely cautious one. If she'd been cautious, she wouldn't have gotten into this mess to begin with.

Fortunately, they only had to shimmy through about twenty meters of duct before they reached their destination. From the very quiet grunt behind her, she assumed the journey was not a comfortable one for Christopher.

At their exit air vent, she paused to study the room below. A storage room for electronic equipment and old filing cabinets. There were some tall metal shelves lining the walls. And a few giant photocopy machines currently taking up the center of the room.

Removing the vent from this angle was a little trickier. It was screwed into the wall from the outside rather than the inside. But no actually locks in here. No motion sensors. No cameras.

Just a very handy window.

She bent some of the metal on the screen, giving herself enough room to reach her hand through, and went to work on the screws with her little screw driver, pulled from yet another pocket. She glanced back at Christopher as she worked. He was frowning at her.

"How many pockets does that vest have?" he murmured.

"So many pockets," she said with happy sigh. "So. Many. Pockets."

When she got the screws undone, she angled the screen around to bring it back inside the duct and set it to one side. Then she poked her head out of the open vent to get a better look at the room. All good. Empty. No sounds from any direction to indicate someone had figured out their prize dragon shifter had been stolen.

Yay, her.

The vent opened over one of the metal shelves, which made climbing down both easier, and potentially noisier. So she took a moment to set up a sound dampening spell before crawling out of the vent feet first and easing down the shelves like a ladder.

By the time she reached the ground and turned around to gesture Christopher down, he was already out. He jumped down from a higher shelf than she would have risked and landed next to her in a crouch. They both held still, listening. And when no alarms sounded, he rose to his full height.

Which felt like it took a long time.

"You afraid of heights?" she asked, still keeping her voice low.

"I can fly. I'd make a piss poor dragon if I was afraid of heights."

She snorted a laugh. "Didn't answer my question, though, did you?"

"I'm not afraid of heights."

"Good. How about scaling buildings along thin ledges? That bother you?"

"You were going to do that with a kid?"

"No. I had a different plan. But that won't work with you." She gestured at him. "You're too big."

She couldn't read the expression that crossed his face—a scowl or a repressed smile or just confusion —so she didn't try.

"This is an adjustment to the original escape plan," she said. "My original plan involved more air ducts and a convenient elevator shaft."

"You were going to take a youngling into an elevator shaft?"

Ah, now she could read his expression. That was definitely a scowl of anger. "I wouldn't have let a youngling get hurt," she said. "The elevator was the easiest way down. But the section of air duct we would have had to go through is too narrow for you. So we're making some adjustments."

"Where does the thin ledge outside the building lead?"

"So many questions." She shook her head. "It leads to a room that we can't access through the air vents, but which is in a part of the building not controlled by the group who stole you, and so is an easier room from which to sneak out to a stairwell." She raised a hand. "Before you say it, I've taken care of the cameras and everything inside the stairwell as well. This isn't my first rodeo. But we can't reach the stairwell easily without moving outside the building for a bit."

"Why did you fix the cameras inside the stairwell when you intended on taking the elevator shaft?"

"Because I'm a careful thief who plans for multiple contingencies," she said, hands on her hips. "Are you finished and can we go now? They will notice you're missing sooner rather than later. And that is a complication I'd rather not deal with."

"Have you planned for it?" He sounded smug, like he'd issued a gotcha.

"Of course, I have." She shrugged. "It's just...not a great plan. Better not to have to use it." Also, she'd planned on discovery while moving a child through the building. The fact that Christopher was not, in fact, a child, had really limited her alternative options. "Let's go."

She stalked to the window, trying to ignore the very large dragon shifter at her back. She supposed once she opened the window, he might be able to just shift and fly home. Except they were in the middle of New York City and someone was bound to notice the flying dragon before he could cloak his presence. The dragons weren't exactly a secret, but one flying through the New York skyline would be noticed and draw a *lot* of unwanted attention. Raising questions Myra knew the dragon king didn't want to answer.

Also she wasn't sure how fast a dragon shifter could shift. If it wasn't instantaneous, he might just hit the ground before he achieved flight.

That idea gave her a shiver.

"You okay?" he asked.

The question surprised her. "Yes. Why?"

"You shivered. Are you afraid of heights?"

He'd been paying enough attention to notice her shiver. She wasn't sure what to make of that. "I'm not afraid of heights." She grinned. "Actually, I love heights." And tall men. But that wasn't the point. "Scaling heights is second nature to me."

Which was true. She'd been climbing around where she shouldn't have climbed since she was a kid. The magic that made her so good at thieving also seemed to have given her a slight adrenaline addiction.

She studied the window. It wasn't one of the usual sealed ones most high-rise office buildings had these days. This was one of the old school ones that pushed up and could be tipped inside for cleaning. There was a screen over it. And it was locked shut. But neither the screen, nor the lock, were much of a deterrent to her.

Pushing the window up without making noise was actually the hardest part. She used a little "grease" magic to quiet the initial squeak, though that initial sound made her wince and Christopher hiss.

The hiss was an interesting sound. A sound that was very *not* human. And reminded her of his father's court. There'd been a lot of very quiet hissing. Only a handful of dragon shifters there. There simply weren't that many in the world. So it wasn't like she'd been surrounded by hundreds of them. Less than half a dozen. But when they're dragon shifters, that's enough.

One is enough.

The one at her back waiting on her to inspect the ledge outside the window was more than enough.

She pulled back inside. "Big enough for me. You'll fit but I hope you have cat-like balance." She asked that last as much as stated it.

He grunted.

A real non-answer answer. Have to do. They didn't have time to argue.

"We're going to the left. We're walking around a corner. And then there will be another window like this one." She didn't mention the other window was a more traditional high-rise window that didn't open. She had that covered and they didn't have time for his questions. "Ready?"

Another grunt.

"Alrighty."

She slid out the window.

Chapter Four

Myra mostly ignored the drop and the view as she moved out onto the ledge outside the high-rise window. She liked adrenaline, but she also knew how to measure it out so she didn't get shaky. Staring down at the street when she was sneaking out someone who's skills in ledge-walking were in question was a good way to overjump her adrenaline with fear. Wouldn't help anybody with that sort of spike.

If she was alone, she might have enjoyed the view up here. The streets of Manhattan below. The closely backed collection of high-rises. All glass and steel and stone and mostly dark windows rising around her as shadows against the nighttime. The glow of soft pink streetlamps far below. The star-like pattern of occasional window lights scattered over the horizon.

The clouds overhead brightened to near orange by the city lights.

This part of Manhattan was mainly business buildings with only the occasional residential place. So at two in the morning, it was quieter than some might think for a supposedly twenty-four-seven city. There was still the occasional bump of cars below, and the releasing air of a bus stopping and opening its door. The cold burn of metal, cement, and tar from a nearby construction sight lingered in the breeze that cooled her cheeks. And a heady punch of salty Hudson River stench caught the very edges of the night air.

Yeah, if she wasn't worried about the very large dragon shifter stepping out onto the very thin ledge next to her, she'd have really enjoyed this view.

Fortunately for them both, this building was one of the old ones with beautiful stone architecture and lovely designs that included things like ledges and decorative carved stone accents. Across the street was one of those smooth steel buildings with nothing but windows and a slick drop to the streets below to recommend it.

She secretly hated the new constructions but not because they made breaking and entering from outside the building harder—she didn't mind that. She had her ways of dealing with that, and she liked the challenge. She just didn't like the aesthetics as much as the old-school stone work and uniqueness of these older buildings.

She inched along the ledge, sliding her feet to ensure she pushed away any potential obstacles that could trip them up, keeping her gaze on their path and destination.

"You doing okay?" she asked, without looking back at him. She took his slightly louder grunt as an "okay."

Adult shifter, used to flying, she reminded herself. This wasn't sending him into a panic. She hoped it wasn't. Fact he was still behind her was a good sign. She hoped.

Going around the building corner with was a bit tricky because of one of those decorative stone curlicues she loved so much sticking out just a little far. She showed him what to do by turning so she gripped the stone, her stomach to the decorative swish, and inched around it while holding onto it. She risked a look at him long enough to see he was following her lead. On the other side, she was able to turn again so her back was to the large gray bricks once more. She waited to make sure he managed the maneuver, and when he did without issue, she let out a long breath. Yeah, she hadn't needed to worry. Apparently, dragons did have cat-like balance.

The window that was their target was two more down. When she reached it, she used the lip over the top of the window for balance as she pulled out yet another tool from her vest pockets. This one a cutting tool. But not just any cutting tool. This one had a little magic in it so the cutting was easy, silent, and the glass wouldn't break.

She stuck the central part of the tool to the window by an also magically enhanced suction cup, then stretched out the wire with the cutting tip at the edge and slid the sharp blade around the dark tinted glass. She cut a bigger circle than she normally would to accommodate the large man with her, then slipped the circular chunk now attacked to her cutting tool through the window, setting it down gently on the carpet inside. She slid the rest of the way through the hole, going head first and rolling to get back to her feet. Before Christopher could slip through, she scurried back to move the circle of glass out of his way. She needed that to fix the window and she didn't want the piece cracked.

Christopher came through the hole head first, too. Slithering inside, rather than rolling over his head and back to his feet, as she had. He just crawled inside, down the uncut part of the window and onto the ground like crawling around on all fours was natural. He stood as gracefully as he'd slipped inside, rising to his full height like he did this kind of thing all the time.

Okay. She was impressed.

"Good job," she murmured.

He scowled.

Fair enough. "Sorry for the slight condescension. Wasn't intended."

Another grunt.

"Not a big talker, are you?" she said as she lifted the circle of tinted glass, using the suction cup stuck to the center as a handle. Carefully, she settled the circle back into the hole she'd created, and keeping it in place with one hand on the suction cup, she used her other hand, which she no longer needed for balance on the window sill, to slide the cutting tool at the end of the wire backward over the cut, sealing it this time.

When she stepped back and detached the suction cup, winding the tool back into a small ball she could return to a vest pocket, she admired her handy work. No visible signs of the cut. Even the tinting had smoothed back together without leaving any telltale lines.

"I'm impressed," Christopher said, sounding surprised.

"He speaks!"

She ignored his scowl to examine the room they'd landed in.

There was a large conference table in the middle of the room, with three rectangular shaped gadgets in the center used for, she assumed, audio-visual presentations or whatnot. The table was surrounded by tall-backed swivel chairs. One wall had a screen pulled down. And there was a small cart against the wall, the purpose of which she had no idea, though the faint stale coffee smell made her think a place for setting up coffee service during meetings. Fortunately, this wasn't one of those conference rooms with an entire wall made of glass. And the door was closed.

This was part of a law firm, one of the few other businesses on this floor, and as far as Myra had been able to tell, the firm had no connections with the group that had kidnapped Christopher. Though, the group who'd had the hutzpah to steal a dragon could have hidden their links to the law firm, she supposed. She'd managed to dig pretty deep into the law firm's computer files, though, and there didn't seem to be any ties.

She motioned toward the closed door. "There's a short hallway beyond that and a door just to the left that leads to a set of stairs. There's an alarm on the door. Do not open it. Let me do that." She lowered her chin to give him a look.

His expression never changed.

She assumed that meant he'd listen to her and continued. "We're only going down six flights. Then we'll come back out into the building and take another set of stairs."

"In case they follow our scent?"

"Your scent. Yes." Hers was still disguised by her handy spell.

"Why not go up?"

"Because this is a high-rise, and I don't have a handy way to get us to the next building for an escape."

"I have wings."

"Yes. I'm aware." When he continued to just stare at her, she shook her head and said, "No flying. Too much chance of being spotted. The point is to get out without being spotted. Your dad prefers knowledge of this whole mess doesn't get out of immediate dragon circles."

She reached for the doorknob, but stopped, hand on the knob, her instincts making the hair on the back of her neck stand up.

She lifted her free hand for silence, but Christopher had gone still the minute she did. They both stared at the door. Then she set her ear to the wood. She didn't have shapeshifter hearing or anything. But she did have a little eavesdropping spell. Which she used on the door.

Inside the office, not at the door yet, but still... Someone inside the law firm. Moving around, pushing things that bumped over carpeted floors. A whispered curse.

"Check all the closed rooms," someone said.

She met Christopher's gaze. "Change of plan," she mouthed.

She sent a locking spell through the doorknob. Then scanned the conference room again. Another air duct.

This one was smaller.

She hurried to the side of the room under the duct and whispered, "Boost me up."

She didn't have time to mess around with wall climbing grips or ladders or even the rolling conference room chairs—though that's what she'd have used if she was alone or had an actual child with her. Instead, she had a very large dragon. Strong enough to give her a lift.

The ceiling here wasn't nearly as high as it had been in the room where the kidnappers had kept Christopher. He lifted her—with an ease she'd have to ponder later—and set her up onto his shoulders, which put her at eye level with the duct screen.

No alarms here—she touched the screen to make sure—so she simply had to unscrew the bolts. There was room for her, but barely enough room for him to squeeze in.

Gonna be tight. "Set me down. You first. If you can't fit, we'll have to go back out the window."

Which she didn't want to do because hanging out on a thin ledge when people were looking out windows for you was a lot more precarious than hiding in a vent. Vents had other exits. The only place to run on a building ledge was...off.

Again, with a shocking ease, he lifted her off his shoulders and set her on the ground. Then he boosted himself up to the vent, his arm muscles flexing under his much-damaged shirt. And wasn't that just rude since they didn't have time for her to admire all those lovely muscles at the moment.

To her surprise, he slipped through the opening easier than she would have assumed. Great. So he fit. Now she just had to get up there. But with the lower ceiling, jumping up and grabbing the edge of the duct was within her skill set. She lifted herself into the vent, head first, her feet finding purchase against the smooth wall as she clambered inside.

The vent wasn't large enough for him to turn and face her, so she was looking at his bare feet and his just-barely-angled head so he could see her. She could move enough to get the screen back in place, but she had to use a little magic to hold it up since bolting it back into the wall wasn't an option in such a small, cramped area.

Once she had their trail covered, she motioned him to move. He slid forward on this stomach, pushing against the steel duct with his feet, and managed to move through the narrow space a lot easier and faster than she would have expected. She scrambled after him, going over her mental layout of the building, looking for a good escape option.

They were about to turn a corner in the vent system when she heard a sound from the conference room behind them. She set her hand to Christopher's ankle to stop him. He froze. She did too, her ears straining to hear more than murmurs.

"...telling you they took the stairs."

"Got the cameras back up in there. No one's..."

"...past the alarms. Can get..."

"Shhh."

"He breathes fire, man. This was a bad idea."

Well, Myra thought, at least someone recognized that. Stealing a dragon was a piss poor idea, no matter what they had intended.

She was going to conveniently ignore the fact that she was *also* stealing a dragon. This was entirely different.

Knowing they'd figured out her hacks and gotten the security systems turned back on was irritating. How the hell did they find those so fast? Also meant they not only knew Christopher was missing already, they'd have the entire building monitored and maybe even locked down while they hunted for him.

She didn't *think* they could lock down the entire building. Too many other people here. Other businesses. Even if it was two in the morning. But the kidnappers could make getting out without being spotted impossible.

Damn it. So much for getting Christopher away before they knew he was missing.

She wasn't sure how they'd managed it, but she was mightily annoyed they had.

CHAPTER FIVE

Myra held still as she listened to the people in the conference room moving around and shoving at things and then the room grew silent. She held perfectly still for another five minutes. Making sure they hadn't just gone quiet to listen for noise. Even the most patient of people eventually gave in and made sound when they were listening out for a possible thief. So she'd just learned how to outlast most people.

Though, she also had not always been this patient.

Fortunately, Christopher didn't make any sound either and he didn't try to rush her. He was so still that if her hand hadn't been on his ankle, she might have thought he'd slithered on ahead in the narrow air duct.

As she grew more certain the people searching for them had left the conference room, she became increasingly more aware that she was still gripping Christopher's leg. His skin wasn't as hot as she'd have expected from a dragon shifter, but warm enough to feel good. She removed her hand from his ankle.

He met her gaze and she nodded, motioning him to move forward around the curve in the duct. The darkness closed around them, then, making it impossible for her to see, but she'd memorized the layout of these ducts and could tell where they were heading—maybe a little of her magic helped with that, too.

This direction led them to a section of wider vents, but also brought them back in the direction of his captors and that wasn't the direction she wanted to go. The stairwell was no longer an option. And the way she'd gotten in—through a service elevator, after taking care of security sensors accessible from outside the building, and then carefully sneaking through gaps in the guards' routine until she was in a position to disable the rest of the security system from the inside—was not an option now since she had Christopher with her and he was a lot harder to *sneak* around with given his size.

Her disguise magic was good. She might have been able to slip a child-sized person past the guards and into an elevator. Maybe. A child-sized person she could hold close enough to encompass them with the magic that kept her hidden. But a person as large as Christopher, even held close, was...

Yeah, that wasn't going to work.

When they reached an intersection of vents going in a few different directions, she stopped Christopher with a hand on his ankle again. She was sure no one would see the tell-tale light now, as they were deep enough in the ducts it shouldn't travel, so she cracked one of the thin light tubes she had in an inner pocket of her vest and wrapped it through a fabric tab near her collar. The green glow was enough to allow them to finally see, but not enough to attract attention. The bigger ducts meant they now had enough room they could move around to face each other better, too.

They needed to talk.

"Okay, so," she said, keeping her voice at a whisper. "We need to decide what we do next."

She leaned close enough she was speaking into his ear. Sound carried in vents, farther than light, and she wanted to minimize that. But leaning in so close to him, she was way too aware of his warmth, which was really nice, and also maybe a little too aware of the fact that he hadn't showered in a few days. He still didn't stink as much as she would have expected. He didn't actually *stink* at all. Which was weird. Or maybe she just didn't mind the sweaty smell of him? That was even weirder. She'd write it off to him being a shifter and leave it at that. No reason to investigate why she might sort of half like the smell of him all sweaty.

She blinked hard a few times and said against his ear, "They've blocked the next two options I had for getting us out. Stairwell security is back on. And if that's on, then their elevator security is back on."

"How did you get in?" he asked, also moving so he was speaking against her ear to keep his voice low.

His breath was very warm, too. "Service elevator, disabled security for that from outside. If they found the internal hacking, the found the external hacking."

"So the air ducts?" He looked around, his scowl fierce.

That expression should probably have scared her. He could breathe fire and he looked really really pissed. She wasn't particularly scared. That was probably a character flaw of some kinds. Chalk up another one.

"Probably back to being monitored closer to their section of the floor," she said. "They didn't have the entire story rigged, though. Too hard to do with the other businesses. But if we keep going that way —" she nodded to one of the branching ducts, "— we'll crawl right back into their motion sensors. We go that way—" another nod toward a different branching duct, "—we go in a little circle that dead ends back at the law offices and the conference room."

The fact that the people after them had gotten into one of the other businesses to look for them was...worrying. She'd been relying on them not wanting to draw attention by breaking and entering on those other businesses.

"There's a vertical duct that way—" she motioned with her hand down the third directional option they had, "—one that connects multiple floors and runs alongside the elevator bank."

"But?"

"It's made up of sheer, slick metal walls and a forty story drop to the ground floor."

"No ladders?"

"No ladders."

"Don't suppose you have something handy for forty stories of climbing in that vest of yours?"

She smiled. "I actually do have something in my vest that can help with a vertical climb."

"That vest is...impressive."

"So is the person who packed the pockets," she said, waggling her eyebrows.

"Yes," he said, a very faint smile cracking his scowl. "Very impressive."

She snorted, and turned away so he wouldn't see how much she wanted to preen under that compliment. "So the problem is," she said when she felt she could whisper in his ear without getting weird about it, "while we won't have to worry about motion sensors in the vertical vent—old building, no one thought about installing them yet—we do have to worry about sound carrying. That shaft connects to the vents on each floor and the way sound carries, we might attract some attention. Any attention risks attracting the attention of the people after you."

"So...we just don't talk?"

She rolled her eyes. "Can you climb down forty stories using rubber hand holds like rock climbing and not grunt or make noise? That's what I'm asking you."

"Yes."

"Good. Because you're going to have to do that."

"This wasn't an option if I was an actual youngling, was it?"

"No."

It had been on her contingency plan, of course. Which was why she knew it was an option at all. But she had really really not wanted to have to use this option with a kid. First time all night she was more grateful than irritated that Christopher wasn't a kid.

Because they didn't have time to fart around, she motioned him down the direction to the vertical air shaft. She conveniently didn't mention that she only had enough of her handy climbing grips for the distance of a few floors, so she'd have to remove them and place them as they went. She didn't want him to worry unnecessarily.

They'd have time for that when they reached the shaft.

Chapter Six

Myra looked down the length of the dark, smooth air shaft, letting the movement of air cool her face. Sound seemed larger and more echoey here, even without her and Christopher making any noise. The space felt open after the air ducts, but also...deep. Very very deep.

Deep enough she couldn't see the bottom in the darkness.

She wasn't afraid of the height, or the climb down. She'd done this a lot—not air shaft climbing, though she had done that, but rock climbing up and down very large, flat mountain faces because it kept her in good shape and kept her climbing skills sharp for just such an occasion. So she wasn't afraid to go down this shaft.

On her own.

Having the son of the dragon king with her, on the other hand...

"Sure you can do this?" she murmured near his ear as she cracked another light tube and tied it to her vest so they'd have a way to see as they climbed down the dark shaft. The old one had faded to a barely-there green glow.

Christopher nodded. "Dragons can climb, you know?"

"I did not know that. Why would a being that can fly need to learn how to climb?"

"Wings are big and get in the way in some spaces. We don't use them all the time." He glanced at her, and his usual scowl softened into something *almost* like a smile. "How much do you know about dragon shifters?"

"Less than I thought I did," she said without hesitation.

Like that fact that even having gone without a shower for at least a week, his sweat still didn't smell horrible. After being close to him this long, she was kind of used to it, and might even not mind it.

When she started wondering what he'd smell like after a shower—or maybe in a shower—she blinked hard a few times and said, "Let's go."

She pulled out some of her climbing grips and leaned into the air shaft to place the first few on the wall. She startled a little when she felt Christopher catch hold of the back of her vest, holding it as she leaned farther down.

She grinned up at him over her shoulder. "'Fraid I'll fall and leave you stranded?" she mostly mouthed since she didn't want to make much sound.

He grunted a reply. Which was just as well. Silence right. They wanted silence.

But it was hard to ignore the little flutter in her stomach. She was supposed to be here getting him out, and here he was making sure she didn't plummet to her death. To be fair, his actions were probably more pragmatic than altruistic or even gallant since she had the vest with all the good stuff in the pockets. Still, it was nice to know he didn't want her to fall and die.

With his hold securing her, she stretched even farther into the shaft and placed an extra few climbing grips to give them a little more room. Then she pushed back inside the vent, or rather she started to push back into the vent and then Christopher just lifted her with an easy, one-handed tug.

Impressive. Little scary. Also a little sexy.

She silently cleared her throat. Then next to his ear, said, "I'm going first, so I can place the cups as I go down. The ones above you that you no longer need? I'm going to have to...call those down to me. I only have enough for about thirty feet."

"You need me to remove them and hand them to you as we go?" he asked, also against her ear.

She enjoyed the warm brush of his breath, which did not smell like sulfur and that was probably very good because they didn't need him breathing fire right now. Though she almost laughed as an image came to mind of a scene from the movie *Die Hard* of fire roaring up an elevator shaft. If there'd been a dragon behind that fire instead of a C4 explosion, they could reproduce that scene.

Not that they had time for that.

"Not necessary," she said, answering his question. She wiggled her fingers. "Magic. I've got this. But don't panic when you start seeing the way back up the shaft disappearing? And remember, absolute silence. Grunt in your head."

When she pulled away from him to look him in the eyes, he was back to frowning. But he did nod. So she assumed he'd be good with all this and swung her legs out into the shaft. Smiling a little when he blinked suddenly and reached for her, only checking himself with his hand almost on her vest.

Decent reaction time. Not as good as hers. But decent. And she'd just learned her reaction time could beat a dragon shifter's. That was handy. Especially when she returned to his father's lair and had to deal with him again.

She started down the shaft, falling into the rhythm of climbing easily. She paused far enough down to give him room, then looked up to watch him move out of the shaft and take his first tentative step onto one of the climbing grips. She wanted to tell him not to worry, they'd take his weight—even his substantial weight—because magic. But since they weren't even supposed to be grunting now, she kept her mouth closed and waited.

After his first few, testing steps onto the climbing rocks, when they held his weight, he moved fully down into the shaft, climbing a lot easier than she'd feared. She let out a long, silent breath and started climbing again.

She paused when she needed to, to place more grips. And when she got low on the ones in her vest, she stopped long enough to mouth a return spell. The grips above vanished and reappeared in her pocket.

The first time she did this, Christopher looked down at her with his brows raised and eyes wide. It was the first time she noticed his pupils were huge, almost encompassing his irises and making his blue eyes look black. She'd bet cash money he could see in the dark shaft better than she could. Lucky. The green glow from her light tube only traveled so far. The bottom of the shaft still felt very far beneath them and was shroud in darkness.

It occurred to her that dragons probably did need good night vision, given so many of them liked caves. Even the shifters liked having a "cave" somewhere to hoard things. And dragons of all shapes and sizes were super protective of their hoards, which she learned the hard way. So she probably shouldn't have been even a little surprised by good night vision.

She really didn't know nearly as much about dragon shifters as she probably should have before getting on his father's bad side.

Live and learn.

As they passed another air duct feeding back into the building three floors below where they'd entered the shaft, she started to breathe easier. The farther down they went, the closer to escape. Even if they had to leave the shaft before reaching the ground level, it would be a lot easier to escape the building from one of the lower floors without anyone noticing.

So long as their escape plan wasn't discovered *this* time, they were home free.

Cockiness. Her Achille's heel.

When the first flash of blue lightning zipped past her, she cursed that cockiness.

She should have known better.

CHAPTER SEVEN

Another sizzle of blue lightning flashed into the dark shaft as Myra flattened herself against the wall, trying to make less of a target. She looked up, in the direction the magic shots were coming from, but couldn't see around Christopher.

"Who?" she hissed.

"The kidnappers."

"Shooting magic?"

"Have a wizard with them."

Great.

The dragon king hadn't mentioned magic. The possibility of there being shifters among the kidnappers, yes—though he hadn't specified what kind of shifter—but he had absolutely not mentioned magic. And he really should have mentioned magic!

No wonder they'd found her security hacks so quickly.

Another zing of electricity arrowed down the shaft, making a mockery of her little green tube light. She squinted against the glare, and said, "Down. Next duct."

They were still ten feet above the duct beneath them, but going back up to a closer duct seemed like a bad idea when that was the direction the dangerous magic was coming from, so down it was.

She heard the sounds of shouts and a howl, which was interesting, and there was a lot of cursing —some of which came from her. She set and called the climbing grips as fast as she could while still moving downward as fast as she could go. Blue magic ricocheted off the smooth metal walls inside the shaft. Her heartbeat pounded hard.

A grunt from just above her.

She looked up in time to see Christopher leaning awkwardly back, his hands slipping from the climbing grip.

"No!"

She grabbed his hand on the way past, clutching his forearm as he wrapped his fingers around hers. His skin was slick with sweat, and he weighed a ton. Not good for her hold. She squeezed tight to his hand and held her body against the wall to aid her hold on the climbing grips. And because she needed it, she added a little magic to keep her own fingers from slipping.

"Let me go," Christopher said. "I'm too heavy. You'll fall."

"Shut. Up. Let me concentrate."

She glanced up again. Now she could see the wizard leaning out of the air vent three floors up. His features were hard to see from this distance, though she suspected if she'd been a shifter of some kind, she would have made out more than the dark hair and vaguely pale skin. Even the *he* part of her assessment might be wrong. Didn't matter. The wizard fired more blue lightning down into the shaft, this time aiming at the wall opposite, angling the shot like a ball on a pool table, trying to hit on the ricochet.

"That's cheating!" she shouted up at the wizard.

There were more howls behind him and then another head poked out of the vent.

"Thirty-seventh floor," the head said. "Go. Get them."

"Let me go," Christopher said again.

She was straining to hold him and not lose her grip, hard enough when he was holding onto her. When she felt his hand loosening, she cursed. "Stop that! I'm not letting you fall."

But she couldn't climb like this. And the duct was still too far below, and they were going to have company there soon.

"I'm placing more grips. Get ready." She hated doing this purely with magic because she couldn't ensure they were secure setting them this way. But beggars couldn't be choosers.

She narrowed her eyes to concentrate and focused on moving the climbing grips around, sending all the ones left above her to a ragged ladder like line below her.

"Take hold of one." She grunted when she felt Christopher gain purchase, easing some of his weight from her. "Make sure it holds before you let go of me."

"Got it," he said, releasing her arm.

She looked down and let out a breath, seeing him once again holding onto the grips. "Down to the vent," she ordered, then looked up again.

In time to see a blue sizzle of lightning arrowing right for her. "Shit." She flattened against the wall, moving as far to one side as she could while still holding the grips.

Wasn't far enough. The magic shot hit her arm, sending a shockwave of electrical pain through her limb.

Her body jolted. Her fingers loosened. Her vision darkened.

She let out a pissed off gasp when her body didn't respond. Her stomach tumbled, but even that felt distant and out of her control. She couldn't scramble to regain her hold. She couldn't even curse. She couldn't do anything.

But fall down the nearly forty story air shaft.

The last thing she saw before the darkness swallowed her was Christopher, hand outstretched, reaching for her.

Chapter Eight

Myra snapped awake, suddenly, but held herself perfectly still as she scrambled to remember why she was unconscious. Cold wind hit her face before she even had her eyes open. Looking down, she blinked. The cityscape of high-rise buildings rolling past *below* her was...unexpected.

Without looking away from those passing buildings, she murmured, "This is going to require some explanation."

"Soon," Christopher said from above her.

The feel of arms around her back and under her legs, the air so cold and wind so sharp it made her eyes water, the heat pumping off the body she was cradled against. A lot of disorienting sensations hitting her all at once. Including the height. She wasn't afraid of heights. Normally. But usually, she had some sort of control on just how high she was.

She forced herself to look up. Christopher's face, still in human form above her, his gaze out over the city, his eyes glowing a little in the darkness. The very large wings sprouting from his back and shoulders were new.

He'd had a shirt on when she'd broken him out of his cell. The shirt was gone now. Not even scraps to show for it. And his bare skin was a good deal warmer than it had been earlier in the night. That heat kept her from shivering with the cold at this altitude. There was a sweep of purple and yellow scales over his skin now. The color of the scales blended into the wings, which had strong bone ridges with a thin purple membrane between bones. They reminded her of a bat's wings. Except the wing span was easily...twenty, thirty feet. Hard to tell from her angle dangling in his arms under him. Like a fish in a hawk's talons. Except this hawk was a lot bigger. And his talons were holding her in a warm, comfortable cocoon.

And she was pretty sure Christopher didn't intend on devouring her. In the bad way.

"I'm not splat at the bottom of an air shaft," she said. And though her voice seemed to whip away from her on the cold air, he apparently heard her just fine because he answered.

"No."

"You can do partial shifts?"

"I can do partial shifts."

Handy. "The wizard and the others?"

She'd swear he winced. But it was hard to tell at this angle and with the overall fact that they were flying and he was concentrating on that.

"I might have left some...crisped shifters and a very crisped wizard in the air ducts after I saved you."

She nodded. Skipping right past the part where he'd saved her—she was probably going to need solid ground under her for that one—she said, "That's going to stink up the place. Imagine the maintenance crew are going to be a little surprised when they discover what's causing the smell."

His mouth ticked up in an almost-smile. It was a nice almost-smile.

She was very tempted to kiss that mouth, and that almost-smile. But she didn't want to distract or startle him while he was flying.

He dipped his wings to one side, picking up a new air current, and banked to the left toward one of the tallest buildings around. Fascinated as she was by the sight of him, she turned away to assess where they were. Everything looked different from this angle, of course, but she was pretty sure they were somewhere in Mid-town, higher end, getting close to the park. Since it was the middle of the night and the park would be empty but for the unsavory types, she wondered if that's where they were heading. What did a dragon shifter care about unsavory human types, right?

But no, the tall building seemed to be his target.

Another of the older buildings, with excellent stonework, a mix of red brick and white stone balconies and accents. This one had a flat roof, with the usual old water tower and raised building where a stairwell would be. The edge around the roof was about waist high with lovely carved crenellated details. Landing on that roof in the arms of a dragon when those kinds of details reminded her of castles was as interesting as waking up high in the air with the city racing past below.

Interesting seemed to be her go-to word tonight.

She was trying to decide if she liked interesting or not when Christopher touched down on the roof. She normally liked interesting. Usually interesting meant fun. Glancing up at Christopher as he continued to hold her in his arms and stare down at her, she thought this might just be fun. She also thought his expression fascinating. And she was very tempted to touch his jaw and see how he reacted.

Then she frowned. "How old are you, really? In dragon terms." She raised her eyebrows. "Like, if I were to kiss you, would that be some sort of...child molestation?" The idea horrified her.

His expression turned into a scowl. "No. Of course not. I'm not *that* young." His scowl softened, but his frown didn't go away. "You really don't know much about dragon shifters, do you?"

"Nope." She shrugged and started to pat his chest so he'd set her down, but the feel of warm muscles and solid shoulders momentarily distracted her. So she let her hands linger on his skin. And because she was watching, she saw his eyes whirl from nearly black with a golden glow over them to something with a more purple glow. None of it like his blue eyes from earlier that night, but fascinating to watch.

"So..." she murmured. "Age-wise for a dragon?"

"Old enough," he said, his voice deeper now and his gaze more intent.

Her stomach tingled and tightened at that, a little tremor of excitement running through her. And again she thought the word *interesting*.

With a great deal of reluctance, she patted his shoulders and said, "Better set me down before you get tired."

Not that he showed any signs of that. He seemed to hold her like she weighed little and could do this all night. Which was a thought one step farther than her brain could handle at that moment.

He did slowly release her legs so she dropped to the ground, but he kept an arm around her as she got her balance. For which she was grateful, because the wobbly feeling she got standing on her own caught her off guard.

"So, what happened?" She vaguely remembered

getting hit by the wizard bolt, and the sensation of falling would stick with her for years. But then the blackness and... And that was it.

"The wizard was tossing around magic designed to render us unconscious, and they didn't care if you fell and died."

"Would you have died if you fell?" she asked.

"Not died. Just been wounded."

Still. "Glad none of that happened." She nodded to his wings. "You shifted in the air shaft?" His wings actually looked too big for the space they'd been in, so... "How did that work?"

"I can adjust the size of my wings," he said.

That earned him an eyebrow raise. "Wow. Might have been useful to know that earlier in the night."

"You didn't want me to shift."

She gave him a look.

"How did you end up working for my father if you know so little about dragon shifters?"

She waved a hand in the air. "Lost a stupid bet. Long story."

"We have time now."

She sighed. This was embarrassing. "The brief explanation is that I assumed when I broke into your father's hoard, I'd just steal the least valuable thing there was. No one would miss it. I'd get out and win my bet. No harm no foul. Except, I sort of underestimated how pissed your dad would be just by me getting into the hoard."

"Because no one should have gotten anywhere near his hoard," Christopher said, sounding both aghast and, she thought, maybe a little impressed. "Were you supposed to steal something in particular? Who hired you?"

His sudden intensity on those last two questions had her raising her hands, a defensive gesture. "First, no one hires me. Most of the time. I steal for myself. Not for other people. And I don't steal from people who would miss what I took. In fact, most of the people I steal from have so much stuff, they've forgotten most of it exists. Do you know how much *stuff* people collect?"

"I'm a dragon. I have an idea."

She both winced and smiled at that. "Your dad's hoard was pretty impressive." At his look, she said, "I wasn't there for anything in particular. Just a trinket to prove I'd managed to get in. It was a bet. A dare with financial backing, if you will. Old rival. We're always testing each other. I figured this one was easy money." She shrugged. "Who knew?"

"Anyone who knows anything about dragon shifters would have known."

"We've already established I don't know nearly as much as I should have." And really, she needed to rectify that situation. Or stop dealing with dragon shifters. Either way.

Except, as she looked up at Christopher, with his magnificent wings folded against his back, and that very interesting purple glow in his eyes, and his warm, solid shoulders, she knew she didn't want to stop dealing with *all* dragon shifters.

He crossed his arms over his chest. A gesture that emphasized his shoulders and chest muscles. She narrowed her eyes. Had he done that on purpose? He'd done that on purpose.

Then he spoke and she changed her mind about his motivation for crossing his arms.

"The shifters and wizard who kidnapped me? They wanted something from my father's hoard."

Shit. "I...didn't know that. Was that why your father was so pissed?"

"My father would always be pissed about someone breaking into his hoard. It's supposed to be impossible."

"Compliment? No? Okay, so... What did the shifters and wizard want? And what kind of shifters were these? Your father failed to mention the species." And the wizard. But she wasn't going to get into that part now.

Christopher skipped over the species question, too. "My father has a magical artifact that could turn shifters into indestructible monsters."

"That sounds bad."

"Which is why my father keeps it secured in his hoard where it's supposed to be safe from thieves."

"Oops?" She wasn't sure what to say to that. Breaking into the hoard had been challenging, but not impossible. At least not for someone like her. And frankly, she was a little proud of that. Even if it had gotten her into some trouble.

"The shifters couldn't find anyone to break in, no one capable of it anyway. They hired the wizard to help. He failed."

She wanted to wince again, but also wanted to preen.

"Did this rival of yours ask you to bring out something specific?"

"Nope. Nothing. Just something to prove I'd been there." But she was starting to see why this all looked very suspicious. "Why did your father send me to steal you back rather than kill me? He had to think I was part of all this."

"You weren't?"

"Of course not." She put her hands on her hips and glared at him. "I told you already, I wasn't going to steal anything of value or even anything specific. A coin or something would have done."

"But it could have just been a test run. Your rival setting you up to steal something larger for them later?"

She let her arms drop as she considered that. Damn it. "Possible. He's a real asshole. That wouldn't be beyond his machinations." Made her feel stupid for falling for the trick, though. She was going to have to repay that asshole. "Except I'm not a hired thief. I only steal for myself." She shrugged.

"Mostly for the challenge. And because I'm good at it." At his look, she said, "What? It's fun."

"Could he have 'bet' you that you couldn't steal something like the artifact? Would you have tried then?"

"No idea." At his scowl, she said, "If I didn't know what the artifact was, how valuable it was, or what it could do, I wouldn't agree until I'd done some research. Does that help?"

"And when you discovered what it could do?"

"You mean when I learned it could magically turn shifters into unkillable monsters, would I still steal it and hand it over to an asshole rival? No. Of course not."

She wanted to be offended that he'd asked. But to be fair, they'd known each other a few hours, and she was here because she'd broken into his father's hoard, and really, she didn't have a lot of moral ground to stand on when it came to thieving. Still. She wasn't the kind of thief to want indestructible shifters loosed on the world. That would be bad for everyone. Thieves included.

Christopher stared at her for a long moment, his arms still crossed, before he finally said, "My father must have seen that strange thread of honesty in you."

"Strange?"

"For a thief."

Okay. She'd give him that.

"Or he wouldn't have sent you to break in and free me."

"I am good at stealing things. Even things that have already been stolen." Which reminded her. "How on earth did they manage to steal you? Being as how you're..." She gestured at him, the sweep of her hands taking in the wings and vaguely referring back to the fact that he'd turned the shifters and wizard in those air ducts into burnt husks.

"Why do you keep referring to what happened to me as me being stolen and not me being kidnapped?"

"I don't deal with kidnappers. I'm a thief. I deal in stolen things."

"Semantics."

"But it works for me. So how did they manage to get to you?"

The faint color on his cheeks, high on those already cut cheekbones, was probably the most charming thing she'd ever seen.

"I was...tricked," he said, turning his head enough he was no longer meeting her gaze.

"Tricked?"

"They set a trap for me." His jaw locked tight on that.

She raised her brows. "Trap?"

"I might have a problem with..."

"With?" Her instincts rose and she stilled. What the hell did a dragon shifter have a problem with that it made him so nervous? Couldn't be anything good.

"I... I can't abide a..." He muttered the last few words so she couldn't hear them.

"A what?" She leaned in closer to hear him better.

"A damsel in distress," he barked out, without meeting her gaze.

She nodded, staring up at him for a long minute. "A dragon. Who worries about...damsels in distress? That's..."

"Interesting?"

"I was thinking more along the lines of ironic and funny, but we can go with interesting here." She felt a smile tugging at her lips and pressed them together so she didn't laugh out loud. "Spotted a woman in trouble. Swooped in to save the day. She was part of a trap. You got clobbered by the wizard's anti-dragon magic."

"Something like that."

"Oh, I have to hear this."

He huffed out a breath and she'd swear there was steam on the huff. He seemed to be radiating a little more heat, too. But it was really the rosy color in his cheeks she found most delightful.

"Mostly...it was like you guessed. She was a shifter, a lion shifter. Not in any danger in the end. And the wizard... They had the containment collar on me before I knew what was happening. Knocked me out. I woke up in the cell."

She nodded, her lips pursed, waiting for him to meet her gaze. He didn't. So she nudged his chin with her fingers. His skin was scorching hot, but it felt weirdly good and that was something she'd think about at some point in the future.

When he finally met her gaze, she said, "That's the sweetest way I've ever heard for someone to get trapped. No reason to be embarrassed."

"It's...not something my dragon brethren understand."

"I imagine. What with eating virgins and all that."

He scowled again and it wiped away some of the mortification in his expression. "That's real dragons. Not dragon shifters. And even real dragons don't always do that. And haven't done that in centuries."

"Told you I don't know much about dragons." She shrugged.

"You don't..." He let out a breath. "You don't think it's a weakness?"

"Not even a little."

"Got me captured by people who want to blackmail my father and steal an artifact to create monsters."

"Shit happens."

His charming smile cracked through his scowl. She returned it with a big grin. Bumping his shoulder, which was still really warm, she wandered closer to the edge of the roof, so she could take in the view.

"Pretty risky, you shifting, even partially, to rescue me. You could have let me fall."

"You did just hear what I said about damsels in distress, right?"

She chuckled. "Fine." She eyed the wings on his back, folded tightly over his spine, but the tops rising several feet above his already impressive height. "Still, pretty risking. Flying out over the city like that. Don't care how late it is, someone probably saw you."

"I cloaked—yes, I can do that—but people in the city wouldn't be expecting to see a partially shifted dragon, so even if they did see me, they wouldn't believe what they were seeing?"

"Probably think you were Batman or someone."

"You think my wings look like bat's wings?" He spread them out, puffing up in a way that was supposed to be impressive and succeeded spectacularly.

"Is that insulting to a dragon? I feel like you found that insulting." She laughed and said, "I like your wings."

"Hmm." He gave them a little flutter before folding them in tight to his back again.

She looked out over the dark cityscape, at the surrounding high-rises with their occasional lit windows, the dark shadow of Central Park a few blocks away, the lines of car lights running up and down the square Mid-town blocks. The wind was a lot less cold when they weren't flying, but it was still crisp and chilly on the rooftop. A sharp contrast to the heat pumping off the man next to her.

Not just man. Dragon.

So much she didn't know about dragons.

She gave him a look from the side of her eye. "Do you have a hoard? Like your father's."

"If I do, would you steal from it?"

"Nothing you'd miss," she said with a shrug.

His mouth twitched. Then more seriously, "What do you do with the things you steal?"

"If I need the money, I sell my take through a very cooperative auction house that likes the caliber of items I bring them. They don't ask too many questions of me or the purchasers, no one is really stuck on provenance, and we're all happy with the financial outcome of the exchange. If I don't need the money..." Shrug again. "I usually return whatever I stole the next night, or the next week."

He blinked down at her. "You return stuff you've stolen?"

"Sometimes. Depends. Why?"

"That's..."

She smiled. "Interesting?"

"That's a good word for it."

She nodded, her gaze skimming the skyscrapers, and the spectacular view of Manhattan from this height. "It is my go-to word tonight. Interesting."

"Speaking of." He moved just a little closer, his

gaze moving over the view like hers. "I seem to recall you saying something about kissing me."

"I did, didn't I?" She swallowed.

"You never did, though. Kiss me, I mean. Even though I'm old enough."

Her cheeks heated at the reminder of her worry. "I never did. I wasn't sure... I thought you might object."

"I wouldn't object."

She glanced up at him just as he glanced down at her. "Interesting," she murmured.

He smiled. A smile that sent a lot of trembly sparks through her body. A smile she could really get used to.

They leaned in at the same time. Meeting in the middle. Her going up on her toes. Him leaning over, a hand on the low wall circling the roof. His lips were incredibly soft. The kiss was very gentle. And her insides danced in such anticipation, she melted closer.

"Interesting," he murmured when he pulled back.

"Mmm." Yeah. The kind of interesting she'd like to indulge in more.

This close to him, she realized his scent was... different now. The flight or maybe the partial shift must have worked like a shower because there was no longer that low-level stress sweat smell. Now he almost smelled like...

"Why do you smell like sugar cookies now?" she asked.

He raised his brows. "Do you like sugar cookies?"

"Love them. But I've never smelled a person who smelled like sugar cookies." It was one of those sweet vanilla scents that made her want to get closer and draw more of it in. Subtle. Not overpowering. But there. Teasing her and making her a little hungry.

His smile did something more to that hunger. A hunger that had nothing to do with food.

"You should probably start to learn more about dragon shifters," he said.

Sounded like a threat and a promise at the same time.

Like a dare.

She was a sucker for a dare.

"Maybe I should." Her gaze dropped to his mouth. To that smile. Then she met his gaze. The purple glow over his blue eyes drew her like a lure. "We should probably let your father know you're out now."

"Probably." He glanced out over the skyline. "Want to fly there?"

She grinned and looked out over the skyline as well. "Sounds..." She gave him a look. "Interesting."

He laughed, the sound making her heart do that fluttery pounding thing. Then he swept her up into his arms so fast she gasped. She wrapped her arms around his neck. Feeling surprisingly secure like this.

"Hold tight," he murmured next to her ear. Then he bent his knees and launched into the sky, his wings snapping open and taking two powerful downbeats before he caught an air current that brought them higher.

Myra laughed even as her stomach dropped to her toes and a thin edge of fear sent adrenaline into her blood. She loved that feeling.

She glanced up at Christopher, just as he smiled down at her.

Yeah. She definitely needed to learn more about dragon shifters.

She had a feeling she was going to be spending a lot more time with one of them.

Now Pick a New Genre

Romantic
Suspense

CHAPTER ONE

Who steals a dragon?

That was the question Terri couldn't stop asking herself. Who the hell would steal a dragon?

Terri knocked on her ex's front door as she stared at the text. The quiet area in the middle of farm country in Connecticut was even quieter in the middle of the day. The surrounding houses built far apart, leaving enough land and space to give the illusion of privacy. There were some cows mewing in a field not too far away. The smell of grass and manure strong in the early spring air. It wasn't cold, which was good. But it wasn't warm either.

Harold would be very unhappy in this weather.

She looked up when the door in front of her opened and tried not to react. She hadn't seen Jim in a few weeks. Probably the longest they'd been apart in five years. She was still adjusting.

He looked good, though. Not particularly tall, but tall enough for her. Wide shoulders, a nice chest, good forearms. He worked with animals, so he stayed fit. But the thing that kept her silent a moment too long on his doorstep, the very first thing she'd noticed about him in that bar in New Haven five years ago, was his eyes. He had lovely dark brown eyes that reminded her of chocolate. Kind eyes. He'd always had kind eyes.

Blinking, she brought herself back to the present. They weren't together now for a reason, and she had to remind herself that reason was valid.

"I got your message," she said, straightening her shoulders. "What happened?"

"Terri," he greeted, his voice a deep rumble. "Thanks for coming."

She noticed the circles around his lovely eyes then. And the furrows in his brow and bracketing his mouth. "How long has Harold been missing?"

Harold was a twenty-year-old Komodo dragon who normally lived in a specialized enclosure in the back of Jim's house. Owning a Komodo wasn't safe for ordinary people, and violated laws without the right permits, but the people who'd bought Harold thought he'd be a fun display pet.

Until Harold had reached his full size and eaten some of their other pets.

Jim's animal rescue team had saved the dragon. But Harold, raised in captivity his whole life, couldn't be sent back to a more appropriate island nation and freed. He'd just die. And at the time, there hadn't been any sanctuaries for him, or zoos with room in their Komodo facilities.

So Jim had built the dragon a home in his backyard. He had the skills and the knowledge to keep the dragon safely, the connections to get the right permits for housing a Komodo dragon. And a love for the old guy that made doing anything else unthinkable.

Terri and Jim had been together then, and she'd helped him settled Harold. In fact, they'd moved Harold into the habitat on her and Jim's first anniversary. Every anniversary after that, they'd included Harold in the celebrations too, in whatever way they could.

She had a hard time not thinking of him as *their* dragon. She adored the big old Komodo as much as Jim did.

Jim gestured her inside. "As far as I can figure it, he was taken last night sometime."

"You're sure someone took him? He didn't just break out of the habitat and go for a walk?" She followed Jim down the long central hallway of his house, straight through the kitchen and out into the backyard. Which was ten acres of land, mostly grass with clumps of maple and oak trees, and a narrow creek running through the back five acres.

"He didn't break out," Jim said. "There was a note."

"A note?"

"I'll show you." He waved toward the habitat.

The building was large enough to give the Komodo room to wander around, about half the size of Jim's house. Filled with savanna scrub areas mixed with tropical forest, and most of the ground covered in sand, there was a skylight that let in a lot of natural sun, and lots of windows to keep the enclosure bright. But everything was reinforced to accommodate a Komodo dragon's strength. The temperature inside was kept at a balmy eighty degrees year-round. And there were timed sprinklers to simulate rainy and dry weather.

There were also rooms for storing Harold's food and medical supplies, the cleaning equipment for the habitat, and a smaller room for Harold to wait in when the habitat was being cleaned or when he needed medical attention. A local vet who'd retired from working at the Brooklyn Zoo came regularly to check in on Harold.

It had taken money and time to get the habitat right. Jim was justifiably proud of the work he'd put into the facility. She tried not to take it personally that he sometimes forgot how much she'd helped build it, too.

"The note was left taped to the observation window in the front," Jim said. "I haven't called the police yet. It said not to. But also, I don't think they'll care unless Harold gets free and starts eating pets."

"Animal control will care. Have you contacted them? Maybe the people at the rescue center?"

She'd been as close to Harold as Jim was, so leaving had meant leaving the dragon as well. She wasn't entirely sure why Jim had contacted her, of all people, and not animal control or his friends at the rescue center, but she was glad he had. She'd have been devastated to learn about this through the grapevine.

"The note warned he'd be killed if I contacted anyone but you," Jim said.

She frowned at that. "Me? Why me?" And while she was glad he had, the fact that whoever had kidnapped Harold had mentioned her was...weird?

They walked into the warm facility, the temperature more suited to the dragon than to her spring jacket. She slipped out of the jacket and hung it on a hook by the door, a move so habitual she only realized she'd followed the habit after it was done. And since thinking about old habits and her time with Jim left her sad, she pushed the thoughts away. They had other things to worry about.

She noticed Jim watching her, frowning a little,

but she couldn't read his expression. Or maybe she just didn't want to.

"Obviously, whoever kidnapped him knew about your...relationship with him," Jim said.

"Which means it's someone we both know? Not a stranger thinking they could extort money from you?"

"Not a stranger. But who do we know who would do something like this?" He led her into the storage room holding all the freezers and cabinets of supplies.

The entire facility had a pungent reptilian smell to it, which she found hard to describe to people. Sort of musty and musky, but also clean. Very uniquely reptilian. The storage room seemed to collect that scent and strengthen it, which meant this room in particularly was always more pungent than the rest of the habitat. Maybe because there weren't any trees and plants to offset the smell of dragon.

Jim stopped at the work table against one wall, under a series of shelves with boxes of medical supplies and various tools for handling Harold and his food. Jim picked up a piece of paper and handed it to her.

"I found that when I came out to feed him this morning. It took me some time to make sure he wasn't still in the habitat. A crackpot could have left it and not actually taken Harold."

She nodded. "Good precaution."

His slight smile made her want to smile back. Instead, she looked at the note.

The person who'd created it had gone with the cliché of cutting out letters from a magazine to make the note. Which seemed laborious when they could have just printed it up on any old printer. Printers were so generic nowadays Terri couldn't imagine they'd be easy to trace. Also, she kind of agreed with Jim. The police weren't likely to be interested in a missing Komodo dragon unless it started eating things it wasn't supposed to. They certainly weren't going to pull out a lot of forensic tests to hunt for Harold's kidnapper.

She didn't think animal control worried about forensic tests either.

But still, the kidnappers had written the note in those letters cut from paper magazines, pasted to a piece of unlined computer paper. It said:

We have your dragon. Contact your ex-girlfriend. She's the only one. If you call anyone else, we'll kill the dragon. Bring $10,000 by 8pm or the dragon dies

The kidnappers added a location for the meet-up below the threats.

Terri frowned at the note. "Why ten thousand? Why not more? Why eight pm? That's a weird time. Shouldn't it be midnight or something?" She held up the single piece paper. "They went to all the trouble of the note cliché, why stop with that one cliché?"

"For the note and time, I have no clue. The money, though, is probably because they know I couldn't get my hands on any more. That's what's left of the last grant I got for Harold's care and feeding."

Taking care of a Komodo dragon properly wasn't a cheap endeavor. That was the reason zoos and proper sanctuaries mostly took in these kinds of cases. Jim had used a combination of donations and grants from some science institutes to build the facility and ensure there was money for Harold's food and medical care. Jim had two different donors that gave regularly, sort of financially adopting Harold even as she and Jim had adopted him. But the rest came from once off donations and various grants.

At her suggestion, they'd set up a website with a webcam inside the facility to follow Harold and a "donate" button at the bottom of the screen. So people could enjoy watching Harold go about his day, and if they were so inclined, throw a little money toward his food. That idea had worked out really well. Nothing that would make Harold—or Jim— rich. But enough to supplement the other income sources.

She and Jim had both been so excited about the

way the website worked out, they'd celebrated with Chinese take-out and a movie night.

She shook off the memory. "So not only someone who knows us well enough to have you contact me, but someone with some knowledge of your financial situation? That's not good."

"No," he agreed.

"Any ideas?"

"I'm pulling blanks. Anyone I know who might have all that information would never risk taking Harold from his habitat."

Because Harold had been raised in captivity, he was actually pretty friendly with humans. Right up until the moment he wasn't. He was a great dragon. But not the kind of animal you turned your back on or got complacent with. And anyone who knew anything about the dragons knew that.

"Is any of his stuff missing?" she asked. "His collar and lead? Any of the catch poles?"

Jim blinked. "I didn't think about that. I was so worried searching for him, and then calling you, I forgot to check."

He hurried to the storage closet where they kept the catch poles and Harold's collar and heavy-duty chain leash. Again, thanks to a captive upbringing, Harold was used to a collar and lead, just like a dog, but he was so strong, it all had to be made from thick leather and heavy-duty chain links instead of softer fibers. And even then, it was entirely possible to pull anyone holding the leash off their feet without much trouble. Harold only walked on a leash when Harold was in the mood to walk on a leash.

The catch poles were for the moments when Harold didn't want to walk on a leash but they still needed to move him around for some reason—like habitat cleaning or a husbandry session.

"The collar and leash are missing," Jim said from inside the closet. He leaned back out and stared at her. "They knew where to get the collar. And Harold let them use it."

"Or you would have found a body instead of a missing dragon."

He raised his eyebrows and nodded. "I know it was nighttime and he's slower when we let the temperature in the facility drop, but still. He had to be okay with whoever took him putting that leash on."

"More and more like it's someone we know." But who did they know that Harold also trusted? Who would know all these details. Including where to get the leash. "The list of possible suspects shouldn't be that big," she murmured. "Who knew all this stuff. Who did *Harold* know that knew all this stuff?"

"Adam Wren?" Jim suggested.

Adam was one of the volunteers who helped them...helped *Jim* look after Harold. It was a never-ending job, caring for a dragon, and Jim did have work and times when he needed a break. Bringing in

Adam had been her idea. Well, not Adam in particular. But a volunteer or two to take up the slack so Jim wasn't running himself ragged. She'd had to pester him for six months before he finally gave in. Adam had been working with Harold for three years now. Which meant Harold would trust him.

But... "Adam doesn't seem the type to do this. Even a little bit."

"I know. That's the problem. No one I know seems to be the type to do this."

She frowned at the note again. "Can you get the money?"

"I already have it. I went and got it before texting you."

"You knew I'd come?" When she'd left, she'd wanted to make a clean break. Leaving had been hard enough. So she had asked him not to contact her unless it was an emergency.

"You said only in emergencies," he said, his voice quiet. "I wanted to...honor that request. This is an emergency, though, so I thought you'd come." He smiled a little, though the expression didn't quite reach his eyes. "It's Harold after all."

She picked at the edge of the note. "It's also our... our anniversary." Not that they *had* an anniversary anymore.

He nodded. "I didn't forget."

One thing he never forgot, she acknowledged. So many other things he did. So many other things got ignored or forgotten or overlooked. She got forgotten and overlooked.

But he'd always, at least, remembered their anniversary.

She looked down at the note so she didn't have to look at him. Looking at him in that moment hurt, and she wanted to worry about something else. She'd spent the last six months hurting over Jim. "Says we need to go..." She squinted at the lettering. "That field where we used to go, the one not far from West Rock Ridge State Park? That's a strange place to have the drop."

They'd met at a bar, but their first date had been a night stargazing at that field. There'd been a whole group of people. Not a quiet, romantic night necessarily. It had been an event planned by the university's astronomy department. And she'd mentioned when they met at the bar that although her specialization was biology, she loved astronomy, too. So he'd taken her to watch stars on their first day.

She pressed her lips together to hold in the rush of emotion from with that memory.

"They probably wanted someplace open. Someplace they'd know if we called the cops or animal control of something."

She shrugged. She'd never kidnapped a Komodo dragon before. She had no idea why they'd pick a big open field. But it was away from most houses. Pretty private, really. That's why the astronomy group used that particular area. So, she guessed that part made sense.

"You have Harold's cage loaded?" she asked.

"Ready to go."

He had a van that was big enough to slid in a cage to hold Harold securely. They would need that to get Harold back to his habitat.

She looked at the note again. Her worry for Harold growing. It was all so very strange.

But all she wanted was to get the dragon back. After that, Jim could worry about contacting the authorities. If he even wanted to.

"We'd better hurry," Jim said. "It's getting close to the meeting time."

They worked together to gather some things they'd need for Harold, like water, food, catch poles and safety harnesses for ensuring they could get the dragon safely into his cage for the trip home.

On the way out the door, Jim turned to her. "Thanks for...all this. For helping. For coming back."

"I'd do anything for Harold, you know that."

He smiled. "I was worried I'd screwed up so much, you wouldn't want to help me. Even for Harold."

"I don't hate you, Jim. That's not...not what happened." She sighed. "But we've had that conversation too many times. Let's go get our boy." She didn't want to talk about what had gone wrong between them anyway. She still hurt too much.

They loaded up the van quickly, heading out with enough time to reach their destination a half hour early. One of the things they'd always had in common—they both hated being late.

And this was one time when being late wasn't an option.

Chapter Two

The field was empty when they arrived. Since the kidnappers were expecting them to be there waiting, they didn't make any effort to hide their presence. They pulled into the middle of the field and parked.

The grass was mostly trampled and scraggly, a few snack wrappers caught in the weeds, evidence of the last astronomy club night. It wasn't exactly a scenic spot. At least the field itself. But it was perfect for stargazing.

The sun was just setting as they parked, so the stars weren't out yet. The gibbous moon would be up later in the night, which meant an early stargazer might get some good viewing in before moonrise. A breeze blew past the van, strong enough to shiver the vehicle briefly. It was going to be a chilly night, but at least it was dry, no signs of rain. Cold wasn't great for Harold, but at least he'd be easier to move across grass that wasn't muddy.

All she wanted was to get the dragon back safely to his habitat. Still, she couldn't help think something felt weird about all this. Something seemed off.

The person or people who'd kidnapped Harold had to know Jim, had to know her. Had to know the habitat well enough to locate Harold's gear. Know the money situation well enough to know how much money Jim could reasonably gather to pay a ransom.

All very very weird.

"Why?" she murmured as they sat in the van, staring out at the sky as it turned orange and purple.

"Money," Jim said with a shrug. "Why else?"

"There are easier ways to get money."

"Ten grand in a twenty-four-hour period? Not many ways."

"But kidnapping a Komodo dragon is dangerous. Who would think of that as their go-to for making a quick ten thousand? The dragon could kill them before they got around to collecting the money."

Harold was actually pretty tame around humans since he'd been raised by them. But he was still a wild animal with instincts. And if he was in danger, those instincts would drive him to lash out at the threat.

"Maybe whoever this is just didn't have other prospects for making quick cash and they really really need the money?" Jim didn't sound any more convinced than she felt.

"Still seems like a weirdly dangerous plan for so little money."

"So little? Ten grand isn't exactly falling from trees."

She rolled her eyes. "You know what I mean. Don't kidnappers usually ask for a lot more?"

"From rich people who can afford it? Probably. But I'm not a rich person who could afford a lot."

"Which I'm sure whoever this is knows. So why not kidnap or bribe or blackmail someone who's rich?"

"No opportunity," Jim said.

"A Komodo dragon isn't much of an opportunity either. And he's potentially deadly. If they don't know how to handle him properly, he could eat them. Most kidnapped people are not more dangerous than their kidnappers."

"How would you know that?" He gave her an amused look.

"I watch TV and listen to podcasts. You learn things."

He grinned. "Still listening to true crime, huh? I never got that. Doesn't it scare you? Knowing what *could* happen?"

"A little. Mostly, it makes me feel prepared. Plus, they're mysteries. I like mysteries."

"You like solving mysteries."

"True." She smiled.

For a split second, she completely forgot about the last six months. Really the last year. The moment felt like *them* when things had been good. When they'd been relaxed and easy with each other. When they'd still spent a lot of time together and no one had crawled into their work and forgotten other parts of life even existed for weeks and months at a time.

The split second ended in a melancholy sigh. She missed those times. When things had been good. She didn't miss being ignored.

As they waited, the silence started to feel uncomfortable. In the beginning, she hadn't minded their silences. Those had been as easy as the conversations. But eventually, when the silences carried more weight and meaning, when they'd started to last hours, sometimes days, she'd grown to hate them. Now, with all that history and baggage, the silence just felt awkward.

"How're the new volunteers working out?" she asked, desperate to fill the quiet.

Just before she'd left, Jim had taken on two new volunteers to help with Harold's care and feeding. One was a biology major at the university, looking to get into veterinary school and needed some good experience on her CV. The other was a young woman who purported to be an environmental activist and former member of PETA who'd grown disillusioned with the group and was looking to learn more. Jim had had his doubts about her. But Angelica had proved to be hard working and quick to learn. Gretchen, the future vet, was a steady hand with Harold, too. Which meant Jim had had enough help. Terri had hoped that would rectify things in their relationship.

It hadn't.

But she did want to know how the new volunteers were working out, if they were still there, or if he'd taken on new volunteers. While she and Jim weren't together anymore, she still hated the idea of him working himself into the ground.

"Great," he said. "Angelica has turned full PETA hater, so we've been able to work well together."

Terri laughed.

"And I think Gretchen will be a great vet. I'll be sorry to lose her when she starts school in the fall. She's taken over almost all of Harold's husbandry duties. The two of them get along well."

Terri felt a little pang at the pronouncement, and she wasn't sure why. Harold had never been just hers and Jim's. Yet knowing Harold like another person that much...

But she was the one who'd left. And it was good Harold like the person looking after his health needs.

"Good," she said, trying very hard to be sincere.

"I'm really glad they're working out. You needed the help."

"I've been trying," he said softly. "Learning how to...let other people do things so I can focus on what's happening around me better. Trying not to lose my whole self in the work."

"You're dedicated. That's not a bad thing." She felt like she had to make that clear. It was never his dedication to his work. It was the fact that he used work to ignore everything else in life. Including her.

"It's a bad thing when work is all I let in. I..." He stared out the front windshield for a moment. "I hid in my work. A lot. I thought, if I wasn't completely obsessed with it, maybe I didn't care enough. Maybe I wasn't the kind of person I should be in order to do the conservation and rescue work I wanted to do. Like, if it didn't consume my life, I wasn't...real." He winced. "Wow, does that sound ridiculous when I say it out loud."

"Not ridiculous," she said. "Just wrong." He looked at her sharply. So she said, "You were always good at what you do, caring and dedicated enough. Obsession isn't necessary and never has been. You're better at your work when there's a balance in your life." She glanced away this time, looking out the window. "Work was just an excuse."

"One I shouldn't have made."

She didn't look at him, just shrugged.

"I didn't understand what I was losing, Terri. I didn't get how much I was hurting you."

She tried to wave that away. "It's done now. We've moved on. It's better this way."

"It's not, though. Not better at all. And I haven't moved on. I keep walking through the door, opening my mouth to talk to you, realizing you're not there anymore... And I hate it with every fiber of my being."

"Funny. You never used to try talking to me that much. At least not in the last year. That was the problem. You wouldn't walk in and talk to me right away. You'd brood and ignore my presence."

And it had never been mean. Never snapping at her to leave him alone or getting irritated if she talked to him. He just drifted off when she made an effort at conversation, his attention turning to things other than what she was saying, or he never made the effort to talk to her. She was pretty sure he'd had no idea what was going on in her life that last year. No idea what she was doing, or going through, or thinking. He'd never been mean, or purposefully cruel, though. Just treated her to a benign sort of disinterest that was impossible to live with after a while.

"And I didn't listen when we did talk," he said. "At least not when you talked."

She pressed her lips together, shrugged. He was right. What could she say.

"I finally got that when I started missing the sound of your voice and realized I had no idea what you were doing."

She couldn't help the bitter little laugh that escaped. "You didn't know what I was doing even before I left."

"And I realized that, too. After you were gone." His voice dropped to a whisper. "I didn't like that realization. Didn't like it at all."

She didn't know what to say to that, so she didn't say anything, just kept her gaze on the rough grassy field, the deepening night.

"I've missed you," he said. "And I'm sorry."

She closed her eyes. Tears gathering even as she tried to will them away. "Miss you, too," she murmured around the thickness in her throat.

"Terri, I'd hoped, maybe... I wanted to contact you, see if you'd be willing to try, maybe just, maybe try a date. Let me try to prove I can do better. Be there for you. The way you are for me."

"I don't know. I don't know." A risk, giving in and trying again. No real reason to think he wouldn't go right back to ignoring her once she was in his life again. He missed her now and so would make an effort for a while. But what happened when he got tired of making the effort?

He opened his mouth to say something but headlights from across the field stopped him. They both turned to face the rumbling truck heading their way.

Jim murmured something under his breath, and when she glanced at him, he was frowning.

"What's wrong?" she asked.

"That truck is familiar."

"We thought it had to be someone you knew, who knew us."

She looked at the truck again. Late model Ford, in a pale color she thought, but it was hard to tell in the dark with the headlights pointing at them. The truck wasn't particularly familiar to her, but that didn't mean much. She hadn't been around for six months.

"Do you know who it is?" she asked.

Before he could answer, the truck cut its engine and the headlights, plunging the clearing into darkness again. Terri could just make out a person shape behind the steering wheel, but couldn't see any identifying features.

For a long moment, no one moved. Then the person in the truck opened their door. Terri glanced at Jim. They opened their doors and climbed out of the van simultaneously.

The person in the truck stepped out next.

A woman, Terri could see now. Tallish, wearing an oversized coat and leggings, boots that looked sturdy. She wore a wool cap, which covered most of her hair but not completely. Enough, though, that Terri couldn't see her hair color. Her features were shadowed. In the dark, at a distance, Terri didn't recognize the woman at all.

But Jim sucked in a sharp breath and cursed quietly.

"Who?" Terri whispered.

"Gretchen," he said.

Chapter Three

Terri frowned at the woman standing just beside the Ford parked not fifty feet away as a cold breeze brushed her cheeks. The night had descended fully, leaving the grassy, open field dark except for the truck's headlights.

Gretchen. Jim said that was Gretchen. The kidnapper was one of the volunteers working with Harold? The one headed to veterinary school?

Well, they'd known the kidnapper had to be someone who knew Harold and his habitat pretty well, but still... Gretchen hadn't seemed like the dragon-kidnapping type.

"Why is Gretchen ransoming Harold?"

"Money," Jim said.

Terri supposed that made some since—the woman had asked for money. But... The whole thing felt weird. If the money was for college, ten grand was a drop in the bucket. Hardly worth the risk since Jim would obviously know her and could turn her over to the police. Hell, he could even contact her university and get her expelled from the program. Why take this kind of risk for money that wouldn't even begin to pay for veterinary school expenses? Especially when kidnapping Harold was an extreme risk all on its own.

The only good thing was that, "At least she knows how to handle a Komodo dragon."

Jim's mouth flattened into a line, but she couldn't interpret his expression.

Gretchen moved forward enough she stood in front of her truck, but didn't get any closer. The headlights at her back threw her into shadows and made seeing her face and expression difficult.

After a moment's hesitation, Jim started forward and Terri kept pace. They stopped still a hundred yards away. Gretchen didn't look to be carrying a weapon, but her coat was large enough to hide a hand gun. And she did keep one hand in a pocket.

Jim was the first to speak. "Why?"

"And how is Harold?" Terri added.

"Harold is fine," Gretchen said.

Answering the most important question first as far as Terri was concerned. She appreciated that, even if it was Gretchen's fault Harold was in danger to begin with.

"I would never hurt him," she added.

"Then why take him from his home? Why risk injuring him, or yourself?" Jim said. "If you needed money, you could have asked."

The irony is that Jim would have worked with Gretchen to get money for college. Grants or scholarships or whatever it took. That was the kind of person he was. At his heart, he was a very good man. Which was one of the many reasons Terri had stayed as long as she had, and why leaving had been so hard. He wasn't a bad man. And never had been. In fact, he was generous and kind. The type of person who would absolutely have tried to help one of his volunteers get the financial aid they needed for school.

He'd just been...so very absent from their relationship. There was only so much benign neglect she could take. But his kindness and generosity were never in question.

"You really don't understand, do you?" Gretchen asked. "But you have to know, you have to realize."

"I don't have a clue why you're doing this," Jim said. "Or why you'd bring Terri into it. You don't even know her."

He was right. They'd met maybe two or three times, just before Terri left. Why would Gretchen even think to involve her?

Again, Terri got the feeling something was really off about all this. It couldn't just be about money.

"Can we see Harold?" she asked as worry for the dragon got the better of her. She was restless and edgy wondering if Harold was actually in the back of that truck or not. They hadn't seen or heard him yet. Was he really okay?

"You can see him in a minute. I've given him a light sedative. To keep his stress levels down."

Terri wasn't sure if that made her feel better, or more worried. Gretchen wasn't a vet yet. And sedatives for Komodo's, for any animal, could be tricky.

"First, we all need to talk," Gretchen said. "This was the only way I could think to get you both in the same place."

That...didn't make sense. Or sound good. A shiver of apprehension moved down Terri's spine.

"What are you talking about?" Jim asked. He took a half step closer to Terri.

That small move felt protective and strangely reassuring in this very bizarre situation.

"I'm talking about us, darling," Gretchen said. "Until you let her go, until she lets you go, we'll never be free to be together. We needed to all talk this out like grownups. But whenever I mentioned her name, you shut down. It's important we make peace. And Harold was the only thing that would put you both back in the same room. So to speak." She gestured at the field with a little wave of her hand.

"Darling?" Terri raised her brows at Jim. She

hadn't realized he'd started seeing someone new. Not that it was her business anymore. But it seemed like something he should have mentioned earlier. Especially after he recognized Gretchen.

And the punch of hurt and sadness she felt was of no consequences. She'd left. He could move on. It had been six months. They were both *supposed* to be moving on. Right? Right.

But Jim's expression gave her pause. He didn't look chagrined or annoyed or anything she might expect of a man whose current girlfriend pulled this kind of stunt. He just looked confused. Truly baffled.

"What are you talking about, Gretchen? What 'us'?"

"Darling. Don't be coy. It's important she knows. That our love is acknowledged in front of her so everyone can move forward. Honesty in these situations is very important."

"And I'm honestly just confused. There is no relationship between us, except for work colleagues. I'm not even sure how you might have gotten that idea."

"Jim. I know you love me. It's obvious. But I also know you're still harboring some unresolved feelings for Terri. We're here to resolve those feelings."

"No, I... I don't know what you're talking about, Gretchen,"

He looked and sounded so sincerely confused, Terri believed him. This wasn't an act on his part. He wasn't that good an actor. He literally had no idea that Gretchen had feelings for him. In fact, Terri was absolutely certain, knowing Jim as she did, that even if Gretchen had been blatant about her feelings, Jim still wouldn't have noticed.

She wasn't sure whether to be appalled by all this or angry. The irony of the situation was not lost on her, though.

"I'm not sure I'm supposed to talk here," Terri said, "but he really doesn't understand. I'm afraid unless you've heard him declare his feelings out loud and in person, he doesn't have them. He's not a subtle man."

"Thank you," Jim said. "I think."

"Not an insult, I promise. Just a truth." She sighed a little. His straightforward approach to life was one of the things she'd fallen in love with. No games. But also, no ability to notice subtleties. At least in humans. He'd always read Harold's body language better than he'd ever read hers.

Speaking of which, "May we see Harold. Make sure he's okay."

"Not until this is settled." There was a bite in Gretchen's voice now. A hiss that hadn't been there before. "I know you love me, Jim. You need to admit it. And make sure she hears you've moved on. It's the only way forward. For both of you."

"Gretchen, I'm so very sorry. I don't know how you got the impression I had feelings for you. I never meant to give that impression. I'm so sorry if I did."

Terri's heart twisted a little. He sounded so genuinely upset. And of course he was. He was a good man who didn't *want* to hurt people. Yet, somehow, he still managed it through unawareness.

He looked at her, his expression pained. "See the problem is, I'm still in love with Terri. And... And that's it. I'm still in love with you." This last he said to her directly instead of speaking to Gretchen.

"Jim." What a horrible moment for the admission to come. Especially because she felt the same. She hadn't yet been able to stop loving him. Loving him had never been the problem.

"This wasn't what I was hoping to do today," he murmured quietly. "I'd intended on inviting you over and talking, and... And I got you an anniversary present, and I was hoping to convince you to give me a second chance. With all the conversation and counseling and whatever we needed to make things work this time."

"You..." She swallowed. "You want to get back together?"

"I never want to be without you again. But I know I have work to do. I need to learn how to...to pay attention. And how to listen when you tell me I haven't been. I never meant to ignore you. I can learn to do better."

Tears made her vision blurry. She blinked a few

times, trying to clear them without letting them drip down her cheeks. "Okay. Okay. We can talk. We can work on it."

"No!" Gretchen shouted. "That's not what's happening here. Jim loves me. I saw the gift you got me."

"That's for Terri, Gretchen. Why did you think it was for you."

"You told me it was! You said it was for me!"

His brows bunched. "When did I do that?"

Terri wondered the same. He might be forgetful, and he might be very bad at noticing the people around him sometimes, but he wouldn't have lied about something like that. In fact, she couldn't even imagine what he could have said to give Gretchen the wrong idea.

Either one of them was lying—and if it was Jim, he'd become a much more devious person in the last six months than he'd ever been—or Gretchen was maybe a little delusional.

An idea that made Terri's stomach tighten, anxiety spiking in her blood.

Some hissing and movement from the truck drew all their attention. Harold, moving around. He must be coming out of the sedative Gretchen had given him. Terri hoped that meant he was okay. She knew he was alive now at least. A relief that made her knees wobbly.

"We need to check on him," Terri said. "Make

sure he comes out of the sedative okay and doesn't hurt himself in the cage."

"No!" Gretchen snarled at her. "We're not finished here yet."

"We have to be," Jim said. "This was all a misunderstanding. A mistake. But we can walk away. Forget it ever happened."

"No. No, you're lying. You're lying to her. Why, Jim? Just admit the truth and we can all move on,"

More movement. Then some knocking around in the back of the truck. Enough to worry Terri. "He might hurt himself," she said. "He'll be confused. We need to check on him."

"He'll be fine," Gretchen snapped. "We have to settle this."

"It's settled," Jim said. "I'm truly sorry I misunderstood what you thought was happening between us was more than colleagues. I'm sorry I gave that impression. I did not mean to hurt you, and I am sincerely sorry for causing you pain. But I am in love with Terri. Still. Always. And that's all there is to it." He spread his hands out, in a kind of surrender. "I don't know how to be any clearer."

"You're lying," Gretchen said, her voice low. "I don't know why you're lying to me. To her. But you have to stop. Now."

More bumping from the back of the truck. A hiss. A rattle of bars. The truck rocked behind Gretchen.

Panic started to kick in. Harold was going to hurt himself. They needed to get to him. He'd had such bad experiences in little cages before Jim's group rescued him. The dragon finding himself in a small cage again was likely to cause a huge amount of stress. That was the kind of stress that could kill an animal just coming off sedation.

"We'll have to deal with the misunderstanding later," Terri said. "Harold needs attention."

Jim started toward the truck, and Terri hurried to follow.

"No!"

CHAPTER FOUR

Gretchen threw herself at them so suddenly, Terri didn't even have time to react. One moment she was rushing to help Harold in the back of the pickup truck, and the next, there was a screeching woman hitting and kicking her.

Instinctively, Terri covered her head, ducking down as Gretchen swung wildly at her, scratching her arms, pulling at her hair.

"He loves me! Not you. He's mine."

"Gretchen, stop. Stop!" Jim there, somewhere.

The pummeling and slaps stopped abruptly. Terri looked up to see Jim had wrapped Gretchen up in a hold from behind, keeping her arms pinned at her sides. Gretchen kicked out and flailed against Jim's hold, screaming and cursing.

"Are you okay?" he asked Terri.

"Fine." She looked at her arms and hands. "Few scratches. I'll need some antibiotics I think." She was probably being petty with that comment. But honestly, humans were dirty. The last thing she needed was an infection from scratches given to her by a jealous romantic rival. Not that she'd known she was anyone's rival for Jim's affection.

"I've got her," Jim said. "Go check on Harold."

Terri nodded. On the way past, she almost asked if they should call the police now. But she didn't want to set Gretchen off until they'd checked on the dragon. Gretchen was thrashing around enough against Jim's hold as it was.

In the truck bed, Gretchen had a large transport cage, the kind with solid metal sides instead of bars. This kind of cage made it harder for the dragon to hurt himself and also made him harder for outsiders to see—probably would have been hard to drive around with a Komodo dragon in the back of the truck without someone noticing the giant lizard. Anything or nothing could be in the solid cage. It was braced with nylon straps clipped to the corner hooks in the truck bed's walls. Seemed to be solid enough, so the cage probably hadn't bounced around when Gretchen was driving. A least Terri hoped.

She lowered the tailgate as the thrashing inside the transport carrier got louder. "Shh, big guy. Shh. It's just me. Terri. 'Member me?" She made soothing sounds as she crawled up onto the gate to look inside the cage window. She was greeted by a low hissing sound. "Yeah, big guy, I know you're upset. No fun being kidnapped and drugged, huh? Don't worry. We'll get you home. Jim is here. We're here to take care of you."

She kept murmuring quietly until Harold stopped thrashing so much. His face appeared near the carrier window bars and his tongue flickered out, a long taste of the air. She stayed close enough to the cage he'd be able to taste her scent. Before leaving, she'd been sure Harold knew her. He'd responded to her voice and seemed content to have her around. But after so many months, did the Komodo even remember her? They weren't dogs or cats. He hadn't been her pet, in any traditional sense. She couldn't be sure he'd even know her still. But she really hoped the sound of her voice was familiar enough to settle him.

He stopped hissing and issued a little rumbling sound. He didn't throw up his last meal—when had he last eaten?—and he definitely sounded calmer.

"Good," she said quietly. "Good. We're here to take you home." She gave the cage a pat as if she were patting Harold in reassurance. "I'll be right back. I need to talk to Jim about transferring you to the van so we can get you home."

She slid off the tailgate and returned to the front of the truck. "He's okay," she told Jim. "We just need to get him home. I can't tell if he's injured or not."

Gretchen had stopped kicking and bucking

against Jim's hold, she was now looking up at him with this sort of besotted expression that was hard to look at. Terri tried not to. Jim was a handsome man, but the naked adoration and obsession in Gretchen's expression was painful.

"We need to call the police now," Jim said.

Gretchen's eyes rounded. "What? No. Why the police? You love me. Everything will be fine now."

"You kidnapped and endangered a protected animal and potentially endangered other lives if he'd escaped," Jim said. "And you tried to extort money from me for him."

"No. I never wanted the money. That was just to get you both here. She understands now, darling. You can let her go."

Terri sighed. It was as if Gretchen hadn't even heard the earlier conversation, or the way Jim had declared he still loved Terri. There was no reasonable way to end this without the police if Gretchen refused to acknowledge reality.

"Would you let us take Harold and just go?" she asked. Just to see if there was any way out without involving the authorities.

"Jim isn't going anywhere without me," Gretchen said, scowling at Terri. "You see how he's holding me? How we are together? You have no place here. Leave him alone. He's mine."

Terri raised her brows at Jim. He shook his head.

"Call the cops," he said. "Let them know we have Harold here so they don't freak out."

"They'll want animal control here, too." She pulled out her cellphone and dialed 911.

"So long as animal control doesn't interfere with our handling Harold, we can deal with them."

"No!" Gretchen started thrashing in Jim's hold again, so hard she got her whole body off the ground as she kicked out.

Jim grunted with the effort to hold her. Terri looked into the truck cab as she spoke to the 911 operator, explaining the situation and that the Komodo dragon kidnapper was struggling—that's what all the screeching was about. Terri paused, her mouth going slack as she spotted the gun on the truck seat.

"Don't let her go," she said to Jim, but let the emergency operator hear her. "She has a gun in here."

"There's a firearm on site?" the operator asked, her voice calm and professional.

"Yes. On the seat of the truck driven by the dragon kidnapper."

"Is anyone in immediate danger?"

"No. But get the police here quick."

"They're on their way."

Terri heard some tapping on the other end of the line and a calm, "First time I've typed dragon kidnapper."

Terri wasn't sure whether to laugh or groan at that. "Weirdest call ever?" she asked.

"No," the operator said. "But close. Police should be there in five minutes. I'll stay on the line until they arrive."

Given there was a gun in the truck, and Gretchen was struggling hard against Jim's hold, Terri murmured her thanks to the operator.

CHAPTER FIVE

The sounds of approaching cars—no sirens as Terri had requested so they didn't upset Harold further—rolled into the open clearing a few minutes later. The wash of all the headlights lit up the usually dark field, blotting out the spectacular star speckled night sky above. The breeze had died down in the last few moments, but the air still had a cold spring bite.

Gretchen fought against Jim's hold harder when the police cars appeared, screaming. "No. No. This isn't right. He's mine. Why did you call the police?"

Terri ignored her to talk to the cops. They took over from Jim so he was finally able to let Gretchen go. But she never stopped shouting and protesting, even after the police had secured her in the back of one police car.

The next hour involved a lot of giving statements, and after animal control arrived, verifying permits and moving Harold to Jim's van. The cops sat in their cars during the transfer. But Harold seemed so relieved to see Jim, he let him put the collar around his head and neck without even a hiss. The two animal control officers helped Terri lift Harold from the back of the truck as Jim stayed at his head. Then helped her get him into the van, though on that side, Harold helped climb up into the van himself, so there was a lot less lifting necessary. The dragon seemed as eager to get home as she and Jim were to get him there.

A few more questions answered before they could leave. The police bagged the gun in Gretchen's truck—it was a real gun, not a stun or dart gun for Harold, but an actual gun with a full magazine of bullets. Terri shuddered to think what Gretchen had intended with that. Any possibilities she could come up with involved bad things for Terri, Jim, and Harold.

Jim debated pressing charges, but the presence of the gun seemed to be his deciding factor. He agreed to come into the station after they'd gotten Harold settled. Terri had to come in to, but she agreed to take turns with Jim, so one of them could stay with the dragon.

By the time they got Harold home and resettled

in his habitat with fresh food and the quiet heat of his shelter, Terri was exhausted. But some of the exhaustion was relief. Relief Harold was home. Relief things hadn't been worse. Relief Gretchen hadn't had the chance to use her gun.

So much relief, Terri found herself collapsing into a chair in Jim's kitchen, a hot cup of tea on the table in front of her, her whole body trembling as the adrenaline finally drained away.

"You okay?" Jim asked, sitting next to her and taking one of her hands in his.

She laughed weakly. "Fine. Shaken. Coming down off all that fear and worry."

"Some way to spend our anniversary, huh?" He looked at their hands, his expression sheepish. "This wasn't exactly the plan."

"But you had one," she said in wonder. "You had a plan for today."

"A more romantic and groveling plan. Yup."

"Groveling?"

"Begging forgiveness. Promising to do better. Telling you all about the counseling I already started so I could ensure I didn't sink back into ignoring you when I got overwhelmed by external factors demanding my attention."

"You're...you're seeing a counselor?"

"It took me a while to really hear what you'd said when you left, what you'd been trying to tell me before you left. I thought you were being too sensitive. Unreasonable." He winced at her scowl but didn't release his hold on her hand. "I know. I know. But I had to talk it out with a neutral person to work through all that. So I did. I wanted to win you back, and I knew that wouldn't happen if nothing changed. But I had to figure out what I needed to do to make you happy, to keep from hurting you in the exact same way all over again."

"I can't believe you did all that. For me."

"I love you, Terri. Still. Always. I hadn't intended a kidnapping to be how we reconciled." He winced again. She tightened her hold on his hand. "But the one thing I can say about Gretchen's actions was it brought us back together. And, I hope..." He swallowed. "I hope you'll, maybe, give me a second chance?"

She stared into his beloved brown eyes. At the man she'd loved since their first date in that open field watching the stars. Could she risk her heart again, and hope for better, for a relationship with more communication and less benign neglect? He obviously wanted to try, wanted to do the work enough, he'd even gotten counseling.

If he was that serious about giving their relationship another try, she could take the risk too. In fact, she thought the risk might be very worth the reward in this case.

"What present did you get me?" She narrowed her eyes and watched him smile that familiar, beloved smile.

"The new astronomy book by your favorite author. Signed. Had to go all the way into Manhattan for it."

"You got me a signed copy." She sighed and let her own smile out. "Our second first date sort of leaves a lot to be desired, though." She leaned forward so they were face to face.

"Not an anniversary tradition I think we'll adopt," he agreed.

"Think we'll tell this story in the future?"

"How we found each other again when someone kidnapped our dragon?"

"Seems only right. Harold has been with us from the beginning. Seems appropriate he'd bring us back together again."

"I'll be sure to add something special to his next meal in thanks."

"Starting over?"

"Fresh start."

"Okay. Okay."

He smiled. And kissed her gently. Even exhausted and emotionally wrung out, the kiss felt wonderful. Like returning after a long trip and wrapping up in her favorite blanket. Like coming home.

"Happy new anniversary," Jim murmured.

Terri smiled, and kissed him again, and decided this was definitely an anniversary for the books. One she'd never forget.

Now Pick a New Genre

Contemporary
Romance

Chapter One

Who steals a dragon?

Jake reflected on that question yet again as he walked into his third pawnshop of the day. This one was a little more open than the last. Less dark. Not quite as dusty. There was still a chaotic jumble of stuff everywhere, but this place looked more like an antique store or a collectibles store than the last pawnshop he'd been in which had smelled like smoke and despair.

The despair was still here, in the obviously large number of items people had to pawn over the years, but at least there wasn't that ground in cigarette smell permeating the air. This place just smelled like old stuff, a little musty. That weird combination that came with too many things sitting around collection dust. But at least the place was well-lit and open. If the dragon was here, he'd be able to see it.

Which brought him right back to the question... who steals a dragon?

It's not like the little gold medallion charm was particularly valuable. Not more than an inch across, and gold-plated, not solid gold. A European dragon, with thick body and wings, sitting in the center of round disk. There was some tiny writing around the edges, an old saying he hadn't looked at in years. The charm was just something that had amused his little sister. Passed down from their mother, who'd also just kept it as a fun token. His sister, Mary, had kept it on her for luck over the years. When she moved to England to marry the love of her life, she'd left him the charm so he'd have some good luck of his own.

And instead of luck, the charm got stolen.

A part of him was tempted to just leave it. Mary probably wouldn't even notice if he had it on him or not. She was swept up in the newlywed life and had bigger things to think about—like finding a job and a place to live that wasn't her husband's tiny flat.

Besides, he wasn't interested in finding a relationship of his own now anyway. The last one had ended badly. He wasn't in the mood to put himself through that drama again. Nice quiet life. That's what he wanted. The last couple of years of quiet had been...great. Perfect. Just him and his dog Chester and nothing at all to worry about.

Except now for the missing dragon.

He went straight to the jewelry cases and started hunting through the various pieces set out under glass, the things people had pawned and weren't coming back for. He wasn't sure where else to look if this place didn't pan out. Maybe the thief had kept the charm? It wasn't really worth enough to sell. At least he couldn't imagine it was worth that much. Mary had gotten it from their mother who'd gotten it from her grandmother, so maybe because it was old someone thought it was worth a lot?

But people at a pawnshop would know a piece of tin from a real valuable piece of jewelry, wouldn't they?

"Can I help you find something?"

The soft, quiet, unexpected voice made him straighten so suddenly, he bumped his head against a rack of gold chains hanging over the glass counter.

He winced and rubbed his head.

"Oh, sorry," the soft voice said. "Didn't mean to startle you."

He turned to face the woman, not entirely sure what he was expecting. Whatever it was, though, the expectation fell short.

Carmen Fuentes?

Holy hell, it was Carmen Fuentes.

Older of course. He hadn't seen her since the end of their sophomore year of college, that last year he'd lived in Vegas before moving to California to finish his degree. Definitely not since then. But the years had been more than kind to her.

He cleared his throat, but couldn't quite managed words yet. She looked amazing. Tall as he remembered, almost as tall as he was, which meant he was looking her directly in the eyes. Eyes which were a surprising shade of purplish blue. He wasn't sure he'd ever seen eyes that color in real life anywhere else. That one movie star was supposed to have purple eyes, but they just looked blue to him. Carmen's eyes definitely had some purple inside the blue, around the iris. Impossible to forget, despite his best efforts.

Her striking eyes were in a striking face as well. Pretty wasn't really the word for Carmen, though. She wasn't conventionally pretty. But...striking. The kind of woman that made you stop and look closer. Her dark, nearly black hair was pulled up into a functional, neat bun, and she wore a red polo shirt with the logo for the pawnshop on it.

That logo brought him back to his surroundings.

The pawnshop. The stolen dragon. And a woman he hadn't seen in years standing behind the counter. After he'd just made a fool of himself bouncing his head off gold chains.

Given the last few days, he really should have expected this.

Did she even remember him? Probably not. Why would she? He was the dorky writer who'd had a crush on her throughout high school. And they'd become friends for the two years of college when he'd been here. But they'd never dated or been anything other than friends. He'd been too terrified to ask her out, to let her see his crush.

Or maybe it had been more than a crush. Hard to say for sure after all these years. Based on the way his heartbeat was hammer and his palms were starting to sweat, he was going to say probably more than a crush.

But she'd been a valuable friend who'd gotten him through those first two years of college. He would have dropped out and ended up working some go-nowhere job if not for her. He definitely wouldn't have taken the chance on going to California and trying to get a job writing for TV and film.

He'd been terrified of fucking up that invaluable friendship by admitting he wanted more than that from her. So he'd kept his crush to himself.

Unfortunately, when he'd moved to LA, the friendship didn't survive the distance. Time and life happened. The emails and calls faded away. When was the last time they'd talked? Eight years ago? Nine? Closer to ten, actually.

A long time. Long enough, he wasn't surprised there was no spark of recognition. He couldn't imagine their friendship had been nearly as important to her as it was to him. Her face was imprinted on his soul. He'd have recognized her anywhere. Yet here they stood with a glass counter between them and her looking at him like he was a stranger.

Maybe that was for the best.

"Is your head okay?" she asked, with a little smile as she reached up to steady the swinging rack with the gold chains.

Smiling at him. But in a distant, shop clerk-to-customer sort of way. Not a "hey you're my long-lost friend" kind of way.

"Fine," he said. Cleared his throat. Why did his voice sound strained? He tried to stay on track, though inside he was reeling. Of all the places he might have randomly bumped into her again, this was not what he'd expected. She'd had dreams too, back in the day. None of them had involved the family business. "I'm looking for a particular medallion." He formed a circle with his fingers. "About this size. Gold. Has a dragon in the middle of it."

"What kind of dragon?" she asked.

He blinked. "You have medallions like that with more than one type of dragon on it?"

"We have a lot of things, sir." Another small smile.

The "sir" caught him off guard. That distant, professional tone coming from Carmen hit him wrong. He glanced around. "Yeah. I noticed. Does anyone come back for their stuff after they've pawned it?"

"Not often." She shrugged. "But they get the money they need and the new owners of the items get something they want. Win-win for everyone."

"Including the pawnshop owners who make a profit."

"Couldn't stay in business if we didn't make money." She responded with complete equanimity, not rising even a little to his sardonic comment.

He admired that. She'd been that way in college, too. Clear about the realities of life. And unapologetic when she lived according to those realities. "May I see the dragon medallions you have?" he asked, dragging his focus back to the reason he was here. If there was more than one medallion, he might as well see them all rather than trying to describe his sister's dragon.

Funny how he thought of that charm as his sister's rather than their mother's. He'd never seen his mother wearing it, whereas his sister wore the charm from high school until last week, the week before her wedding when she'd passed it to him.

Carmen reached beneath the glass case and pulled a few boxes out from underneath. The fact that there was more than one box coming out made his eyes widen. How the hell was he going to find *his* medallion in all that?

But after pulling out four boxes, she glanced

inside three of them and put them back. She looked up and smiled again. "Always the last box you look in, right?"

He nodded, but he was caught up in her smile and not sure how to respond. She had a really lovely smile. She had always had a smile that captivated him. In fact, it was one of the first things he'd ever noticed about her. And such a soft voice, too. Not high or squeaky or even wispy and light. Just...soft. Like a gentle caress.

Shaking off the distraction that mingled with old memories, he looked into the box she pushed across the glass case to him. Inside were about a hundred little medallions. The range and selection were impressive. Everything from old fashioned cameos with silver edges, the image inside a silhouetted of a dragon instead of a woman, to simple silver designs with only the vague outline of a dragon, to solid gold medallions with dragons and saints fighting on them. What was that saint again...? George someone, right? Fought the dragon? He couldn't remember.

He must have mumbled the last out loud, because Carmen answered. "Saint George. You had it right."

"Thanks," he muttered, a little embarrassed she'd caught him mumbling to himself about saints. "There are a lot of dragon medallions and charms here." An inane comment, really, but he hadn't seen so many in one place before. "I've been to a couple of other pawnshops and none of them had this many. A few places didn't have any at all."

"No dragon medallions or no medallions period?"

"No medallions period. That was one of the smaller shops, though. I think he specialized in used musical instruments and didn't have a lot of jewelry on hand."

"Justin's place," she said with a knowing nod. "He doesn't understand jewelry and is always afraid he'll overpay. He understands vintage guitars."

For some reason, her knowledge surprised him. "You know a lot of other pawnshop owners?"

"It's my business. I know all the players." She smiled again, but it was harder around the edges than the last one. Strained, like he'd offended her somehow.

He hadn't meant to, but for the life of him he couldn't figure out what he'd said wrong. It was true she hadn't dreamed of working in a pawnshop back in college, but her grandfather had owned a pretty prosperous one before retiring. Maybe she'd kept up with the business more than Jake had known. Maybe her desire to avoid it had changed over the last ten years. Dreams changed.

He of all people should know that.

And if Carmen was even remotely the same person he remembered, she'd have gone into the business with everything she had, giving it a thousand percent. If she wanted to be the best damned pawnshop clerk in Clark County, she'd do it. Maybe she thought he was doubting her commitment?

Because he didn't know how to apologize for whatever he'd done to offend her, he buried his attention back in the box and started sifting through the charms.

"Is it okay if I put some onto the counter so I can see in the box better?" he asked, glancing up.

Her attention was on the box as well. "That should be fine." She didn't look up at him.

That probably shouldn't bother him as much as it did. She didn't recognize him. She didn't know him. And he needed to just get on with things and get out of here. Bringing up a long-ago friendship she'd obviously forgotten felt like a bad idea. Especially since it obviously hadn't been important enough for her to remember. He'd make a fool of himself. And he felt like he'd done enough of that already.

Time to move on.

It was only with that thought that he realized... He hadn't ever really moved on from Carmen Fuentes. She'd been in the background of his mind all these years. A part of him waiting for this moment even though he hadn't really thought it would ever happen.

Now that the moment was here, and she

obviously didn't even know who he was, he realized just how differently he'd hoped a reunion between them would be.

And admitting that, out loud, now, would just be humiliating.

No. No. This was better. Her not remembering him.

This was better.

Chapter Two

Carmen watched as Jake started laying different charms in a small pile on the counter sorting through them. He fished around for the gold ones, examined them, then set them aside. The process involved a lot of sifting through the non-golden medallions and trying to find the glints of sparkling yellow.

She could hardly believe she was seeing him again. After all these years. And here of all places. This wasn't exactly the reunion she'd imagined with the college crush who'd broken her heart. Not that he knew he was her college crush who'd broken her heart. They'd always just been friends. She'd been terrified of losing his friendship so she'd always been very careful not to reveal her real feelings.

In the end, she'd lost him anyway. So she sometimes regretted her earlier restraint. At least if she'd admitted her feelings for him back then, and he'd left anyway, she'd have some sort of sense of closure. Instead, she had this vague sense of things undone for...what, nine, ten years?

Although, having him standing there with no idea who she was... The fact that he'd never realized she wanted more than friendship from him was probably a small mercy. One less thing to be embarrassed about now.

She wasn't embarrassed to own the pawnshop. It was her family's business, one she and her brothers opened again after her father refused the business from his father. And she loved working with her brothers. This had turned out to be a great career. Unexpectedly so. She was damned good at it, too.

But this wasn't exactly the thing she'd spent college talking about, not the business she'd originally intended on opening.

Screw it. She was great at her job. She had a good eye, especially for Vegas kitsch, and she was always fair with both buyers and sellers. Theirs was one of the best pawnshops in Vegas. She had no reason to be embarrassed. The modern business wasn't even like it had been back in the day when her grandfather had his shop. There were reality TV shows about this industry and everything now.

Besides, pawnshops were a lot more profitable than bookstores. She could do a lot more with the money she made here than she could with a barely-getting-by indie bookstore.

"Feel a little like a dragon on his hoard," Jake said with a chuckle, gesturing to the pile of medallions growing on the glass counter in front of him.

"There'd be more precious stones involved if you were a real dragon," she said, trying to force a lighter tone. It wasn't his fault she was sensitive about her work sometimes. Maybe even a little defensive. He wasn't actually standing there judging her. Just going through piles of medallions looking for the specific one he needed.

"I imagine you've got some precious stones around her somewhere," he said, smiling, his attention still on the box of medals. He had a nice smile still. "Any dragon would be delighted by this place."

Well. That was a compliment she found hard to resist. When he looked up, she was grinning at the image of a dragon curled up on top of their shop, guarding it from all comers. He seemed very pleased with himself that he'd made her smile. His expression had her resentment wavering.

So she gave in a little and went with the joke. "If we never sold anything, there'd be a case to be made that we are dragons, hoarding all our treasures. But we pay for them. And some of them are trinkets more than valuable loot."

He laughed.

Ah, it was a good laugh. Another thing that brought back way too many memories.

While the laugh was the same, not everything about him was as she remembered. He wasn't as fresh-faced as he'd been in college. The years had started to drop onto his face, just a little, in a few creases around his eyes and on his brow when he scowled at a silver charm with another image of St. George fighting the dragon on it. But she liked the signs of age on him. If anything, he was more handsome now. His dark hair was maybe a little long and in need of a cut. His eyes were still that surprising blue that used to make her heart beat a little harder. He was thicker now, filled out, his face not so lean and hungry. And it suited him.

There was maybe a little more cynicism in his expression. But that was to be expected, she supposed. She was a lot more cynical now than she'd been in college, too. Even if her brothers did joke about her being too accepting. Wasn't her fault she liked the eccentric people who came in and out of their shop. She'd always liked a good character.

"I feel like I should ask your name," Jake said, almost to himself.

The comment stuck a surprising knife into her gut. She tried to ignore it. "Carmen Fuentes. You?"

His hands tightened on another medallion and he kept his gaze down when he said, "Jake McGuire."

The awkwardness of introducing herself to someone she already knew made her cheeks heat. Fortunately, he hadn't looked up. She watched his hands as he sifted through all the gold and silver disks. She used to love watching his hands. She was a little embarrassed to realize she still loved watching those long blunt fingers moving through perfectly ordinary tasks.

She cleared her throat. "Anything yet?" she asked, nodding down at the box even though he wasn't looking at her.

"Nothing so far. Lot of similar ideas, but not the one I'm missing."

Missing? She hadn't thought about why he was looking for a specific medallion. She asked aloud, "Missing?"

"A few things were stolen from my hotel room two days ago." He kept his attention on the box. "Not much. The only thing with any value was the medallion, and even it's not worth much. Just a sentimental piece. But... Well, I'd hate to lose it."

"You assume we'd buy stolen goods?" she asked quietly. It wasn't a unique assumption. And unfortunately, it did happen. She was trying hard not to be offended. But it was a touchy subject. She and her brothers tried to be very careful, a lot more careful than their grandfather had been. They wouldn't take anything they thought might be hot.

Unfortunately, things still got through. And it bothered her every time.

Having Jake here, not so much accusing but assuming she'd have stolen property in her store... that bothered her. Probably more than it should.

He flinched, his shoulders tightening. But he said, "How would you know? Especially with something like this. Not like there'd be an announcement on the news. 'Stolen dragon medallion. Thieves on the loose.'" He made a face and glanced up at her. "Sorry. I don't assume you'd buy stolen goods on purpose. But honestly, how would you even know?"

He was right. She had to give him that. They obviously couldn't always know, which was why she was touchy about the subject. Still. "We won't buy anything we suspect is hot, on purpose, but... Things get through." She winced, and then sighed and leaned against the counter.

"There's a story in that sigh," he said, as he went back to sifting through all the dragon medallions.

Because he wasn't looking at her, and because this was Jake and even after so many years she felt compelled to tell him things about her life, she admitted, "Just had the cops in here a couple days ago, looking for a piece of jewelry stolen—ironically—from a hotel room. The woman who'd sold the necklace to us had had a great story and one of those innocent faces that fools men real easily. My associate, a man—" not one of her brothers, fortunately for her brothers, "—bought the piece. He assumed the diamonds on the necklace were fake, didn't check properly. Turned out to be quite valuable and the diamonds were real. Police confiscated it. I'm still not sure we'll see our money back from the insurance company. So... Little touchy on the subject of stolen goods. Sorry."

"I'm sorry that happened."

He sounded so sincere she felt her muscles relaxing.

"Was that the first time?" he asked, glancing up again.

"No. As you said, how can we know? Suspect... yes, sometimes. Then we don't buy. And we're supposed to check things that may or may not be precious stones. Even if they aren't stolen, that affects both the price we pay and the price we can sell the things for. But whether something is absolutely stolen or not...we can't *know*. We're not an auction house that demands documents proving provenance. Still a pain in the ass. And not great for business."

He glanced around the large room and she followed his gaze over the racks and shelves of nick knacks, the cases of jewelry, the stacked boxes and tables piled with all sorts of things people might sell for money. She wasn't sure what he saw, but she saw a few things that needed to be rearranged. And a few racks her brothers had let get dusty.

"You take in anything?" he asked. "No specialties like...the vintage guitar guy?"

She looked at him deadpan when she said, "Jewelry is our specialty."

His brows raised and she watched the realization wash through his expression. "Which is why you're so angry about the stolen necklace. You assume your associate should have known better?"

"He should have. Especially with something like a diamond necklace. And now here you are looking for a stole piece." She shook her head. "We're getting sloppy if this is twice in one week."

And that was a conversation she was going to have to have with her brothers. One of the big things they'd decided when agreeing to reopen their grandfather's shop was that they wouldn't traffic stolen goods if they could help it. Jewelry was her specialty, and they knew they wanted that to be the store's specialty. But they also recognized it was risky. Having two incidents of possible stolen property in her store in a week bugged her. A lot. *Especially* stolen jewelry.

"I'm not sure if this helps," Jake said quietly, "but I haven't found my medallion yet."

She sighed. That wasn't helpful for him at all. And she felt a little guilty that it actually did make her feel better. "I'm sorry. I shouldn't have told you all that. Not really your concern. I hope you find your medallion in there somewhere. I do. It's just been a week."

And to top it off, she was having a whole conversation with a man she knew, who she'd been in love with years ago, and he had no idea who she was.

Talk about the shitty cap to a pretty annoying week.

CHAPTER THREE

Jake studied her carefully as he plucked out another few medallions to set on the counter. She looked very annoyed. He was a little surprised by how familiar that expression was to him. How...nostalgic it made him. Seeing Carmen pissed off hadn't been a regular occurrence in college. She was slow to anger. But when she got ticked off, she got ticked off and didn't bother to hide it.

He probably shouldn't still know her expressions this well.

"I get that," he said, to her comment about having a bad week. He'd had a bit of a week too. And walking in here and seeing her and her not knowing him wasn't helping.

"You were staying in a hotel," she said, her soft

voice going brisk as she changed the subject. "Not from the area? Here for work or vacation?"

"First a wedding. And then work." He skimmed over the part about not being from here. He hadn't lived here for ten years. So technically, he wasn't from here.

"What do you do?" she asked, idly moving some of the charms and medallions he'd removed from the box into another pile.

"Business writer. I'm reporting on a conference here in town."

"Actuaries or investment brokers?"

"Investment brokers." He raised his brows in a silent question.

"I keep up to date on which conventions are in town. You'd be surprised who wanders in here after coming in for a conference, then losing their money at the poker tables or slot machines. They have to sell something to get home. As many people have that happen as people here on vacation gambling away too much. Might be worse. The ones supposedly here on business lose track of their spending quicker."

He nodded thoughtfully as he turned back to the box of medallions. The glints of gold were getting harder to find. "I've seen a little of that at this conference. Too much drinking in the evenings. Too much throwing money at the tables. Those new cards for the slots, where you're not putting in actually money, just spinning down money on a card... Those seem dangerous."

"Oh, that's the point. You don't know what you're spending. Easy to overestimate your wins and underestimate your losses that way. Easy to play just one more game."

"Seems kind of boring. I preferred the quarters pouring out of the machine when something hit."

He hadn't played the slots often because, well, they were just part of the background when you grew up in Vegas. They were in the grocery stores and convenience stores and the sounds of them pinging were ubiquitous. But when he'd turned twenty-one, he'd spent a couple of twenties enjoying some time at the slot machines, getting free drinks, pretending he could afford to lose those twenties. The sounds of quarters hitting the metal trays had been...fun.

"You said...you were here for a wedding before the conference? Not yours I take it?"

The joke sounded a little awkward for some reason, but he ignored that. He suspected a lot of people came in here right after Vegas weddings too. Or when those wedding didn't happen and the engagement rings were sold.

"My sister," he said, keeping his attention on the dwindling gold in the box. "She married an English guy. Left for London right after the ceremony."

"To live or for the honeymoon?"

"To live."

Silence, then, "Is that good or bad?"

He frowned a little when he looked up.

"I just mean, you sounded a little...sad. Like you'd miss her."

"I will," he admitted with a shrug. "We're close. But he's the love of her life. I couldn't really begrudge her the move. And he's a good guy. I know they'll be happy."

"Nice," she said, her quiet voice even quieter. So quiet he almost didn't hear her.

A brief silence passed, with just the sounds of moving metal against metal between them as he ran his hands through the remaining charms. Then she said, "What else was stolen from your room?"

"Only the medallion and the plug for my phone. I didn't have anything remotely valuable in there. I'm not sure why anyone would break into my room in the first place."

"What did the hotel say?"

"Ask if I wanted to file a report with the police." He rubbed a hand across the back of his neck. "Didn't seem important enough to go to all the hassle. Like I said, nothing very valuable."

"Didn't just...misplace them?"

When he looked up scowling, she raised her hands. "I'm just saying... You claim nothing else was stolen and the medallion wasn't worth much. The only other thing missing was a phone charger? Why would someone risk breaking and entering for...nothing."

"Like I said, I have no idea. But the medallion and charger are missing. Not misplaced. I searched the whole room, and turned everything inside out and upside down looking for that medallion."

"Sentimental piece," she murmured. "I'm sorry it's missing."

Her soft voice took the sting out of his defensiveness. "I've been searching pawnshops because... I didn't know what else to do." He met her gaze. "Feels a little pointless, to be honest. The thief probably dropped the medallion and charger into a dumpster somewhere." He sighed.

"Don't give up just yet. There are still a few more gold ones in there."

He nudged around a few of the charms. "I can't believe there are so many with dragons on them. Enough you have a whole box."

"Dragons are a popular motif. You'd be surprised what has dragons on it."

"Probably." He'd never really thought about it before. Except for his sister's medallion, he never thought about dragons. He lifted the box and slid the remaining contents around a little, hoping to uncover anything he'd missed.

"If you can't find it in there," Carmen said quietly, "there might be one more place to check."

"Another pawnshop?" He looked up, not feeling

particularly hopeful. He got caught in her uniquely colored eyes, her gentle gaze. That expression sent him back ten years. And he had to clear his throat to force himself back to the present.

"Not...quite," she said. "But she collects all things dragon. Everyone in town knows that. If someone wanted to sell something with a dragon on it, they might just go to her instead of a pawnshop." She rolled her eyes a little. "Less worry that Ama will ask if it's stolen."

"She doesn't care?"

"She doesn't care." Carmen shrugged. "But she'll also give back something stolen if the owner shows up. She's sort of a... Things with dragons find their way to Ama and then stay there, until it's time for them to go somewhere else."

"That sounds a little woo-woo, coming from a pawnshop owner."

She smiled and it was a spectacular smile. A smile that made Jake blink and left him a little breathless. She'd always been able to take his breath away, but in that moment... She was the same and yet different. A grown woman now, where they'd been kids in college. And that aging, that maturity had only made her more spectacular.

"You'd be surprised what pawnshop owners encounter," she said.

He imagined he would be.

Jake considered her offer as he finished going

through the box of charms. While a few came close, none were his dragon. He let out a resigned shrug as he put the medallions on the counter gently back into the box.

"Guess that's the end of that," he said.

"Ama next, then."

He wasn't sure he wanted to go to all that trouble. His sister would be pissed that he'd lost the charm, but he'd spent two days looking for it, and this was the closest he'd gotten—at least Carmen's shop had dragon medallions. He should probably just give up. The medallion was lost, likely on its way to landfill, or maybe taking up someone else's pocket space. But it was gone. And wasting more days looking for it seemed a waste of time. He'd extended his stay here too long already. He needed to get home, finish his article, get back to work.

Glancing at Carmen, he considered admitting the truth to her before he left. It was...surprisingly good to spend time with her again, even if it was just a few minutes and she had no idea who he was. For the sake of that old friendship, she should probably tell her who he was, that they'd known each other once upon a time.

But then what? He was on his way back to LA. She'd stay here and run her business. What would come of admitting anything now? Except embarrassment for both of them.

And spending any more time with her would

only get him thinking impossible thoughts again. Best to protect himself. Leave now. Let the past go along with the dragon medallion.

"Thanks for the information and the offer," he said, sliding the box back to her. "But I think I'll just leave it. It's a small thing, not worth much. It's not going to turn up anywhere."

"Don't give up yet," she said, reaching over the counter to hold his hand.

The contact startled him into complete stillness. The gesture had been meant to comfort, but... Now that they were here, he wanted to turn his hand over and grip hers. And not let go. Never let her go again.

A surprising enough thought he couldn't move at all.

She blinked a few times, hard, like she was startled, too. She looked down at where her hand covered his. He followed her gaze. She had long-fingered hands, with pretty nails painted in a pinkish color that probably had a precise name, something like blushing rose or something. His sister would know. All he knew was that the color suited Carmen.

And she wasn't wearing any rings.

That didn't mean much these days. Still, he noticed. Ten years was a long time. She might not be single. All the more reason to keep the past to himself. But the feel of her hand over his, warm and almost, but not quite, familiar left him...restless. Left the truth, the admission, on the tip of his tongue.

Not just that they'd known each other. But that he'd loved her then. He couldn't believe how hard he had to work to keep all that truth in.

Carmen didn't move her hand away when she repeated, "Don't give up just yet. Not until you've seen Ama."

She looked so earnest, so hopeful. How could he say no to her? How could he not go wherever she asked?

"I'll take you to her," she said, suddenly, as if the idea had just occurred to her. "If Ama can't help..." She shrugged. "Well, we'll figure something else out. You said the piece was sentimental. We'll find it."

Her hope was infectious. He found himself smiling, hoping. And he wasn't even sure what he was hoping for. Just that, the way she kept referring to them working together to find the medallion, the way she referred to them as if they were a team...filled him with a happiness he hadn't felt in a while. He'd search for the little dragon charm forever if it meant spending more time with Carmen. Even if she didn't know who he was.

He finally turned over his hand and gripped hers. She didn't pull away immediately. "Okay," he said. "Let's go see Ama."

She grinned. "Wait here. I'll be back in a minute."

He let her hand slip away, enjoying the way her soft skin slid against his. She hurriedly put away the box of medallions then disappeared into the store, heading toward the back.

Jake studied the jewelry pieces inside the glass display case, feeling a lot more cheerful now than when he'd come in.

The overall gloominess of his day had just gotten a little brighter.

CHAPTER FOUR

Jake's improved mood took a hit when he saw Ama's house.

The address was out in the desert on the road back toward California. He followed Carmen in her four-wheel drive truck and worried his serviceable but not-designed-for-off-roading Toyota wouldn't make the trip.

But Carmen never led him off paved roads. The paved road just got a little rougher by the time they reached their destination.

Warm late autumn heat seeped into his bones as he stepped out of his car. The sky was a perfect blue overhead, cloudless and bright, but the dry desert warmth, one of the few things he missed about Vegas, left him feeling a little itchy and edgy.

They were very far out in the desert here.

The house, a single-story ranch house, was in the middle of nowhere and surrounded by nothing but scrub desert. Lots of rocks and a few shaggy tumbleweeds caught against the wire mesh fence that surrounded property that was also mostly rocks and desert. The rocks and desert beyond the fence seemed arranged and neat, though, like a tended garden. He thought there might be a design to the arrangement, but from outside the gate, he couldn't make it out. Everything smelled like dirt and dryness, with a little hot tarmac and distant creosote thrown in for good measure.

The wire mesh fence wasn't tall, so it wasn't designed to keep people out. After a moment, following a bellow of deep woofs, he realized the fence was probably there to keep the dogs in.

There were a lot of them to keep in.

"Not afraid of dogs, are you?" Carmen asked, looking a little concerned when he stared at the five —or was it six?—large basset hounds rushed toward the gate.

He had a brief pang at her question. Back in the day, she would have known the answer. But she didn't remember him, he reminded himself. Of course she didn't know how he felt about animals.

"I like dogs," he said. "I have a dog. I just have never encountered so many basset hounds at the same time."

"Ama loves dragons and Elvis," Carmen said with a little smile.

"Elvis?"

"That hound dog song of his? It's her favorite. So she adopts basset hounds."

He glanced between Carmen and the dogs, now aligned at the gate, tails wagging as they stared up at him. Their long faces and excess skin, their ears dipping close to the ground. Hound dogs because she loved Elvis?

Sure. Why not?

"Makes sense from a certain perspective," Carmen said, sounding like she wanted to laugh.

He liked that sound. "From a certain perspective…? Yeah, it does."

She pressed a button on the side of the gate, a button he hadn't noticed, and then they waited. The basset hounds all looked expectantly up at them. One brown and white dog let out a deep woof, and all of their tails wagged faster.

Carmen gave him a smile. Her stunning eyes were hidden behind dark sunglasses now, but he imagined the amused expression went all the way to her eyes. He wondered if she was fucking with him. If all this was some kind of joke. She'd always had a weird sense of humor. And if she'd remembered him, he could imagine her doing this to him as some sort of hazing. A joke played on an old friend because so much time had passed since they'd spoken.

But she didn't know him, and this seemed an awful elaborate joke to play on some random man who'd wandered into her pawnshop looking for a stolen dragon medallion.

Her eyebrows popped up over the top of her dark glasses. "It's not a joke," she said, as if she'd just read his mind. "You'll see when you see the inside of Ama's house."

"You haven't brought me out here to be basset hound food, have you?"

She laughed. "Ama would never feed her babies anything as unhygienic as human meat."

"I'm...not sure that's reassuring."

She patted his shoulder, her hand lingering for a moment before she dropped her arm back to her side. That was distracting enough to get his mind off the basset hounds.

"If the roles were reversed," Carmen said, "I'd be pretty nervous about now, too. But don't worry. Ama is harmless. She just likes dragons and Elvis."

"Her house is going to be bursting with dragons and Elvis stuff, isn't it?"

"Yes it is."

Despite that warning, he was still not prepared for the interior of the house.

Or for Ama herself.

For some reason, he'd been imagining a little old lady with gray hair and weather roughened skin and a shawl over fragile shoulders.

Ama was...not that woman.

She was taller than either he or Carmen, wide shouldered, her arms sleeved with colorful tattoos, her skin around the tattoos a sun-darkened brown. Her hair was obviously dyed black and she wore it in a mile high beehive hairdo the likes of which he'd never seen in real life. She was slim-hipped and well-muscled. She wore black leather pants, which had to be scorching in the desert heat, but they looked well-worn and soft, the color almost gray. Her sleeveless black t-shirt was tied in a knot around her waist and had a heavy metal band logo on the front and a listing of concert dates on the back.

Her age was impossible to guess. She might have been mid-fifties, early sixties. But then she could have been in her early forties or late thirties. There was a hardness to her mouth, that softened when she cooed at the dogs. But that softness didn't reach her dark eyes when she looked at them over the gate.

"Carmen," Ama greeted with a nod. "What brings you all the way out here? Better not be trying to buy my Elvis statue again. I'm not parting with that for love nor money."

"Good to see you too, Ama," Carmen said with a touch of irony in her soft voice. "Not here for anything like that." She gestured to Jake. "He had a dragon medallion stolen from his hotel room. It's sentimental. So we're looking for it."

Ama gave him a once over. He felt a sudden need

to straighten his shoulders and smooth out any wrinkles in his t-shirt. He didn't. But holding Ama's gaze when she met his was disconcerting and difficult.

"Sentimental about a dragon, huh?" she said. He opened his mouth to comment, but before he could, she said, "I like that. I approve. Come in."

The minute the gates opened the dogs swarmed around Jake's legs. A lot of deep woofs and bumping and tail wagging ensued. Jake found himself laughing. A gaggle of bassets was a little overwhelming, with all that loose skin and those long ears flapping everywhere, but they were so happy and eager for his attention they were hard to resist.

He paused long enough to pet all of them, giving them scratches behind the head and saying hi. When he looked up, Ama was standing at her front door watching him. And Carmen was smiling down at him. Her smile caught him in the solar plexus. Momentarily leaving him breathless.

Then one of the bassets bumped him hard enough he almost fell over. "Gotta goes, guys," he murmured, righting himself. "Don't want to keep your mom waiting." He kept his voice low, but Ama must have heard him because she sniffed and turned back inside.

"Did I just fuck up?" he muttered to Carmen as they started toward the house.

"I think you just made a friend," she said back,

still smiling.

He could lose himself in that smile. Blinking back to his surroundings, he said, "Elvis statue?"

"Long story." She leaned in close to lower her voice, and that started his heartbeat thumping a little harder. "I'll explain later."

Later. Implying they'd have a later in which to talk. Even as the thought made his pulse jump, a little niggling of guilt bit at him. He really should tell her the truth. The longer he went keeping the fact that they'd once known each other to himself, the more he felt like an ass for it.

She was right, though. Now wasn't the time. He could tell her after the business with Ama was done. He *would* tell her.

And when she admitted she didn't remember him, he'd accept that the past was the past, *finally*, and take his battered heart back to LA.

As he stepped into Ama's dark home, the transition from bright autumn sunshine to dim interior forced him to pause on the doorstep, blinking while his eyes adjusting. When they did, he continued to blink as he looked around.

There were dragons, and Elvises—Elvi?— everywhere. Hanging on the walls, carpeting the floor, decaled on the ceiling. Stacked onto every available flat surface in view. Elvis against black velvet, golden dragons on blue silk, little pewter statues of fantasy dragons holding colorful crystals, a flying dragon across the ceiling, Elvis bobble heads bouncing next to a dragon whose long neck wove in the bush of air from the air-conditioning. European dragons, and guitar playing Elvis, and Asian dragons, and Elvis in a Hawaiian shirt, and...

A life-sized Elvis statue that looked like the man himself was standing in the middle of the living room just off the front door. Standing next to a curled up dragon the size of a small car sitting on top of a pile of—what he assumed to be—fake gold and jewels.

More blinking as he took in the sheer extravagance of it all. The commitment to all things dragons and Elvis was...

"Impressive," he said.

"I could have gotten a fortune for that Elvis statue if she'd been willing," Carmen said. "Had a guy in looking for something just like it." She sighed.

More than one person in the entire world wanted a life-sized statue of Elvis? That was a revelation.

"The dragon on the pile of gold..." He nodded to the car-sized statue next to the life-sized Elvis. "That's not real gold, right?"

"If it is, Ama's not saying."

"Isn't she afraid of thieves?"

"She can hear anyone getting near her place from a mile away, she's got noisy dogs—"

"Who are disastrous guard dogs," he interrupted. "They'd welcome in a thief."

"But they make noise doing it," Carmen said

without missing a beat. "And besides all that, Ama has both motion detector alarms and almost as many shotguns as she has Elvis paintings. Only a truly stupid person would try to rob her."

He nodded and let his shoulders relax. He hadn't even realized he'd tensed up. "Good. Good to hear."

Carmen stared at him with her extraordinary eyes, a frown forming lines between her arched brows. "You were worried about her? You don't even know her."

He shrugged and made a face and walked farther into the house. What was he supposed to say? He *wanted* her to get robbed? What kind of asshole did she think he was?

She doesn't know you, he reminded himself. Again. She doesn't remember you. So of course she doesn't know whether you're an asshole or not.

Carmen touched his shoulder, lightly, before he'd moved too far away. He glanced at her, trying to rein in his annoyance with logic. And failing miserably.

"I'm sorry," she murmured. "If I offended you. I'm not used to people...being that concerned for a stranger." She shrugged. "Don't see that a lot in my line of work. Concerned for themselves. For family. For someone they're close to. But for strangers..." She shook her head.

"It's not that rare," he said, relenting because she was still touching his shoulder and that was making it hard to stay irritated. Or to think straight.

"I think it's sweet," she said, in that soft voice, her purple eyes dark and luminous in the dim hallway.

He fell into her smile again, and it took him a moment to drag his mind back to his surroundings.

A sudden explosion of Elvis music helped.

He looked around. "Uhm..." Where was that coming from?

Ama came out of a back room and said, "I have speakers throughout the house. Love hearing the King sing in every room."

"Of course," Jake said, nodding. "Can't blame you."

"You like Elvis?" Ama said.

"Not as much as this," he admitted honestly. "But I don't mind his blue suede shoes."

Ama barked out a laugh, the sound booming in the confines of the crowded house. "Medallion you said? That's what you're looking for."

"Gold," he said, hoping to stay on her good side, "with a dragon in the center. A European dragon, thick bodied, wings."

Ama gave him a once over and nodded. "Why's it sentimental?"

He hadn't even told Carmen this yet. He glanced at her when he said, "It was my sister's. And before that my mother's, and before that my grandmother's. We don't know how far back it went."

"Religious?"

"No. Not even solid gold. Just gold leaf. A family heirloom, but a cheap one."

"Know why it was important to your grandmother? Enough she passed down a seemingly cheap piece of jewelry?"

"I...never thought about it. I just assumed she liked it and that's why she gave it to my mom and why my mom gave it to my sister."

"Why'd your sister give it to you?"

"She got married last week and moved to England." He shrugged. "I figured she wanted me to have it so I didn't forget about her." He said the last with a smile, because really it would be impossible to forget his baby sister. She was a force of nature. It would be like trying to forget air existed.

"So she didn't tell you about the charm? Nothing about the legend around it?"

"There isn't one that I know of."

Ama snorted. "Then you don't know a lot."

He frowned. "What are you talking about?"

"Come on." She turned abruptly and disappeared deeper into the house.

Jake frowned at Carmen. "Any idea what she's talking about?"

"Not a clue," she said, also frowning, her gaze on the direction Ama had gone. "But we should probably follow her and find out."

CHAPTER FIVE

They found Ama in a room that had to be a kitchen since there was a refrigerator and an oven against one wall. Lot of cabinets too. And that might have been a kitchen island in front of the fridge and stove, but it was hard to tell under all the piles and boxes and...stuff. So much stuff. And all of it dragon or Elvis.

Ama was one hardcore collector.

She moved some stacks of papers and a few boxes off what turned out to be chairs, placing the stuff against the wall with more stuff.

This room looked more like a staging area. Or a storage area. Where the rest of the house had a lot of nick knacks and collectibles everywhere, all the paraphernalia was arranged neatly and obviously placed to be on display. There was a lot of it, but it was well organized and there was enough room to see what was surrounding all the stuff. Like being in a museum. You could still walk around the displays.

In this...kitchen? Jake supposed kitchen. In the kitchen, the stuff was just in piles, stacked high against the walls and on all the flat surfaces. Even most of the floor. There was a path between all the stuff, which he and Carmen followed to reach the seats Ama had cleared for them. But otherwise, there wasn't an empty surface in the place. His nose twitched at the dust, something that hadn't been evident in the front of the house.

A rustling sound to his left made him think rat, but a smallish basset hound emerged from behind a stack of boxes, gave him a higher woof than the dogs outside, and trotted up to Ama, giving her ankle a headbutt.

Ama didn't even look down at the basset baby as she leaned over and swept the little one up into her arms. "This is Jewels," she introduced. "Only baby here at the moment."

"She's...cute," he said, because Ama seemed to be expecting a response.

"The medallion you lost..."

She moved on from the baby basset and right to business so abruptly, Jake stumbled a little mentally trying to keep up. His senses were overwhelmed by the house, the dogs, and, if he were being honest,

Carmen, so he wasn't exactly quick on the uptake at the moment.

"It's got a story to it," Ama continued. "A good one."

"You... You know my medallion?"

"I've got it." She said that without any hesitance. Without even showing it to him to make sure they were talking about the right charm. He was about to point that out when she continued. "I knew exactly what it was when Ken brought it in to trade."

He had questions about this Ken person, but a gentle touch from Carmen on his forearm kept him quiet. Honestly, a touch from Carmen left him too breathless to speak. Or think. Which in this case, he supposed was good.

"Ken's mother is having health issues," Ama said. "They've been very worried, thought they'd lose her a few times. He was looking for a miracle to help." She shrugged. "He thought I had one, but knew he'd have to bring me something in exchange."

"What do you have that could help with illnesses?" He glanced around the piles of boxes and stacks of paraphernalia. He supposed there could be a whole pharmacy in here and he wouldn't know about it.

"Ken's sister cleans rooms and saw the medallion in yours," Ama said, ignoring his question. "She suspected it was something I'd like. They had no idea what it really was. But the sister thought it would make a good trade and so did Ken." Ama shrugged. "They were right."

"I'm confused." About a lot of things. But also, "Why did she steal my phone charger as well as the medallion, if all she wanted was the medallion?"

If that had been the only thing missing, he'd likely have just assumed he'd dropped it somewhere, or misplaced it, or it had fallen out of his pocket or something. The missing charger plug was what had convinced him the medallion had been stolen.

"Maybe hers was broken?" Ama said. "They didn't feel the need to mention a phone charger. They were more worried about their mother."

If that was supposed to make him feel embarrassed for asking, well... It sort of did, but also, this was a logic hole that was going to bug him. Why steal his charger?

"Anyway," Ama said, getting back to her story. "Your medallion earned them the thing they wanted from me."

"Which was?"

"A dragon's breath charm. Infused with a real dragon's blood."

He stared at Ama. She stared back, not blinking. Sure. Dragon's blood. Why not. There'd been a real Elvis at one point. Why not real dragons?

He shook his head. "Is it helping?"

"They brought me the medallion two days ago."

"Not enough time to know then," he said nodding.

"Their mother made a full recovery yesterday and is back to nagging Ken to get married while scurrying around the kitchen cooking which was always her favorite thing to do. So... Yes. The dragon's blood helped."

"That's..."

He was going to say unbelievable and impossible. But at this stage, he decided to let it go. A lot of unbelievable things had happened that day. Including meeting Carmen again after all these years. Logic wasn't going to help him today.

"Does this mean you will or won't give me my medallion back?" he asked. Then winced. His tone was sharper than he'd meant. He didn't want to piss Ama off, but the talk of real dragons and miraculous recoveries put him on edge. And he'd already been pretty edgy walking into this house.

He glanced at Carmen. She was watching him carefully, with those gorgeous eyes, but she hadn't commented even a little throughout the story.

"You can have your medallion back," Ama said. "I don't keep stolen goods." She glanced between him and Carmen. "Though I have a feeling it's done its work already and you'll be able to pass it on soon anyway."

"What?"

"The legend behind your charm." She said that

so matter-of-factly and then paused without explaining even though she already knew he didn't know about any legend or any of the background of the charm.

None of his relatives had seen fit to pass any stories about the dragon medallion on to him. Including his sister, if she'd known them. He wasn't sure whether to doubt Ama—assume she was wrong and there wasn't really a legend. Or whether to doubt his relatives—did they really *not* know about a legend this whole time?

Ama leaned back in her tall-backed chair and draped her long, muscled arm over the back. "Want to know about the legend, or do you just want the charm back?"

He opened his mouth to say he just wanted the charm back, but what came out was, "What legend?"

He scowled at himself. He didn't need to know whatever story Ama wanted to tell. He wasn't even sure she had the right charm yet. And none of this made any difference to him. He just wanted the family heirloom returned so his sister didn't kill him for letting it get stolen in the first place.

"This particular medallion, this dragon of yours, carries important powers," Ama said, her gaze on his. "It's said the charm will lead the possessor to their future love. Their true and forever love."

He'd been so braced for something cryptically horrible, Ama's actual story surprised a laugh out of him. A sort of rude snorting laugh he regretted the minute he saw Ama's eyes narrow.

He raised his hands in apology. "Sorry. Sorry. I thought you were going to tell me there was a curse on the charm or something. Like the possessor of the charm would meet an untimely end or something."

Ama pulled her chin back and her mouth flattened. "First, did any of that happen to the family members passing down the charm?"

"Well, no—"

"And second, do you think I'm such an idiot, I'd let a cursed dragon charm into my home?"

"No. I— Wait, are there cursed dragon charms?" And why had he asked that since he didn't want the answer.

Fortunately, Ama ignored his question. "You scoff because the charm's magic is soft and positive, not deadly and full of doom."

"No, really, I—"

"But there are many good things in this world that link to dragons. Many dragon things designed for good. This is one of them. The charm will, eventually, lead the owner to their future, to the love of their lives. What the dumb shit who's given such a gift does with that gift is up to them."

Jake flinched, knowing he was the dumb shit in this story. It took a great deal of effort not to glance at Carmen in that moment. An even greater effort not to let Ama's story carry him away on a flight of fancy.

Because... Carmen. She was right there. After all these years, Carmen was sitting right beside him. And he was pretty sure, even though they didn't know each other anymore, even though she didn't even remember him... There was a part of him acknowledging that Carmen was now and had always been the love of his life.

Only she had no idea.

She didn't even remember their friendship. And if he glanced at her in that moment, he was afraid she'd see every single one of his emotions, all that history beaming out of him. Except to her, those emotions would be coming from a stranger.

He forced down a hard swallow, kept his attention on Ama, and said, in an effort to appease Ama, "Thank you for telling me about the legend. I do appreciate the information." Even if he didn't want to believe it.

"Mm." Ama's noncommittal response did not convey a lot of forgiveness.

"May I...have the charm back now? I can pay—"

"If you pull out any money, I will melt your medallion down and return it as a hunk of metal."

Jake raised his brows. "Okay."

He really didn't understand what Ama wanted or expected of him. But so long as he got his medallion back, he didn't care.

"It was meant to be yours, passed down to you by your family. I would never risk the consequences of getting in the way of that." Ama glanced between Jake and Carmen. "But I am glad I was meant to be a part of this journey."

"Journey?" Jake was trying hard not to read anything into Ama's words. Trying to ignore some niggling instinct poking at his brain. The longer he sat here, though, the harder it got. Because he still couldn't get around the fact that, after all these years, thanks to his stolen medallion, he was sitting next to Carmen again.

He risked a glance at her. She was staring at Ama, her brows lowered over her magnificent eyes, her expression...thoughtful?

Ama ignored his question and she stood abruptly, disappearing into the depths of the boxes and stacks of stuff surrounding them.

Jake leaned a little closer to Carmen, tried not to get distracted by the fact that she smelled wonderful —like sweet lemon and something flowery and familiar in an unexpected way—and whispered, "Did any of that make sense to you?"

Maybe he was wrong. Maybe all this legend stuff was nonsense, and Carmen would tell him that, and he would accept her word and just get on with his life. Without worrying that his medallion had...led him to all this.

Because if this had been some sort of destined meeting, wouldn't Carmen at least know who he was?

"I'm not sure what to think," she said quietly, leaning into him too. Which was distracting as all hell.

She doesn't know you, he reminded himself. You can't just take hold of her hand even if that does feel like the most natural thing in the world to do right now.

"But it's just a story, right?" Carmen said. "A little bit of fun to tell your sister after you get the medallion back. No such thing as...true love."

Right. Right. Exactly what he'd expected her to say. All this was nonsense and there was no True Love legend. Very logical. Exactly what he wanted to hear.

Wasn't it?

"Except my sister passed the charm on to me right after marrying the love of her life," he said.

He met Carmen's gaze and she stared back at him with her gorgeous eyes. And for some reason, Jake couldn't quite catch his breath. Or rather, the only thing he wanted to breathe in was Carmen.

His pulse thumped harder and almost against his will, his gaze dropped to her mouth. When she didn't slug him, or turn away from that involuntary show of interest, his heartbeat sped.

CHAPTER SIX

Ama reappeared with the same suddenness as she'd disappeared, forcing Jake's attention back to his surroundings and away from Carmen. He straightened away from her abruptly, coughing into his hand to cover the awkward moment.

Without ceremony, Ama plopped a little golden charm into Jake's lap. He had to scramble to catch it before it hit the ground. He scowled as he brought the charm up so he could see it.

"Is it the right one?" Carmen asked.

Letting out a sigh of relief, his shoulders relaxing, he nodded. "Right one."

There was even the little chip in the gold, where you could see the ordinary tin underneath, in the upper left side, near the dragon's wing. The dragon itself seemed undamaged by the adventures. A little miniature beasty, viewed from the side, its wings raised just enough to give the impression of size, its stocky body crouched low on its four thick legs.

There was a little lick of stylized fire coming from its mouth, which Jake had looked at countless times over the years. He knew he'd seen the shape of that fire multiple times. Stared at it as often as he'd stared at the charm. And yet, he'd never noticed...

"Does the end of the flame form a heart shape?" Carmen asked. "That's pretty."

"Huh. Yeah," he said. "Yeah, I guess it does." And wasn't that strange he'd never noticed that before. Probably all the talk of legends and love that made the heart more obviously this time. Yeah. That was the reason he could see it now.

He glanced at Carmen again.

"Good luck with that," Ama said. "Don't lose it again."

Jake scowled at Ama. "I didn't lose it. It was stolen. Remember?"

"For a purpose, I think," Ama said quietly.

"So you'd give Ken the thing he needed to help his mother." Did he sound a little desperate? No. No. That was exactly why the charm had been stolen. Nothing else. No other reason.

"Sure," Ama said. "You keep thinking that."

Jake's gaze strayed to Carmen again. She was looking between him and the charm, her expression unreadable.

When he looked back at Ama, she was grinning, revealing a row of very straight, very white teeth. She sighed, "Men." And shook her head. "Okay, young people. Time to leave my house. I have some new Elvis purchases I need to catalogue."

Ama walked them to the front door, where the passel of basset hounds met them. They encircled Jake again, looking for attention, so he obliged them with some scratches and pats. The attention was greeted with a few very deep woofs.

At the gate, Ama shooed the dogs aside as she let Jake and Carmen out, closing the gate again before any of the dogs could follow. She nodded at them. "Enjoy yourselves. Be sure to keep in touch when things...happen."

She walked away on that cryptic comment, the dogs following her when she whistled for them.

"What things does she think will happen?" Jake asked, staring at Ama's firmly closed front door.

"Got me," Carmen said. But she was also staring at Ama's house with a thoughtful expression. She gave herself a little shake. "Anyway." She turned back toward their cars, but hesitated, looking at her key fob as she bounced it between her hands.

That's what finally did it for Jake, what pushed

him over the edge. All that talk of love inside. A supposed legend. Seeing her again after all these years.

He just couldn't let her go without telling her the truth.

He had to admit they'd known each other once. He had to come clean. About this at least. He just... he couldn't leave without knowing if she might, possibly remember something of their friendship.

"We've met before," he blurted.

She gaped at him, her expression shutting down.

Damn. Well, too late to take it back now. Full truth. Or as much truth as he could give her. "Actually, more than met. We went to high school together. And college. I know you don't remember me—"

"I remember you," she said, her soft voice very quiet. "I thought you'd forgotten me. That's why I didn't say anything."

He stared at her with his mouth open for a long moment, the hot sun beating down on him as he replayed what she'd just said over and over again in his mind. She... She remembered him. She hadn't forgotten him.

But she hadn't admitted that either.

"I could never forget you," he murmured. "I just... I was really surprised to see you."

"Same. Weird coincidence, huh?"

"Weird." He rubbed his fingers over the charm in his hand, the little dragon with its heart of flame pressing against his thumb. "Been a long time."

She nodded.

"This is going to sound weird," he said, girding himself to take whatever reaction she threw at him. "But I've...missed you."

She blinked. She hadn't put her sunglasses on after they left the house. He could see every emotion moving through those gorgeous purple eyes. He just couldn't tell what those emotions meant.

"Didn't forget me?" she murmured, almost to himself.

"Never," he said. "Never could."

"Did you try?"

The smart comeback sparked a completely inappropriate smile. "Not really. I figured, when the emails stopped... You'd gotten busy with your life and, keeping up a friendship with me wasn't..." He swallowed. "Wasn't important anymore."

"You never answered my last email. That's why I stopped."

"Which one?" He straightened. He'd been diligent about answering every email he got. Even with the physical distance between them, he'd never stopped being in love with her, and if all he could have was their friendship, he'd had every intention of keeping it going.

But she'd just...stopped emailing. When he noticed, when he realized he hadn't heard from her in a bit, he'd accepting the inevitable. He'd known that moment would come. The time when she'd outgrow him, move on to other things. So he'd tried to let her go. Tried not to be the stalkery ex-friend she no longer wanted in her life.

Except he was starting to realize...maybe he'd got that wrong?

"The one congratulating you on getting the job in that TV writing room," she said. "Your dream." She smiled, but it looked forced. "I was really proud of you. Going after what you wanted." She glanced away and slipped on her sunglasses. "When you didn't get back to me, I assumed you were too busy. And then... You know. Time passed." She shrugged.

Jake's heart was hammering so hard he could barely breathe, barely make sense of what had gone wrong. All this time... A simple missed email? That was why their friendship died?

"I never got that email," he said. "I figured you were busy with your bookstore and didn't have time for me anymore."

"What? No, that's..." She stared at him again, though he could no longer see more than a vague outline of her eyes behind her sunglasses. Then she let out a long sigh. "Well, shit."

He felt the exact same way. All this time...

He straightened his shoulders and faced her fully. "I know this will sound weird. We don't know each other anymore, and after ten years, trying to pick up a friendship or... Well. It's just that..."

He stuttered to a stop. He didn't know how to say any of this. He wasn't going to tell her right here, right now that he'd been in love with her all those years ago. That he might, possibly, still be in love with her. But he couldn't let her go again either. He couldn't let any more time pass without at least...trying.

"Would you like to have dinner with me?" he asked.

"Don't you have to get back to LA?" A faint pink crept over her cheeks but he couldn't tell if it was a blush or the heat.

"I'm in no hurry," he said. "I'd just... I'd love to spend a little time with you." He shrugged. "Maybe... I don't know. Just. I'd like to spend more time with you."

A slow, careful, hesitant smile turned up the corners of her mouth. "Yeah. I'd like that, too. Dinner sounds good."

He resisted the urge to shout and dance around like an idiot, but only barely. He was pretty sure his grin looked a tad maniacal. "Mexican food?" That used to be her favorite. Their favorite together.

"I know a great place." Her smile was soft and warm.

"You always did know the best restaurants."

Jack followed Carmen back into town, trying not to let his relief and excitement get the better of him. But this was Carmen. And he couldn't imagine anything better than spending the evening with her, eating Mexican food, catching up, and maybe, just maybe seeing if he could finally admit the entire truth to her. Not right away. He didn't want to scare her off after all this.

But soon. Someday soon.

He gave the little medallion a glance where he'd placed it in his car's consol. Was it strange that he was this happy about his charm getting stolen? Probably. But if it hadn't, he probably wouldn't have met Carmen again.

Might have let the love of his life get away.

Thanks to Ken and his sister stealing the charm, Jake had a second chance at something he'd let slip through his fingers. He had no intention of letting that something special go again so easily. He'd gotten the dragon back. And he was about to have dinner with the gorgeous woman he'd adored since high school.

Life felt full of possibilities in that moment. Full of potential. Potential that made his heart thump hard with anticipation. Potential he hadn't hoped for in almost ten years.

And he had his little legendary dragon charm to thank.

Now Pick a New Genre

MYSTERY
HEIST

Chapter One

Who steals a dragon?

Me. I'm the who. I would absolutely steal a dragon. Especially one worth a small fortune from people who shouldn't have it in the first place. Not that I'm one to talk. I've... acquired many things over the years that I shouldn't have had in the first place. But to be honest, I do it so I can give them back to the people they belong to.

Yeah, I know, a walking, talking Robin Hood. Or in my case, Rose Hood. That's me.

With maybe less of the stage musical cast surrounding me.

The dragon in question is a little bobble that for a long time, no one realized was super valuable. A little golden statue that sat on the mantel of a nice woman whose family stole it from China during their missionary years. That was a long time ago, and the dragon had been passed down for several generations, so the woman hadn't the first clue it was worth more than the gold it was made of. And even that she thought was just gold plate, nothing worth a lot. A tourist trinket if you will.

Except that it came from a time before tourists. And after doing a little research, the woman realized that several of her inherited bobbles from those missionaries were actually really valuable artifacts from ancient China. Some of the big dynasties, if I remember the story right.

I'm a thief, not an expert in Chinese history, so I don't know much about the dynasties, their time periods, and what is and isn't valuable from those dynasties. I do know that my current client decided to take some of these pieces to one of those giant antique collection shows, just to see how valuable the pieces really were. She was pretty clever about it, played dumb, didn't let on that she knew more than that her missionary ancestors picked the pieces up in China.

The show expert in Chinese history confirmed my client's suspicions. That most of the pieces were super valuable artifacts. Valuable enough that not all of her sequence aired on TV. They couldn't for several reasons—liability, international incident, that kind of thing—but the biggest reason was that, while most of the bits and pieces were worth a few thousand, some of them closer to the tens of thousands—and wasn't that just a revelation for everyone involved—but the dragon...

The expert estimated its worth as roughly eight million dollars and thought it would fetch more if it went to auction. But said expert also warned that this was a piece the Chinese government would claim was stolen and demand back. Some symbol of one of the Emperor's or something like that. Something pretty important to Chinese culture anyway. And not something they'd let a white American lady whose ancestors had stolen it just randomly sell at auction without raising a fuss about it.

At least, this is the story my client told me when she asked me to steal the dragon.

Who has it now and how did it get stolen away from her? Well, there's another story. And it's not the lighthearted, someone stole it to return it to its rightful owners story either. Nope. These were people from the antiques show, who overheard what the dragon was worth. And up and stole it before the end of the show. Went missing, despite all the attention on it, and for a short time, my client thought it was gone forever and she'd be screwed as soon as the Chinese government found out about the piece.

She doesn't have four million or anything like that to compensate the Chinese, and frankly, no one was sure they'd be looking for financial compensation. I mean, it's a chunk of their history. That's worth more than money to folks, right? So my poor client thought she was doomed to be in the middle of an international incident she hadn't a clue how to maneuver and didn't have the financial resources to make right or even really defend herself.

Enter...me.

I reacquire things that get stolen. I was at that antique show, too. For...reasons. And I heard the scuttlebutt through the whispers and rumors circulating the show. Antique collectors and dealers are a gossipy lot, and for someone like me, that's worth more than gold. So I hear about my poor client being officially in over her head thanks to some religious ancestors who didn't believe their own hype —what else would cause you to steal relics except for coveting thy neighbor's stuff? Or something.

Anyway, Gloria was in trouble. And I stepped in to help.

It's what I do. What can I say? Robin Hood, right?

So the people who stole Gloria's golden dragon—or I should say the Chinese people's golden dragon, but they'll get it back from Gloria once I get it back from the thieves so for now, since she's my client, I'm calling it Gloria's dragon. The rest will get sorted out in the end.

Anyway, the folks who stole the dragon are a couple of clowns who've made their living acquiring "impossible pieces for the most select, exclusive buyers" or some such bull. They own a little auction house in New York City. Nothing the level of Christies or the like, but a nice little place with exclusive access for like...international billionaires and stuff.

They run the business out of a brownstone on the Upper East Side, with top of the line security throughout—would pretty much have to, right?—and a whole lot of buffers between them and the riff-raff. Including a security company that hires out goons the size of small buses just to make all the security really obvious out front of the place as well as inside. Apparently, the billionaires like that sort of thing.

Now, remember how I said I don't have the full stage musical team around me? Well, I do actually have a team. They're just not musical theater ready. They are, however, extremely good at their various jobs.

Andy is the master hacker. Can't do thieving these days without a hacker. Everything's attached to computers and some such. Without a computer person, you're in hot water. And Andy is our computer person. An extraordinary computer person at that.

Andy's job was to find me a way into that

brownstone that didn't involve setting off every alarm in the building. He got us the layout of the place through hacking some architectural records. A decent sized, five stories building. The top floors mostly offices, the middle two floors the auction house proper. And the basement level, the specially built vault room. Unlike a lot of brownstones, there was no outside doors leading down into the basement level directly. The only way in or out of the place, for an ordinary person, was through the front door. Which was good for security purposes, but paranoid person that I am, the idea of having no real alternate ways out of a building creeped the hell out of me.

The surrounding brownstones were tight against the building, no gaps to slip between. Most of them had at least tiny postage stamp-sized outdoor spaces. But our particular brownstone did not have such an amenity, and so, no back door to take advantage of.

So it was the front door, the fire escapes, the roof garden door, or nothing.

Yes, this place had a roof garden. Upper East Side. It's fancy.

And also the home of crooks.

Which, now I think about it...

Anyway, back to my not-musical-theater-ready team. There's also the delightful Luiz, who is one of those kinds of people who can be anyone, anywhere. Seriously. Especially here in New York. Luiz can be moving through your garden, and you just assume he's supposed to be there. Walking through the party with a tray, assume he's staff. Fiddling with some appliance, he must be the repairman. Carrying a canister of poison, obviously the exterminator. People overlook him all the time. He blends into the background.

And I cannot tell you how conveniently handy that skill is. It's amazing what a clever man can do when no one's paying attention to him.

Then there's Marisa. Marisa's got the long con down like nobody's business. We met when she tried to con me. Little misunderstanding. We worked everything out over drinks. We've been fast friends ever since. And we work good together. Even when all I need is a B&E, Marisa's conwoman skills are next level helpful.

Finally, there's Juno. Juno is our jack of all trades. Need something built? Ask Juno. Need something taken apart? Ask Juno. She's the one who built a duplicate of the brownstone vault room literally overnight for me. I got the job. Andy hacked the brownstone's vault's plans. I told Juno I needed a replica to practice in. Day later, I'm walking into the place. Beautiful work. Just beautiful.

Now, me. As I said, I'm the thief. I'm the lock picking, sneaking around, sliding between the doors, climbing the side of buildings, grabbing the thing and getting out without being noticed kind. I used to do it for the thrills—and the cash of course. You need money to live. But it was never really about money for me.

Well. Okay. Some of it was about money. I like to do a little more than just live. I like to be comfortable.

But after a while, the money's just building up and not doing anything special for me. There's only so much I need to live comfortably and indulge my, maybe a little excessive, habit for pretty shoes and books. I'm not a yacht and mansion kind of person. Too high profile. Someone starts looking into how you got all that money. Someone wants to know if you're paying your taxes or not. And if not, if you're doing it legally. Cause yeah, there's lots of legal ways not to pay taxes.

Me, I pay my taxes, because I don't need the IRS looking at me. I'm meticulous about it, and I don't do all the stuff I could do to avoid it because, for me personally, keeping a low profile is the thing.

There's a thrill in being that person living next door to all the ordinary, working people, living their lives, never having a clue that nice neighbor girl with ever-so-slightly expensive tastes in shoes and a lot of packages with books delivered is actually a master thief. I like that delightful little secret as much as I like stealing things out from under the noses of assholes.

And, wow, do I love stealing things out from under the noses of assholes.

Which brings me back to the brownstone.

Takes practice, breaking into a vault. And planning. And frankly, poor old Gloria didn't have a lot of time before someone spilled that she was in possession—or at least had been—of a priceless Chinese relic—or well, there was a price on it, but you get the point. So unlike some of my other difficult thefts, I didn't have as much time to get everything in place with this one.

We still managed.

Invitations for the sale of the dragon went out the day the clowns stole it. So we knew when the auction was happening. They weren't waiting around for the Chinese government to come calling either. The sooner they got the piece sold and pocketed the money, the sooner they could wash their hands of the whole thing, and let Gloria take all the blame. The buyer certainly wouldn't rat them out. Who wanted their newly acquired priceless artifact confiscated by customs officials because it was a stolen relic belonging to someone else? No one. Especially the multi-millionaires and billionaires who frequented these kinds of underground sales. No one asked provenance questions, no one talked about provenance issues.

So we had the date and time for the auction. And since it was happening within days of the clowns stealing the dragon, we figured that was our opportunity. We'd have a lot harder time stealing it from the eventual buyer than we would the auction house. Plus, during an auction there's all these people around. All these potential distractions, ways in, and options for setting up my team.

Marisa's got lots of contacts that move inside these big-wig crowds, just to keep abreast of the latest valuable-things markets. Helps with cons to know what's what. And Marisa is good at knowing what's what. Thanks to her connections, she not only got us the right time and date for the auction, she also managed to get us a single invitation.

And Luiz, who's just a genius at going unseen? He's outstanding at passing for hired labor. No one even thinks to question him. He shows up in the right clothes, with the right attitude, and people just *assume* he's part of the staff. He's so good. Future generations of thieves and con artists should really study him.

In the days leading up to the party, while I practice in Juno's replica vault, Luiz got into the brownstone posing as cleaning crew and managed to tag both the upstairs offices and the auction hall floors with listening devices. When someone sees a short guy in the cleaner's uniform wiping down door handles and wooden surfaces with polish, they don't tend to notice him pressing tiny little metal disks into the creases in door frames and underneath various tables.

Juno and I, with help from Andy, found me the best way to crack the vault. And Andy found us a way through the security sensors and cameras leading into the vault. But that took him a good forty-eight hours to work out, and he had to, unfortunately, get in touch with a former colleague to get some keys. Unfortunately, because the colleague hadn't talked to Andy since Andy transitioned, so there was this whole thing with deadnaming, and misgendering and stuff Andy had to deal with. He's letting it go— he's a better person than me. I'd have smacked the guy. But I have that kind of leeway.

Still, it was a thing. So Andy's getting a bonus after we get the dragon, just for putting up with that crap.

Marisa's finagled invite to the auction came pre-fit with a good cover story. Because of course it did. She was going in as a billionaire's "buyer" with the implication that she was also his mistress, and no one wants to piss off a woman in that kind of position when she's got her hands on a billionaire's purse strings. The clowns who stole the dragon knew where their bread was buttered.

And with that, we had everything in place. We were ready for the big day.

At least, we had a plan.

CHAPTER TWO

On the day of the auction, Luiz went in early and blended right in with the catering team. Dressed in his crisp white shirt and black pants, he hustled around during set up, getting his instructions, then picked up a tray and started circulating flutes of champaign. And, of course, no one even thought to question who he was and how he got there.

With the listening devices in place, we knew where everyone was, which made for some interesting eavesdropping. The gossip you can pick up during one of these swanky, underground events. If I were the blackmailing sort—frankly, too risky for my blood—I'd have been able to make four fortunes on just that one night.

But I digress. Keeping track of the clowns, the

security staff, and the party guests was vital to our plan. I had a very narrow window of opportunity in the vault itself. And I'd need to know if said opportunity was getting any narrower because people started moving around where they weren't meant to be.

There were other items involved in the auction, not just the dragon. But the dragon was the front and center star. And so, they brought the gorgeous golden statue into the party, under heavy security, for a few minutes. To whet the appetites of the buyers.

That was Marisa's chance to make sure the real dragon was even there. We were pretty sure there were no forgeries involved. Not much time to get one made, for one thing. But since *we* occasionally pulled off the impossible, I wasn't putting it past the clowns to come up with a forgery and make even more money off their theft.

I should probably mention the clowns are brothers named William and Anthony Pike. Their history is an interesting read of peripheral mob connections and a dad who dabbled in very effective Ponzi schemes. They've understood the grift from a young age. And I might have let that sort of thing go —who was I to judge—but they kept grifting the underdogs and the working stiffs in favor of the billionaires who really didn't need any more money or stuff.

That's my Robin Hood complex speaking again.

The Pikes were two average sized white men. William the older, with gray hair that had to be more aggressively dyed to get a chestnut color going. Anthony the younger boasted a full head of blond hair and never let William forget about it, from what we overheard. They're pretty well known around the antiques and collectibles communities. And, of course, people whisper about them. But far as I could tell, no one lobs actual accusations at them.

Listening to them circulate through all the high-rollers at the party before the auction, showing off their most prized possession, I kinda understood. Their connections, their confidence, their command of a room... If I were an ordinary joe who realized they'd stolen my stuff, I wouldn't know how to get it back from them either.

Which is where the real me comes in.

The me who had to get into the building still.

Since the front door was a security nightmare with people coming into the party and guards and everything, and since I couldn't afford to slip in with the catering crew or even pretend to be a guest—we only had that one invitation anyway—I went with the sneaking-in-through-the-roof-garden option.

They had that pretty secure, under most circumstances. But on an auction night, they kept the security up there minimal because they were okay with their guests wandering out there. Let the rich guys take a break for a smoke in a lovely garden on a nice night and they're more likely to bid high on the next trinket they want. So on this particular night, while they still had cameras up everywhere—Andy could hack those so we were okay there—and motion sensors all over the place to keep track of their guests on the roof—Andy couldn't hack those, so Juno built me a replica roof garden so I could practice avoiding them—the actual door into the building was unlocked.

Not unsecured mind you. Just unlocked.

The brownstones next to our target didn't have any side windows of course, and one had a roof with its own security—which made me pretty curious what went on inside that house, but I'd look into it at another point. The other neighbor was less worried about people climbing onto their roof and using it to access their neighbors' roofs. So that's the place I used. Accessing that roof was relatively easy. No garden up here, just a lot of flat, tarred roof and bird poop.

I crept across the tar, avoiding as much bird poop as possible, to the garden roof. It was up a story from my vantage, which meant a little climb. The rope and hook I'd normally use was both too noisy and also might hit one of the non-hackable sensors I had to worry about. But fortunately, with only half a story to climb, I could scale the thick orange bricks. I can actually climb the side of taller buildings, but I don't do that much. Too noticeable, if I'm honest with you. Takes too long, have to be careful, like rock climbing, and there's too many opportunities to be noticed.

So I scale the twelve feet I need to to reach the edge of the garden roof, then peek over the ledge. The garden was impressively lush for the early spring. It had rained last night, so while there weren't any obvious water puddles I'd have to work around, the plants were all happy. The Pikes had gone with comfortably stylish deck chairs and tables, and there were a few marble statues among the various boxes of plants and small trees. Thought I caught a hint of citrus among the greenery, but the smell of tar from the roof below me was too strong and overpowering most of the green.

Slipping over the low wall into the roof garden, I kept low, adjusting my backpack straps as I paused to get my bearings. Listening for guests who'd snuck up here for a smoke, or a quick fuck, or a business call they thought wouldn't be overheard. No sounds beyond my own breathing and the traffic below. Few horns in the distance. Someone yelling about a block away. Even on the Upper East Side, we were still in New York City and the place was noisy.

When a bus on the cross street screeched to a stop and let out a loud hiss, I crept away from the wall, taking the route through the garden that avoided the cameras and the motion sensors that would trigger the cameras. Those particular systems were only connected to internal feeds. Nothing Andy could access. So getting around them was my only option.

The door out to the roof garden was in a little shed-sized building that led to a stairwell and, I shit you not, an elevator. A private house with an elevator. I loved those. So decadent. And to be fair, if I lived in a five-story *house*, I'd probably want an elevator too. Imagine all the hiking necessary just to get laundry done? You don't think about it much until you've lived in a five-story walk-up and laundry room's in the basement, and then you have more sympathy for the rich schmucks living in a five-story house with a basement. Or more sympathy for their staff, since it's probably not the rich schmucks doing the actual laundry, right?

While there was no lock on the door, there was a sensor on it to register when it was open and closed, and an associated camera that would catch anyone moving out—or in my case *in*—as soon as that sensor was triggered. This was another one of those internal loop things that Andy couldn't access. So it was up to me to fritz the motion sensor just long enough to sneak in.

I could probably have waited for someone to come out. But I didn't like counting on chance. That was no way to make a plan. And I was pretty sure the camera would still pick me up sneaking in behind the person coming out. I could have dressed in my party gear and pretended to go back inside with any guest who came up to the roof, but again, cameras and chance involved. I wanted nothing to do with either.

Tweaking the motion sensor was something I could work with. And I managed to get it to disconnect briefly, giving myself a twenty second window to get inside and get the door closed without a camera being tripped.

Once inside, though, I was pretty exposed. Elevator across from me, stairs to the right. Windows on the left to give the little foyer some natural light on good days. Bright overhead light tonight. The brightness was a pain. I was wearing all black, a wool cap covering my normally light hair pulled low, sneaking around and staying hidden in the dark uniform of a good thief. But in that brightly lit foyer with the clean yellow walls and Spanish tiled floor, I felt a little too visible. No shadows to hide in here.

And, to add chaos to mayhem, the elevator dinged just as I got the door to the roof closed, seconds before the motion sensor went back online.

I slipped into the stairwell, hurrying down far enough I couldn't be seen, pressing against the wall to stay even more unobtrusive. Listened hard. Whoever came out of the elevator had a heavy step that echoed in the low-ceiling foyer. The roof door slammed open as they walked out.

Someone in a mood. Glad I'd avoided them.

The stairs stayed relatively quiet, no guests

deciding hiking up instead of taking the elevator sounded good. No Pikes. No staff trying to sneak out for a smoke.

I slipped down to the first two flights, to where the auction house proper was, before having to abandon the stairs to avoid people.

Marisa, over our ear mics, said aloud, "So many fine pieces, Mr. Pike. What a marvelous auction you've assembled this time. Tell me more about this piece."

"Ah, Ms. Hardgrave, this piece is exquisite. I'm sure Mr. Somerset would be most impressed. It's a relic from the Yuan dynasty. Solid gold. According to our researchers, there were only a handful of these made. The golden dragon was a representative of the Emperor and this small version was a special symbol used to mark his favor for his most trusted allies."

I slipped into a storage closet to avoid some staff while I listened to whichever Pike brother Marisa was talking to tell her about our dragon. With the dragon on the floor, not in the vault at present, I had to bide my time. They'd return it to the vault soon, before the auction, when the pieces would only be brought up one at a time for the biding. But for now, the dragon was out of my reach.

"Fascinating," Marisa said, sounding less than fascinated.

"Oh, it is a very rare and valuable piece," the Pike

brother enthused. "We expect the bidding to go quite high."

"Of course." I could practically hear Marisa's tight smile and was a little sorry I couldn't watch her performance from my closet cover. "And what about this piece?"

"Oh, uhm, yes, this is a less rare, but still exquisite piece. Originally from Austria, a comb of the Empress..."

"He sounds disappointed Marisa wasn't more impressed with his stolen dragon," Andy said over our shared ear pieces.

"She's playing it perfectly," Luiz said. "Scanned the room while Anthony was talking, only flashing him a polite smile when he was done."

She was so good.

"William's had a few more enthusiastic potentials," Luiz continued. Then paused when someone got close and chatter in the background got louder. A brief "Thanks" which I assumed was directed at Luiz for the champaign but might not have been since these weren't the kinds of people who tended to thank the staff. Then Luiz was back. "Think there's a little competition going between the brothers to see which of them gets a bidder most interested. They're looking for a big score on that dragon. It's their center piece and they've been talking it up a lot."

"Could you get close enough to William to see

what he's been telling people?" I whispered. There was enough party noise, and staff noise in the kitchen, I wasn't likely to be overheard inside my closet, but I wasn't the sort to take unnecessary chances. Just necessary ones.

"I'll see if I can swing past," Luiz said.

Marisa was still with Anthony so she didn't comment. I listened to her question Anthony about a few more pieces. Never even circled back to the dragon. She really was a consummate con-artist. Even when Anthony brought up the central piece for the auction again, she skipped right past it with barely an acknowledgement.

I love my team.

Luiz hissed quietly in our ears, "Heads up." Then louder, "Drink, sirs?"

The other Pick brother's voice now, and a second unknown man. "It's extraordinary," the second man said. "But there could be issues."

"The provenance is well supported, Forester," William said. "What issues could there be?"

"I've heard things, William. Rumors out of China."

Already? We were trying to beat the news reaching the Chinese government, to keep Gloria safe. Were we already too late?

Not that that changed anything. If we didn't get the dragon tonight, getting it later would be a lot more difficult. Even without the added threat of a government body also trying to find and reclaim the relic.

"Just rumors, Forester," William assured. "There is nothing in the world like the dragon. Nothing that survived the centuries anyway. It's one of a kind. Priceless."

"Yet you've put a price on it."

"It's my job. And it's a starting price."

Forester snorted. "I should just let Allen have it."

"You could," William said. "But you'll never hear the end of it. Every time you see him, he'll remind you of this treasure and how you passed on it."

They moved away from Luiz then, or Luiz from them. Either way, the rest of the conversation and Forester's reaction to William Pikes' taunt went beyond our range. Didn't really matter.

"Not much new," Luiz said. "We know William's pitting the bidders against each other."

"And that the Chinese may already know about the relic," Andy said.

"That's not going to be good for Gloria," Juno said. She was back at our base of operations with Andy, on hand to help if needed, but mostly her part of the scheme was done.

"I'm hearing the same rumors," Marisa said, finally speaking directly to us. "Whispers that the dragon's provenance and ownership will be challenged by the Chinese. That's been both a draw and a discouragement for a bunch of these people."

Draw for the ones who liked to court danger. Discouragement for those who preferred staying under the radar and working their manipulative money games unnoticed. Or those who were just scared of the Chinese. But to be fair, most of these people were rich enough they feared very little in life. Even a big powerful governmental body.

"Doesn't change anything," I whispered, glancing at my wristwatch—the old-fashioned analog kind because I was old school. "Almost time. Let me know when they take the dragon back down to the vault."

"Starting to collect the displays already," Marisa said quietly, then her voice got louder and she was off into another conversation with...sounded like one of the other wealthy guests.

Once everything was back and secured in the vault, I'd make my move in the moments of chaos as they got everyone settled for the auction proper.

My chance came only a few minutes later.

"Ladies and Gentlemen," William's voice, loud enough I heard it without Marisa and Luiz's ear pieces echoing it back to me. "If you'll please follow my brother and I, we'll get things underway."

There was a lot of shuffling and noise, more movement into the kitchen as the caterers prepared to downshift. They'd continue to serve drinks throughout the rest of the evening, but the food portion of the night was over.

When the kitchen noise settled a little, I slipped out and slid down the stairs to the basement and the vault. The entire basement of the building was taken up by the vault with only a small foyer in front of the steel wall and vault door—an actual round, vault door, like the kind of thing you'd see at a bank. The door was thick metal, impossible to blast through without raising the house, and had a rather impressive electronic panel lock in the center. Low lighting, likely to protect the art, gave me a lot of shadows to hide in, including a small dark space next to the back of the stairs near the wall.

I ducked into that spot as the door to the vault slowly eased open and a security person walked out with the first item up for bid. While the guard's back was turned, I slid a thin, black disk along the floor, letting it slip into the vault just before the door closed.

I waited for him to go up the stairs. Listened for a long moment to make sure no one was changing up the schedule and coming down early for the second piece. When things stayed quiet, I hurried to the vault.

From my backpack, I pulled out the little tablet Andy had prepared for me, attached the probes to the electronic lock panel on the front of the vault door, and triggered the code that would disable the lock for me for twenty seconds without sounding an alarm.

Not long, but long enough for me to slip inside and have the door closed before the sensors realized something wasn't as it should be.

The locks slid back, the sound of metal grinding and clicking loud in the otherwise quiet room. Noise from the auction above carried faintly down to me. No change in that noise level so I knew no one had heard. I unhooked my tablet and swung inside the narrow crack in the door, pulling it closed the second I was inside. Little blue lights around the edge of the door confirmed it was sealed and that, as far as the door was concerned, all was well in the room.

I didn't move away from the door immediately. First, I had to make sure the little disk I'd slid into the room worked.

When the door was locked, motion sensors on the vault floor clicked on. If the door was open, they were off, but since we'd hacked in instead of entering a proper code, and since an open door would draw suspicion from the security guard when he came down again for the next item, something had to be done about the motion sensors.

Andy's answer had been rather ingenious. The little disk was a miniature disruptor that shorted out the motion sensors. The minute they came on, the disk's programming counter them. Andy did try to explain it to me. But I have to admit, I didn't understand it. This is why I work with Andy—so I don't have to understand or figure out the technical stuff. I break in and steal the thing. He gets me past the sophisticated security. We made a very fine team.

The blinking red lights around the floor that would have indicated the motion sensors were active were all off. We'd practiced this in Juno's vault replica. So far so good. I took a single step into the room. Waited for alarms. None blared.

"Think we're good," I murmured aloud, so my ear piece would pick it up. The others had been quiet in my ear since I started this part of the run, though I could still hear some of the auction through Marisa's ear piece. That was a quiet background hum I barely noticed now that I was inside the vault—a background hum that remained the same, even after I moved.

No alarms.

"You're good," Andy confirmed.

I didn't waste time. There were stacks of art against the wall, display cases and cabinets with all manner of items on them. But the thing I was looking for, the golden dragon, was in its own isolated case in the center of the huge room. A tall pillar topped by a strong plastic case brought the dragon to eye-level.

The gold sparkled in the vault's low lighting, winking in the single overhead light that was on when the door was sealed. Seeing the piece in person for the first time was a little overwhelming. How had Marisa been able to play it so cool earlier?

The golden statue was about two feet long and a little less than half a foot tall. The dragon was the serpentine types with the long body and tail, quite short legs, and an impressive ruff around its head. There were horns on its head and what looked like a mustache around the raised nostrils on its snout. Individual scales covered its body, thin pieces of gold gently welded into place. The dragon had been given a lowered brow expression, which made it look fierce, and the teeth carved into its mouth were all sharply pointed.

The artistry of the piece was truly impressive. There weren't any added jewels or embellishments. Just pure sparkling gold. Gloria had said that before she'd put the piece on her mantal, the dragon sat at the back of a closet with a lot of the items she'd inherited from her family, dull and dusty from the way it had been stored. Obviously, the statue had been given a good scrub since then, letting the gold glitter. All the better to demand a high price at auction.

The plastic case enclosing the dragon was sturdy bullet proof material that would be impossible to shatter, and it was attached to the pillar so the case couldn't just be removed.

And it was locked.

The Pikes were not taking the security of the dragon lightly.

I studied the lock at the base of the case. This was

the one place we hadn't been able to get much information. We suspected there'd be an extra layer of security around the dragon, an extra lock, but we hadn't been able to determine what that might be in the narrow timeframe we had to work in.

Fortunately for us, for me, the Pikes were relying on the outer sophisticated security measures to really protect the dragon. For this last layer of defense, they'd gone old school with an ordinary key lock. Just a normal lock that required a key.

I was very good at picking those kinds of locks.

But even after I had the lock open, I didn't immediately reach for the dragon, first studying the base and the pad underneath the golden statue.

Yup, more motion sensors. And that was going to be tricky. Not impossible. But tricky.

I gently set my backpack on the ground, my gaze drifting to the vault door. I didn't have a lot of time left before the guard would be back for the second auction item.

From the backpack I pulled out the replica dragon Juno had made for us, based on pictures Gloria had provided. I studied the replica a moment. She'd done a really nice job. Not identical. The replica was just...lacking something from the original. I'd have had to have studied both pieces longer to say what that lack was, but I didn't have the time. For now, the replica would do.

Juno had used gold painted led, ensuring the

weight was as close to the dragon's as we could get without having weighed the dragon precisely. Still, the motion sensors would detect the movement when I replaced one dragon with the other, even if they registered the new dragon as weighing the right amount.

The transfer had to be done quick and efficiently. These kinds of motion sensors were designed to absorb some movement and not go off—there was a rumbling subway under this city that came close enough to this building all the basement motion detectors would be blaring regularly if they picked up every little wobble and rocking motion. So the trick was fooling the sensor into thinking the dragon was vibrating from a passing train, maybe rocking a little, but otherwise not moving.

I had less than a minute to manage this delicate feat.

And if I was caught in here, there was nowhere to run.

CHAPTER THREE

My hand hovered over the real golden dragon for a long long moment as I steady my heartbeat, letting my pulse slow, let my breathing even. The delicacy of the move, the tight timing, the excitement... I had to control all that or this wouldn't work.

I really love my work.

The dragon glistened under the light as I let my hand softly touch the top. The gold was cool, the intricate scales underneath a delicate texture against my sensitive fingertips. I positioned the replica right next to the real dragon, setting it up so that I could move them at the same time.

The train vibrations rumbled through the base of my feet. I could just hear the *ka-chunk ka-chunk* as the line passed beneath the streets near the building.

One last steady, slow breath in. Hold…

Sweep one dragon to the side just as the other touched the motion sensor pad.

I paused, the real dragon in my hand, the replica sitting steadily on the pad.

The sounds of the train faded. The rumbling underfoot stopped.

Everything went very quiet and steady.

No alarms.

The sounds from the auction normal.

I smiled.

Just as the lock on the vault clicked.

Gently, but quickly, I lower the plastic case over the fake dragon, stuff the real dragon into my backpack, and head toward the corner of the room where I knew I could hide from the security guard so long as he only came in for the second auction item.

I ducked carefully behind a pile of paintings that wouldn't be sold at this auction, squeezing between a heavy gold frame and the steel wall. Held my breath again. Mostly to ensure I could stay small enough to hide in the shadows.

I heard the guard moving around. Heard the shuffling of his feet against the steel floor, the sounds of him muttering under his breath. A movement of something. A curse.

The curse had me freezing, not even blinking. I hadn't locked the dragon case yet. No time. And it was sitting in the center of the vault, clear to see from the door. I tried to remember if I'd left anything out of position, if I'd left a lock pick behind, if there was something I'd dropped near the column under the dragon...

Another curse and then a mumbled, "Fucking chest. Who the hell buys this stuff? Not even any gold or jewels."

There was more muttering, but I could barely hear what he said over the sound of my heart pounding in my ears. I breathed out slowly from my mouth, silently.

More shuffling footsteps and another curse. Then the sounds of the vault door closing.

I was so relieved, I almost forgot to toss my second disk to disable the motion sensors into the center of the vault.

Scrambling in my backpack, I snatched up the disk and slid it across the floor just as the vault door clicked into place and the locks re-engaged.

Then let out a noisier—although still quiet —breath.

The disks were a one-shot deal. Once the door opened and the sensors turned off, the disk stopped working. Once the door closed again, the motion sensors reset. And without a second disk to disrupt the sensors again, all of this would have been wasted. The minute I stood to leave I would have triggered the newly reactivated motion detectors.

My heart was still pounding hard. More from the

part where I nearly forgot the disk than from the close encounter with the guard. I'd planned for the guard part. Once I could steady my pulse, I slid out from behind the stacked paintings, careful not to tip them over. The front one started to topple, but I reached it before it slammed against the steel floor. Slowly lifting it back into place and settling it, I glance at the vault door.

Still no alarms blaring and the distant, very faint noise from the auction sounded normal.

My ears rang with the surrounding silence inside the vault as I listened hard to anything I could pick up from outside the door. Halfway to the exit, I remembered the dragon case needed to be locked.

Damn it. Two things I'd nearly forgotten. Getting sloppy.

Relocking a key lock with lockpicking tools is as easy as picking it in the first place. I gave the replica one last look, reassured it was sitting exactly as the original had been. The case was in place on top of the pillar. The case was locked. Nothing dropped or incriminating around the pedestal.

The guard would be back in two minutes for the next auction item. He'd have a second person with him for this one, since it was a heavy vase nearly the size of me. That gave me two minutes to get back out of the vault and into the shadows behind the stairs.

Plenty of time.

I made it with a full fifteen seconds to spare.

There was a lot more cursing over the vase than there had been over the chest. At least from the first guard. The second one was silent and glowered at his associate while his associate closed the vault again.

They grunted as they eased the heavy vase up the stairs, and there was one terrifying moment when one of them snapped, "Careful! We drop this thing, they'll charge us for it. You got two million dollars laying around?"

"Fuck no."

"Me neither. Watch your step."

More grunting and muttering.

And then that lovely silence. Except for the sounds of the auctioneer queuing up the bidders as he explained the history of the giant vase.

I slipped upstairs and made my way carefully back to the roof, ducking into the occasional closet or alcove to avoid staff, and once to avoid a couple who'd snuck away from the auction for a quick bit of fun in an office. They were noisy enough to cover any sounds I might have made as I passed by on the last flight of stairs up to the garden. Luckily, they hadn't decided the garden would be a good spot for their fun. That would have made my job of getting away a lot more complicated.

And as it turned out, my escape was already complicated.

By someone in wandering through the garden.

Chapter Four

I was barely through the door out to the rooftop garden when I heard a scraping sound in the foliage nearby and had to dive behind a planter. In my ear, Luiz asked, "Rose, you almost out?"

I pressed the earpiece tighter against my ear so no one would hear his voice, keeping silent until I could figure out who was on the roof.

Peaking around the edge of the planter, I spotted an older man with gray hair and a sharply trimmed mustache having a smoke, the tip of his cigar flaring in the darkness. The lights from the surrounding buildings illuminated the area, but none of the garden's own lights were turned on. The man stood with his side to me, puffing on his cigar, contemplating the skyline, which was not very impressive from this position. Mostly just the backs of taller buildings.

I waited him out, trying not to curse when I heard Luiz in my ear again, starting to sound panicked. I willed him to be quiet and not worry. But our timing was off now. If I didn't check in soon, they'd all start to panic.

Except I couldn't even whisper yet. The man was too close, and the rooftop was too quiet.

The smell of his cigar drifted to me across the lush greenery, a sharp musky scent that blotted out the other city smells not covered by the surrounding plant life. I heard the subway rumbling past again, deep underground, the sound nevertheless carrying all the way up here. And traffic on the crossroads got noisy when a light changed. Someone laughed loudly a street over.

The smoking man seemed oblivious to it all.

I found myself counting the seconds as his cigar grew slowly, slowly smaller. How long did it take to smoke a cigar? Seemed like this guy was drawing it out. Couldn't he do this faster?

Then another voice from the doorway.

The unseen man said, "Put that thing away. You know what your doctor said."

The smoking man sighed. "I'm not allowed any pleasures?" His heavy French accent rolled the last word.

"I'm your pleasure," the unseen man said.

"Come back inside. That necklace you wanted to bid on is up next."

The smoking man gently rolled his cigar on a wooden planter, snubbing it out. He checked the tip, then slipped it back into an inner pocket of his suit jacket. He straightened his sleeves with a gentle snap, the gesture making his jeweled cufflinks wink. Then he headed back for the door, disappearing from my view.

I waited until I could no longer hear the two men talking as they descended the stairs. Then I rushed to the ledge. No more time to waste. The dragon would be up soon. I wanted to be blocks away before the guards went to get it. Just in case.

In my earpiece, I murmured, "I'm leaving the roof now. Got slowed down by a smoker."

Andy's breath of relief was audible in my ear.

"Dragon's up in three more pieces," Luiz said. "Hurry. I'm on my way out now."

"Bidding is noisy," Marisa said. "See you back at base."

Marisa would stay throughout the auction, even if the dragon was discovered to be a fake. She was really good at maintaining her role, all the way to the end. No suspicions about who she really was would be raised. And that meant her associates inside these circles could continue helping her infiltrate them.

Scaling back down a wall is actually a little harder than scaling up for me. But I dropped onto the neighboring roof without a sound, hurrying across the tarred surface to the stairwell door and another hurried walk down four flights of stairs.

I'd just turned onto a noisy cross-street two blocks away when I heard the auctioneer through Marisa's earpiece.

"And now, for the highlight of our auction tonight..."

I slipped into the subway, heading downtown for my transfer to Queens, losing the rest of the man's spiel.

I MET GLORIA AT THE METROPOLITAN Museum of Art, at the rooftop bar, because that seemed really appropriate for handing over priceless art which would then be returned to its culture of origin. I might have been feeling a little frisky when I made those arrangements.

The bar wasn't particularly crowded yet, not quite happy hour, but wasn't empty either. People scattered around the open terrace, or sitting on the little wooden benches around the high retaining wall encircling the balcony. The sun was out, bright in a near cloudless blue sky. The sounds of traffic from behind the building didn't overpower the lovely view of Central Park and the Upper Westside and Midtown skylines beyond. It was a really magnificent view.

I stood to one side of the terrace, on the raised platform farthest from the outdoor bar with its selection of expensive cocktails, wines, and overpriced snacks, waiting for my client as I admired the view.

"How on earth did you get in here through security without...?" Gloria's voice behind me.

I turned to face her.

She glanced down at the courier bag I had hanging against my hip. It was an army green color and had the stamp of one of our fair city's famous bookstores on the flap.

"They had to search your bag," Gloria said, her voice low, just above a whisper. "How did you...?"

I smiled at the way she kept trying not to say anything out loud. There weren't any other people nearby to overhear. But I did appreciate the discretion.

"I have a friend who works security here." I shrugged. "Made sure they were doing bag checks when I came through."

That was one of the other reasons I picked this location. Besides the great view. My friend was pretty amenable to helping, since she knew the dragon was heading home at the end of all this. She liked the idea of art returning to its country of origin, too, when it was taken out illegally—though my friend was always careful not to call it "stolen" when she talked to me because she didn't want to offend me, seeing as I'm a thief and all that.

"Was there any trouble? Any issue?" Gloria asked, wringing her hands together.

Gloria was a woman in her sixties who looked like a woman in sixties. Her gray-blond hair was cut short, but not in a cute funky style, just that older woman short that makes it easy to take care of and to hide the fact that it's thinning. Her blue eyes were creased with the happy lines of aging. Her mouth was a little pinched, and her nose a little stubby, but otherwise she had a very pleasant, round face. And she sparked my protective instincts because she reminded me, in baring if not in looks, of my grandmother.

Although, my grandmother would have stomped into the Pike brother's place of business and demanded her dragon back or she'd poison them both. Grandma had a mean streak. And access to the most amazing book of poisons.

"No issues," I told Gloria. "No one seems to have noticed the fake. Which means the poor slob who paid ten million for it is going to be pissed when Interpol picks him up for trafficking in stolen goods, only to realize he'd been sold a fake."

There was a nice symmetry to that part. The buyer being out ten million, being picked up by international authorities, and still losing the prize.

"And the Pikes?" Gloria asked.

"Yeah, they're not having a good week either."

An anonymous tip to the Chinese government *and* Interpol *and* the American customs office about a number of stolen items I'd spotted inside that vault meant the Pike's auction house got raided. Just that morning, as a matter of fact. The team and I watched some of the mayhem from across the street. It was pretty entertaining watching Willian and Anthony get escorted out of the building surrounded by very official looking people and one man who looked particularly angry as he followed them. A little snooping confirmed that last man was a Chinese diplomat and the dragon wasn't the only cultural artifact the Pikes had stolen.

Who knew?

Well, technically I did, but not before breaking into the vault.

"So... So I'm not going to get into trouble or owe anyone millions of dollars?" Gloria asked.

"No one will ever know what happened. Even the Pikes haven't figured it out yet. They don't know who we are. There's no way for them to trace any of this back to us, or to you. They'll just think the dragon they stole from you was actually a fake and the expert at the antics show had made a mistake." I grinned again at Gloria's wide-eyed expression. "My team and I are pretty good at this kind of thing."

"May I... May I see it?" Gloria nodded to my

courier bag, then glanced around the terrace to make sure no one was near enough to see anything.

Since I'd been keeping an eye on the dozen people on the roof already, I knew we were safe enough, so I opened my bag, unfolded the additional bag inside holding the dragon, and let her have a look.

She leaned in close, washing me with the smell of her lavender shampoo, which smelled less overpowering that most lavender stuff does to me. She reached out and ran her finger over the golden dragon's long, scaled body.

"All of this for this little guy who'd been in the back of my closet for a decade," she breathed.

"My contact at the embassy is going to meet you at the boat house. She'll pay for lunch—let her! You can hand the dragon over, and she'll preserve your anonymity. The Chinese government is also going to offer you a 'thank you' reward for returning such a priceless relic. Do not turn it down. My contact had to do a lot of negotiating to get you some compensation."

"Oh, but it was my ancestors who stole it in the first place. I really don't need anything."

"And you're doing the right thing by returning it, freely and without demanding payment. Doing the right thing, in these circumstances, should come with at least a little reward. My contact agreed and ensured her government did, too."

Gloria would find out soon enough the "little reward" was a million dollars. That would set her up comfortably for a while if she was careful with it. A good retirement pension for doing the right thing. But I wanted that to be a surprise.

"Encourages others to return relics to their country of origin," I said by way of explanation.

Not that I thought that would happen very often. Too many people finding themselves in Gloria's situation would have just tried to sell the dragon to the highest bidder and run with the money. But it does my cynical heart good to meet people like Gloria, so I want to encourage them in their good efforts.

I handed her the second bag from inside my courier satchel, the bag with the dragon wrapped up in it, an ordinary reusable shopping bag that didn't look like the kind of thing you'd carry a priceless relic in. I'd hidden a tracker in the bag, just in case. First, I didn't want someone to snatch it from Gloria and get away with stealing what I'd gone through so much trouble to steal already. Second... Well, as I said, I'm a cynic. And I work with a lot of con people. I was certain Gloria was on the up and up, but just in case...

I didn't want someone to steal what I'd gone through all the trouble of stealing already.

Her hands shook as she took the bag and looped the long strap over her shoulder. "I don't know how to thank you. You've saved my life. Is there anything...anything I can do for you? You said you wouldn't take money, but...I have a small pension. I could maybe pay—"

"That won't be necessary," I said, cutting her off. "I'm just happy to see the little guy returned to his home."

And also, it was possible I'd slipped another little gem from the Pike's vault that wasn't stolen from another culture, and that, when I sold it, paid for our entire escapade. I have no problems robbing from the crooked to pay for my ability to help the innocent.

Like I said before...Robin Hood complex.

I wished Gloria good luck and watched her leave the roof bar, waiting until my tracker in the dragon bag assured me she was on her way to the boat house. I sent my contact a text to let her know the dragon was on its way.

Then I took one last, long look out over the park and the skyline beyond.

Beautiful.

A nice way to finish up a job well done.

Now Pick a New Genre

SCIENCE
FICTION

Chapter One

Who steals a dragon?

Andy couldn't believe she even had to ask that question. Because really, who the hell *steals* a dragon?

And not just any dragon. No. This had to be the Dragon X-47 B Class with cloaking capabilities that also just so happened to be the flagship of the Gremoren Fleet. Someone decided it was not only a good idea to steal a whole ass starship, but then thought, *You know what, I'll steal the absolute most significant battleship in the main fleet of the deadliest species in the sector because why the hell not. In for a quin, in for a quintal.*

It was quite literally *the* most suicidal thing Andy had ever heard anyone do in her entire life. And she'd been present for the Tenchian Battle at Ominor, when the Mica had dive bombed a battle cruiser in their little Z-pods.

She stared at the scroll of data moving across her view through the feed-link. The conference room on the Absinea was silent, the air ripe with both anticipation, fear, and the same kind of awe preventing her from speaking. Heavy mugs of coffee, tea, and for Zander, pine-juice, sat untouched on the conference room's long, oval table. Everyone in the room had access to the data feed. Everyone was seeing the details of the potential job at the same time as Andy. The room was so quiet, she could actually hear the air refiltering system whispering and the hum of her ship at rest.

Her tracking team was small, but one of the best in the sector. The Absinea crew were known for their ability to find anything. But as she leaned back in the molded airchair—the chair adjusting its temperature to keep her comfortable—and studied the data Gremoren Commander Pxin had dropped into their feed, she had her doubts.

More than the usual doubts, too. Because this wasn't just any stolen ship. This was a flipping Dragon. Someone had actually gone and stolen a Dragon.

She shook her head. Su-i-cid-al.

The flagship of the Gremoren Fleet, known as the Destroyer, took a crew of at least ten just to get it from one point in deep space to another. It wasn't the kind of ship that one person could pilot and jump because most of the systems were not automated and synced. It required coordinated effort across multiple systems just to *move* the ship. This was done on purpose. So no small band of enemies could take it over. And anyone smart enough to get on board and hack into the ship's systems without being killed by the Gremoren crew couldn't overpower the ship through a single port point.

The weakness was obviously that in battle, if one of the required ship systems took too much damage, or the crew in that section were killed, the ship could end up dead in the aether, so to speak.

But since Dragon shields were almost impenetrable to most on-the-market weapons at present, the Gremoren had taken the tactical design risk to offset other potential dangers. They had never been able to fully protect their systems from hacking. Despite twenty years of war advancements in other areas. The Blends, in particular, had always been able to find a way in and access their computers.

Dragons had been designed to counter this. Different systems. None interconnected. Each required to work simultaneously. Each requiring a number of crew working the individual system.

And that was just to move the thing. In battle, even more crew were required.

The whole set up in the B Class was specifically

designed to prevent the possibility of hacking and theft.

And yet...

Someone had not only stolen one of the Dragons, they'd stolen the flagship. Destroyer. Right out from under the Gremoren command crew's watch.

That had to be embarrassing. Gremoren did not react well to embarrassment.

The fact that they wanted to hire Andy and her team to retrieve the ship, rather than go after it themselves was...interesting, though.

That niggling concern over "interesting" was what made her hesitate to take this job. Well, that and the fact that Dragons were also extraordinarily difficult to track. But more, it was her concern over the "interesting" part.

"We really want to get into the middle of this," Mace said quietly, echoing her concern. He was the Absinea's primary engineer and the best tech whisperer money could buy. Thick, bald, tattooed, pale brown skin, and short, most people missed his kind soul and assumed a lack of delicate dexterity from his large hands. But Mace could finesse the finest of gadgetry and make most tech hum.

He was seeing all the same data Andy was seeing. And everything that was missing from that data scroll.

If he was hesitant, Andy knew her own concerns were warranted.

"Not sure either, be honest with you, boss," Kiva said. Kiva could find a specific milliliter of gas in a lightyear's wide gas cloud. Red hair piled in a messy bun, pale skin dotted with freckles, curvy and average height, Kiva was a human equivalent of a blood hound. She found the scent of a missing thing in the data and followed that scent unwaveringly. But she was hesitant to track the Dragon, too.

The growing voices of unease had Andy even more suspicious of this job.

"What are we missing?" she asked the team.

"A motive," Jenx said. A data cruncher and the team's medic, Jenx was tall, willowy, dark skinned, with hair in braids decorated with little silver clips and beads. She was very good at saying a lot with a single raised eyebrow. She was also extremely good at probability analysis. "What possible reason did the thieves have for stealing the Gremoren's flagship?"

"Outside of preventing them from using it in an attack?" Mace pointed out the obvious.

"Well, yeah," Jenx said. "But there's no current war happening. The Gremoren haven't attacked anyone lately. And the sector truce accord has held for the last five, six standards."

"Doesn't mean it'll remain in effect," Kiva said. "Gremoren aren't living if they're not dying in battle."

Mace swiped a hand over his bald, tattooed head. "Such a fucking waste."

Andy had to agree. Wars and takeovers and skirmishes and battles never went well for anyone but a few higher ups. The higher ups managed to get richer and more powerful somehow. Almost everyone else just ended up worse off than before. Or dead. And sometimes, she thought the dead were the lucky ones. But that was her doomspeak side. She tried not to indulge that part of her personality too often.

"You think someone out there knows more than the rest of the sector about Gremoren future invasion plans?" she asked the table.

Jenx gave her a look with that single raised eyebrow and pursed lips.

"Which means," Mace said, "we get that Dragon back, we give the Gremoren what they need for an invasion."

"Not necessarily," Banter said, his gaze still turned inward as he studied the data scroll.

Banter and Zander were twins, average height, variously brown skinned, dark long hair for Banter, blond short hair for Zander, and average builds. They were the Absinea's pilots, and could thread a needle with the ship, flying with an instinctive connection to the Absinea that Andy had rarely encountered in pilots. They were human, but had been raised on Blend with a species that lived, breathed, and worshipped tech code. And while their hacking skills weren't up to the Blends, they were capable of more than most humans.

"Anyone anywhere ever think someone was capable of stealing that ship?" Banter blinked out of the data scroll and looked at the people surrounding him again. "Not just the Gremoren. They're arrogant as a general rule. Probably never crossed their command's mind it was even possible to steal the Destroyer."

"But someone managed it," Kiva said, nodding.

"And if we assume whoever they are, they're the ones the Gremoren were considering attacking..." Jenx said.

"We can assume this was a warning to the Gremoren," Mace finished.

"A shot across the bow, so to speak," Banter said with a little smile.

"So we stay out of it?" Andy asked, because this had to be a team decision. "Or we take the Gremoren's substantial fee—enough to keep us in food, fuel, and luxuries for the next two standards, I will add—and find the ship because the ones who've stolen it have made their point?"

A lot of looks were exchanged around the table.

Mintha, who'd been quiet to that point, said, "I wouldn't mind the fee." A comment met by a lot of grunting affirmatives. "But I'd also love to ask the thieves why they did this, if it was a...a shot across the bow."

Mintha was a soft-spoken former research biologist turned lawyer—a career change they admit to being unusual—who'd been the last to join the Absinea crew. They were almost as tall as Jenx but thicker and with a more flamboyant dress sense. Pale skinned, their black hair cut in an easy bob, today they wore a full body purple jumpsuit covered in large yellow flowers that matched the tiny tattoo on their right cheek. Mintha liked their luxuries and earned their take with a keen, quiet insight, and an insatiable curiosity that asked questions the others didn't always think to ask. They were also a contract shark, which was useful.

"Assuming we'll be in a position to talk to the thieves," Andy said. "If—a very big if—we can find the ship, there's no guarantee the persons who stole it will be anywhere near it."

"No guarantee they won't be either," Mace pointed out.

"We may well have to steal it back, right," Kiva added. "And if we have to do that, we aren't likely getting answers from thieves we're stealing from."

Retrieval of stolen property was always an interesting adventure. Sometimes, they just tracked things and let their clients know where said thing was. Sometimes, they returned said stolen thing to their client. Sometimes, to do that last part, they had to purchase said stolen thing—expense billed to the client, of course. Sometimes, they had to steal the stolen property back.

The Gremoren were requesting, "Return of stolen property by any means necessary."

Andy considered that request. The "any means necessary" did give them a lot of leeway.

"If it was just a track-and-report," Jenx said, "we'd be less likely to get in the middle of a potential invasion situation. But we might also enable said situation."

Andy was not excited about that potential.

"The contract doesn't specify we steal the ship back," Banter noted. "Or even directly return it. We could get away with a simple track-and-report, right?"

"But 'by any means necessary' for Gremoren probably means violence," Mace said. "And they'll argue the fee if we just track-and-report."

"An argument we'd win in a sector tribunal," Mintha said. They'd had to test contracts a few times in tribunal. They'd gotten very good at arguing fine print wording.

"We could just say no," Andy said into a moment of silence. "We don't have to take the job. Leave the problems and moral dilemmas to another tracker crew."

"We're the best," Mace said, without any

arrogance. Facts were facts. "The Gremoren might not take kindly to us turning down their job."

"Specially when another tracker crew is a lot less likely to find the ship," Kiva added.

"So if we don't do it," Jenx said, "it's not likely to get done."

"Is that a bad thing, though," Banter said. "Or maybe a good thing."

"Hard to tell." Jenx shrugged. "Depends on the real reason the ship was stolen."

"Right," Kiva said. "We're just speculating. Could be nothing more than opportunistic joy riders wanting to prove themselves."

"In which case," Mace said, "we'd have turned down a small fortune and simultaneously made an enemy of the Gremoren for nothing but speculation and guesses."

"We're allowed to not take jobs," Kiva said, her mouth pursed. "Gremoren putting us on an enemies list cause we don't want their money seems extreme. And bad for business, holding grudges against anyone who won't work for you."

"But also the Gremoren military are vengeful and sensitive to slights," Jenx said. "Even if all that sensitivity and grudge-holding is bad for business."

"It is good for giving excuses to go to battle," Banter said in a pragmatic tone. "Excuses to go into battle are a higher priority to Gremoren military leaders than business."

Andy sighed. That was, unfortunately, true. And she did not want the Gremoren deciding they needed to go to battle against the Absinea and her crew for a perceived slight.

"We could take the job and fail," Jenx suggested with another of her very telling raised brows. "No shame in that, in this circumstance. And the Gremoren couldn't hold a grudge if we put in sincere effort."

"We'd lose most of the fee," Andy pointed out. "But at least we wouldn't be any worse off."

Their current contracts contained an expenses clause so they were never out of pocket if they attempted but failed to track something down for their clients. In the early days, when they were still establishing themselves, they'd had to eat the expenses if they failed. It had been a great motivator to not fail. But that clause had gone into the contracts the minute they had the clout to enforce it. Mintha had insisted, and Andy had not argued with them.

"No one'd begrudge us the failure," Kiva said. "Not like this isn't a near impossible job on the face of it. Never mind the underlying possible fuckery."

"Would be a face-, and ass-, saving way to get out of this," Mace said with a little nod.

"Only problem with that plan," Banter said. "What if we find the ship?"

And wouldn't that just be their luck. Their own

skills turning around and biting them in the ass. All for a stolen fucking Dragon.

Andy looked around the table at her crew, meeting each gaze, noting the various combinations of worry and inner conflict in their expressions. Zander, who'd remained silent throughout the debate, sipped his pine-juice, expression thoughtful. Mintha holding a large coffee mug without drinking, just staring at the table, lips pursed. Mace tapped a finger against the table next to his mug of tea. Kiva shifted in her seat, looking around at the others. Jenx nibbled her lip and spun one of the beads at the base of a braid as she went back to scrolling the data. Banter ran a hand over his head and twirled his coffee mug with the other hand, an unconscious show of dexterity from the Absinea's pilot.

Her full crew. Only seven humans. Small, because that's all they needed to do the job most of the time. Not really enough of them to move the Destroyer, if they did find it. Given the schematics they'd been given of the ship, they *might* be able to jump it. Maybe. With Mace's ingenuity and Zander and Banter's piloting skills. But with so few people, they wouldn't be maneuvering the Dragon with any kind of grace.

Which meant they could absolutely support an interpretation of "any means necessary" to mean track-and-report. No one, especially the Gremoren, could expect her small crew to actually move the Destroyer.

And the fee was really *very* large.

Without knowing anything about the thieves, though, failure was, for once, the safer option.

So, the choice was, at least for the moment, simple.

She cleared her throat and everyone looked directly at her. Even Jenx turned away from the data scroll. "Decision time," she said. "We take the job and hope we fail, or we turn down the job and risk Gremoren wrath? Those are our choices."

More looks were exchanged around the table.

Kiva started the vote. "Take the job, hope we fail."

"Job failure, but job," Mace said.

"No job, hope Gremoren wrath is exaggerated," Jenx said.

Mintha nodded. "No to the job, avoid the Gremoren going forward."

Banter shrugged. "I think we should do the job. It's impossible. We'll fail. No one can get mad."

Zander grunted, the first sound he'd made all conference. "Job. No way we find this ship. Even if we try." He looked around. "But we'll have to really try to make this work."

Andy let out a long breath and leaned forward, her arms on the table. "Four to two. Take the job."

"How about you, Andy?" Kiva asked. "What's your vote?"

Her vote now wasn't strictly necessary. The majority had already spoken, and frankly, she was always more of the tie breaker if there was one. Otherwise, she tried to stay neutral in the votes. If she thought her crew was off the rails, she held the option to override their decision. But she'd never had to do that. They were a team and went with majority choice.

So her vote wasn't required. Still, with every eye on her, she said, "I vote take the job, hope to fail." She shrugged. "I can't imagine how we'll track this fucking ship. Failure was always the most likely outcome. And it keeps the Gremoren from turning into an enemy we don't need. Take the job."

"Settled then," Mace said. "But Zander's right. We'd better make a good show of trying to find this ship."

Kiva nodded. "Sure and they have to believe we've tried."

"Then we honestly try," Andy said with a shrug. "We do try."

There was just no way they'd actually find the ship.

CHAPTER TWO

They found the ship.

Of course they found the ship. It was the absolute worst possible outcome. So of course it was exactly what happened. Andy should have known. Her team was the best. Even when they were trying not to be.

If they got out of this without any of the worrying possibilities they'd debated before taking the job, she was going to boast about this find to all future clients.

But it was a complicated point of pride she could have survived longer without.

"Can't believe we found it," Mace said, as they all stared at the blue image floating over the viewer at the center of the command deck.

The command deck on the Absinea was a large

circular room, low ceilings, with screens surrounding half of the forward part of the room for sub-jump viewing. In those screens, the Destroyer was little more than a distant dot, and not a significant enough dot to stand out against the distant glow of a planet in this Blend-controlled system. The minute they'd picked up the presence of the Destroyer, they'd all abandoned their places around the smaller circular stations for data, ship diagnostics, piloting, and communications to gather at the central viewer where they could look at the Dragon in the magnified holo-image.

"It's just right there," Jenx said, shaking her head.

The blue image of the ship revealed a glorious war machine. Wide, thick body, shaped like a long cylinder, with sharp stabilizing wings running around the hull. The thrusters were cold, based on the readings they were getting, so the ship hadn't moved in a while. But Dragons could power up fast if the crew aboard knew what they were doing. The image didn't show any of the ship's coloration, but the details of airlocks, port views, cargo doors, and most importantly weapons hatches came up in full 3D detail.

The Absinea was still several hundred thousand kilometers from the ship, far enough to pick it up on their scans, not close enough for it to fire any of its impressive range of weapons at them. But anyone aboard would obviously know the Absinea was there now.

The Destroyer hadn't moved since they'd dropped into the sector. Hadn't attempted contact. Hadn't acknowledged another ship was hovering just outside weapon's range.

"How the fuck we find that thing?" Kiva asked, gesturing at the image. "And why aren't they doing anything about the fact that we found them?"

"Why aren't they cloaked?" Jenx said out loud what they were all thinking.

"Was this too easy?" Banter asked.

Easy was maybe not the word Andy would use. It hadn't been exactly easy. They'd put in a lot of work and time, tracking from last location, estimating possible trajectories, calculating best and worst cases.

Tracking a ship through the vastness of space wasn't like following biological scat on a planet. Tracking through space was more a matter of running probability models and calculating options combined with assessments of the natures of the thieves. What was known about their thinking and behavior. Some ships had tracking beacons, of course. That helped, even when thieves turned the beacons off. Some left residual chemical signatures in their wake before a jump.

Jumps could literally take a stolen spaceship anywhere, but there tended to be more probable options. A logic to where thieves would eventually go. Maybe the first few jumps, designed to throw trackers off, were random and pointless. Just spots in space with no rhyme nor reason for that choice. Impossible to find them in those places because space was huge and ships were small. And if the thieves just went to deep space and never came out, well, the ship wouldn't be found.

But that wasn't the point for most. No one stole a spaceship to then just go hang out forever in empty space. Beyond the psychological issues with that, eventually they had to return to some reference point. A place to sell the ship or it's parts. A place to resupply. A place to get repairs. There were only so many of those places in the sector. Combining modeling algorithms, with all the data about the thieves, the ships themselves —their jump and supply capabilities, their maintenance needs—and the thieves usually gave her and her trackers a decent set of options for locating a stolen ship.

Then it was just a matter of time.

They tracked different things, not just stolen space vessels. Each *thing* had its own set of logic steps and analysis. But with spaceships with jump capabilities, this was the process they'd found most effective.

Andy had never once thought they'd be able to use this process to find a ship that could cloak, though. Especially not in the first logical location they'd determined. No need to hop around, leaving ping tracers at the various options, waiting for another clue. Another data point to bring them closer. Nope. Got it in one.

Which, yeah, if she were being honest, was a lot easier than it should have been.

"Not as complicated," Zander said in his quiet voice. "That's the phrase we're all looking for."

Jenx nodded. "Not nearly as complicated as it should have been."

"I mean, we're good, lads," Kiva said.

"But we're not this good," Banter finished.

"So what now?" Mace asked Andy, looking through the blue image, to where she stood on the opposite side of the viewer.

Andy was still processing that image. That the ship was just...right there.

She roused herself to answer Mace's question. "Now..." She shrugged. "We send the location coordinates to the Gremoren and get paid." She frowned as she said this, her gut tight, anxiety crawling over her skin.

Not her usual reaction to talk of getting paid. Getting paid normally left her euphoric. Getting paid meant a little bit more security. Getting paid put them one more giant step away from those early, hard-scrabble days when life was precarious and survival always in question. Getting paid was both supremely satisfying—they'd done the job and found the thing!—and a huge relief—all immediate, necessary needs would be met!

The anxiety and hesitance clawing at her stomach and squeezing her innards was not the sort of feeling she associated with "getting paid."

"Doesn't feel right," Banter said. "Something's..."

"Off," Jenx said quietly, rolling one of her braids around her finger. The little beads clicked together.

Mace continued to hold Andy's gaze. The blue light of the holo-image reflected off his bald head, turning the ink of his tattoos black. "Our job is track-and-report. Not recover."

"At least that's how we're interpreting the contract," Mintha added, always the lawyer. They'd changed out of their purple, flowered jumpsuit into a bright pink and orange paisley dress. The colors mixed with the holo's blue light made Mintha look like a nebula.

"That is how we're reading the contract." Andy pursed her lips and nodded. "That it is."

"We are absolutely going to check out the ship before we send the Gremoren the location, though, aren't we?" Mace said.

"We absolutely are," Andy agreed.

It wasn't the assignment, wasn't the job. At least it wasn't the job they'd intended to do. If she were being honest, the job they'd *intended* to do was put on a good show before failing to find the ship.

Instead, they'd found the ship and had to follow through.

But this job had been dodgy from the start. And their lives relied on data. They were missing data in this situation. That missing data felt important.

"That will increase the probability of disaster," Jenx pointed out.

Having, Andy was sure, crunched all the currently available data and analyzed the dangers.

"I'm not saying we shouldn't go," Jenx finished. "But our odds of getting deeply into trouble will increase."

"Yup." Andy nodded. She looked away from the blue image of the Destroyer, meeting the gaze of each member of the crew. "Stations, please. Let's go have a look."

No one argued with the plan. Which spoke volumes.

CHAPTER THREE

They took the Absinea in closer to the Destroyer, slow and careful, the twins maneuvering on a wide arc that gave them room to change trajectories if the Destroyer moved into attack mode.

Kiva monitored the scans from the Destroyer, watching for any hint of their weapons array coming up. Jenx and Mintha monitored communications chatter in the area and listened for pings from the Destroyer. With the planet so close, there was a lot to filter through. But Mintha had a good ear, and Jenx could sort through the audio data faster than anyone else aboard. Mace kept close to the Absinea's engineering station, in case they did need to suddenly change strategies.

And Andy studied the scan image in the central

viewer, looking back and forth between the blue light image and the real-time image as they got closer and closer to the Dragon.

When they were within firing range, but still a ways out, Andy started a countdown in her head. Counting how much more vulnerable they got. Waiting for the alarms to blare. The Absinea's shield could take one, maybe two hits from any of a Dragon's weapons, but after that they'd be cooked. And while they were significantly smaller and very maneuverable, the Dragon was faster and just as maneuverable.

They might outrun the Destroyer and jump in time to escape, but that was only because the twins were excellent pilots and Dragons were so difficult to fly without an experienced crew.

The reminder of just how hard a Dragon X-47 B Class spaceship was to handle stopped her downward dread spiral, and she adjusted her threat assessment and analysis to take that into account. The thieves could fly it, or they wouldn't have made it this far, but that didn't mean they could handle it well enough to attack. They hadn't even taken it all that far from the point of theft.

Blend space. They'd brought the ship into a system controlled by the Blend. Who couldn't hack a Dragon.

Yet.

Among other tiny bits of analysis, her crew had

picked this system of all the probabilities because of its distance from the point of original theft, and the location of a near-planet station with all the necessary parts and tech personnel to repair a Dragon. There were only so many places someone could go with this type of ship.

But they'd had to leave motivation of the thieves out of their analysis because they didn't have that data. Just speculation. Finding the Destroyer here, in Blend space, was a new data point. And Andy was churning through possible motives now.

They'd thought this could be a so-called shot-across-the-bow to warn the Gremoren not to launch an attack against...whoever they might attack. But Blend space gave this idea a new angle.

"You think they're trying to learn how to hack the Dragons?" she asked quietly, of no one in particular.

"Been thinking that same thought, boss," Kiva said, her attention never wavering from her station board. "Blend system right away? Seems...meaningful."

"Meaningful," Mace said. "And suspicious."

"Did the Gremoren know, do you think?" Banter asked, most of his attention on piloting the Absinea closer to the Destroyer. "Did they suspect the Blend in all this?"

"If they did," Jenx said, frowning at the image of the Dragon getting larger in their view screen, "why would they hire us and not just come here to take back their ship?"

"That would for sure start a war," Zander said from his seat next to Banter, his blond head nodding up and down as he studied both his piloting console and the view port.

"First," Mintha said in their lawyer voice, "there are treaties all over the place to prevent that."

"But if they were going to violate treaty anyway to attack..." Mace said.

"We don't know that, though, do we? We were just guessing at that," Kiva said.

"A hypothesis," Mintha agreed. "Not a fact. And *if* the Gremoren knew the Blend had the ship, or at least knew the thieves would bring it here—to sell or trade or blackmail or any number of options —and the Gremoren *hadn't* intended to violate treaties, they'd need us to find the ship and retrieve it."

"So as not to start a war with the Blend," Andy said, nodding. "But...why not just send us here directly? Why pretend they didn't know where the ship was? We could have spent months standard tracking the Destroyer to different destinations before finding it here."

"Giving the Blend lots of time to learn how to hack it," Mace said. "Lots of time to learn all sorts of things about the stolen ship, and its possible vulnerabilities, before it was found."

"So why risk that time?" Andy said. "Why not just send us here?"

"Predicated on the Gremoren knowing where the ship was," Mintha said, "my second reason for why they'd hire us instead of coming here directly, was to put a buffer between them and the Blend. A neutral party to confirm the Blend had stolen the ship, and it wasn't just a Gremoren ploy to start a war. That... legitimacy gives the Gremoren legal legs to stand on if they want to hold the Blend accountable for the theft. Legitimacy they wouldn't have had if they'd come here on their own to retrieve the ship."

"Ah!" Kiva said, smacking her forehead. "And that's why they couldn't have sent us here."

Andy let out a soft groan.

"If they'd sent us here directly," Mace said, "knowing the Blend took their ship, they'd lose that legal loophole."

"A loophole that could justify invasion," Jenx added, "not just legal recourse."

"But they'd have to make it look like they had no idea who had stolen the ship first," Mace said.

"Without the buffer of a neutral party like ourselves finding the ship, they'd have to go through diplomatic rather than military channels," Mintha said.

"But they'd still be giving the Blend lots of potential time to learn how to hack their most unhackable ships," Banter pointed out.

"Our reputation is that good?" Mace suggested.

Andy snorted. "No one's reputation is *that* good. They were taking a serious risk."

"Gremoren like their wars," Kiva said.

"We're still making a lot of assumptions," Zander said quietly, most of his attention, like Banter's, still very much on piloting the Absinea.

"All the more reason to check out the ship," Andy murmured. "Any signs of weapons coming on line?" she asked Kiva. They were well within range now.

"Nothing yet, boss." Kiva shifted from one foot to the other, though she didn't look away from the data scrolling across her screens.

"No weapons yet," Andy murmured.

"Might not be able to use them," Mace said. "Might not have enough people. Might not know how."

All possible.

The image of the ship was significantly larger in their view screen now, large enough Andy could see real-time details. The silver and white gleam of the outer hull. The array of weapons hatches circling the long length of the ship. The extraordinarily sharp edges of the small fin-like wings twining around the exterior.

"Hearing anything?" she asked Jenx.

"Nothing from the ship," Jenx said. "No chatter

from the planet or the station to and from the ship either."

"This is all rightly weird," Kiva muttered. "No sign of weapons powering on yet, boss."

"Get closer," Andy said to Banter and Zander. "Close enough to dock, but don't dock yet."

The twins didn't question her as they moved the Absinea up alongside the hull.

"Anything?" she asked Jenx and Mintha. "Warnings? Pings? Anything?"

"Nothing," Jenx said.

"Just silence," Mintha confirmed.

"Is there anyone *on* the ship?" Banter asked. "Maybe it's been abandoned."

"Leave a Dragon X-47 B Class just sitting abandoned in space near the planet of one of the Gremoren's ancient enemies?" Kiva said. "Makes about as much sense as any of this, but also...why the fuck would anyone do that?"

"Whole thing stinks," Andy agreed. "Whole thing stinks a lot."

"Dock?" Banter asked.

"Dock," Andy said. "Let's go in and see what's what." She glanced around the crew. "Full weapons and safety measures. This situation smells worse that a Targelian sewer."

No one argued with her as the twins brought the Absinea close to a docking hatch on the underside of the Destroyer.

Chapter Four

The Destroyer *felt* empty. Not that that meant much. It was a huge ship. One corridor with no one in it waiting to attack them didn't mean the ship was actually empty. Still, the eerie feeling of walking through an abandoned ship stuck with Andy as she, Kiva, Mace, and Banter moved toward forward toward the control station.

The ship's proportions felt awkward to Andy. Designed for Gremoren not human. Tall, narrow corridors. Doorways and hatches too thin to move through easily with their bodysuits on. Screens and data ports a little too high on the gleaming red walls. The floors were a smooth white, and for reasons she couldn't entirely pinpoint, walking on them gave her a sensation like she was about to fall. Like each step was landing a little...wrong, a little farther "down" than she was expecting, causing her to wobble.

She'd never been on a Gremoren Dragon before. Was the strangeness normal, or just her hypervigilance playing mind-games with her?

Probably both.

The place smelled different than a ship dominated by humans, too. Even with good air filters and circulation, there was always the low-level undertone of human sweat on their ships. She thought whatever this scent was, it was likely the Gremoren equivalent. But rather than human sweat and musk, the scent here hit her nose like something faintly fishy, with a little citrus in it, and a bit of overheated ozone. It was a truly odd combination, and didn't smell exactly like the Gremoren did when she'd met them in person.

The air was a lot warmer than was comfortable, too. Especially since she didn't dare take off the thick protective bodysuit they'd all donned to come aboard. The bodysuit and helmets would protect them if they ended up in space, or if the ship's life support systems went down. But they were also useful protection against any dangerous traps left on board. They'd learned that lesson the hard way when she and Kiva had almost been caught out by a poison gas being released through the air system on another ship they'd been retrieving.

When people didn't want their stolen property

stolen back, they tended to leave nasty surprises as deterrents. There were a lot of ways to kill intruders on a ship hovering out in space. So safety protocols meant the boarding crews always kept their bodysuits and helmets on.

But the heat inside the Dragon was so high, sweat trickled over Andy's back. She adjusted the bodysuit's internal temperature to compensate.

"Hot in here," Banter commented.

"And very red and white," Mace said.

"Interesting aesthetic," Kiva said. "But disorienting as fuck."

"That it is," Andy said as she almost trip again from stepping on the white floor that was absolutely even and flat but not where her senses were telling her it was.

"Feels like I'm trying to walk on stairs but when I step down the stair isn't there," Banter said.

"Probably feels normal for a Gremoren," Mace said.

"Wonder what it feels like to a Blend?" Kiva said so quietly Andy barely heard her.

Where the Gremoren were a tall, thin, bipedal species with huge eyes that saw in spectrums humans couldn't access without mechanical aid, the Blend were a heavier-boned, multi-limbed species whose speed and dexterity were belied by their thicker size. The Blend had skin protected by thin, iridescent scales, while the Gremoren were hairless and had a thin layer of mucus they excreted when they needed additional epidermis guard. The warm temperature inside the ship was well suited to both species. But the proportions... Andy, like Kiva, had to wonder if the Blend were bothered too, or if that was just a human issue.

They made their way toward the forward part of the ship, to the control system sector, the Dragon equivalent of a command deck. The systems there couldn't actually control the entire ship, of course. But it was the place those not used to a Dragon might congregate, the place where, on a typical ship, the main flight deck would be located. Dragon configuration meant the control station was in charge of ship-wide coordination. It was the location that ensured all other stations were working in harmony together.

None of the doors they passed were open, so Andy felt the constant tingle of stress, that worry that someone would jump out at them, or they'd be surrounded before they knew what was happening. Their bodysuit scans weren't picking up anyone. But given the cloaking capabilities of a Dragon, she assumed there were other things the Gremoren could cloak. Even if they never admitted to such technology.

They passed one open area that looked like a large mess hall. No one was inside. No bodies. No living beings. Just a few dozen long tables with attached benches, curved in a kind of wave taking up the central part of the room. Couches and cushioned chairs dotted the perimeter. And against the left wall a bank of storage units, some of which Andy knew produced the food. On the Absinea, they called them cookers. But the Gremoren called the cubbies that prepared and cooked their food a word that translated to rotisserie.

There was no evidence the rotisserie had been used recently. No residual food or containers on the tables. No cubby door partially open. Most ships kept their mess cleaned because having loose debris or unsealed cabinets could mean dangerous projectiles floating around if something on ship went wrong—attack, inertial dampeners dropping out, life support systems fritzing... If some sort of emergencies arose, the last thing a crew wanted to worry about was floating drinks containers zooming past.

Despite knowing that, the mess hall still felt... unused. While the journey from their starting point to here wasn't a long one, all the jumps short, it still took time to get here. Time in which the people piloting the ship would have to eat.

The itch between Andy's shoulders and the way the fine hairs on her neck prickled continued as they moved through the rest of the ship. The eerie silence and lack of attack or even evidence of passengers creeped her out. The heat, which she was aware of even though she could barely feel it through the suit anymore, didn't help.

The control station was also behind a closed door, which meant they had to open that door to see if anyone was inside. Andy's suit scanners weren't penetrating the thicker metal here, and the circular door's seal was tight. A panel beside the door opened it—she'd gone over the Dragon's schematics until she had them memorized while they were tracking the ship—but there was a code required.

A code which should have been unhackable. Because, well, that was the point. Thieves still got into this ship, and they moved the ship, so they had to have had access to the control room. So they had to have figured out the code.

The Gremoren military command had been very reluctant to hand over the ship codes to Andy and her team when they'd accepted the job. Andy had insisted. Without them, they wouldn't be able to access the ship to retrieve it—even if they had decided, technically, to just track-and-report. The Gremoren didn't know that yet, and Andy had had to put on a good show when finalizing the contracts.

They'd accepted her logic, after some negotiation, so she had the code to get in.

But...

"How did they hack the doors?" Kiva asked quietly. Saying out loud what Andy was thinking.

"Should be a lot of them somewhere around

here, too," Banter said. "I know it's a big ship, but there should be some evidence of people, right?"

"Like in the mess," Kiva said. "Wasn't any sign anyone had used that place. Don't know of a single being who can go this long without at least taking in liquid."

"Could have left the Dragon and gone planet-side or station-side in a shuttle?" Mace said. "Something they brought with them? Someone who met them here?"

"And leave a ship like this unguarded and just sitting out in the middle of space?" Andy shook her head. "Seems risky."

"Maybe they assumed no other thieves would be fool enough to try stealing what had already been stolen?" Kiva said.

Good point. But until they finished their search, they couldn't hope for any answers.

Andy pressed her palm to the panel beside the door, bringing up the floating terminal. She flicked in the code, hoping the Gremoren hadn't lied to them about this at least. She was certain they'd lied about other things.

A sharp chink sounded, and then the hiss of releasing air. Her team stood to the side, backs to the wall so they wouldn't be immediately seen by anyone inside the control room. The heavy circular door rolled back into the wall, a process that took too many seconds. With each moment the door was partially open but not fully open, Andy expected weapons fire, or a clinking shock bomb rolling out, or some other kind of attack. The Destroyer had a fully stocked armory. Even if the thieves hadn't brought weapons with them, they'd have access to all kinds of goodies after taking the ship.

But nothing happened. The door finished moving into the wall and the room beyond remained silent. Andy took a deep breath, held it, then rolled into the doorway, her own weapon raised.

The room was empty.

She let out the breath and motioned the others inside.

"Creepy as fuck," Kiva muttered.

The silence was starting to ring in Andy's ears too.

The room was active, the low-level hum of all systems running. A large, tall, circular room with proportions still strange to Andy's senses. The perimeter of the room had work stations, and a circular hub in the center of the room would, when up and running, show the entire ship schematic.

Mace went to one of the work stations, running his hands over the screens until he pulled up shipwide visuals. All Dragons were fit with surveillance throughout, which was useful. Multiple screens rose around Mace, and he scanned through the ship's various corridors, levels, and rooms, flicking his hand across the board to switch views as he studied each. The surveillance went into most places on the ship, which left few pockets for anyone to hide.

Still nothing.

Kiva went to the central hub and brought up the ship schematic. The white light image that rose up over a central hub displayed fine-level details across the ship and announced systems readiness in each area with blinking, colored lights—blue for ready and cool, red for ready and hot, green for offline. The green areas were storage and crew cabins. Which meant some of those places had been powered off and the life support there shifted into a low running level that wasn't comfortably habitable.

"They weren't using the crew cabins," Banter noted. "At least they didn't leave them livable."

"Not storing anything that needs environmentally controlled storage either," Kiva noted.

"They stole the ship for something other than housing and storage," Mace said dryly.

"But it's good to confirm that," Andy added. "We're still guessing at motive here."

The sections of the ship marked with red included the room they were standing in and some of the other sectors necessary for piloting the ship. The blue areas, places that were at the ready but in an inactive cycle, were the weapons, strategic, and repair sectors.

"So they had all the sectors important to a fight on standby but not active," she murmured. "Interesting."

"They had to be expecting the Gremoren to come after them," Kiva said.

"Probably surprised they got away without being followed," Mace said.

"If you were certain you'd be followed by other Dragons, which would be able to blow you out of the aether, would you still steal the ship?" Andy asked as she studied the schematic.

"The whole caper's seemed suicidal from the start," Kiva said.

"Sure has," Andy agreed. Which led her back to the why. Why the hell do this? And then...abandon the ship near to, but not docked in, Blend space?

"Any signs of systems being tampered with?" Andy asked.

Banter went to another work station and started flipping through screens of data. Kiva took up a third station and also started filtering through the data. The room fell silent as they worked, while Mace continued to flip through the various views of the ship, and Andy stared at the schematic's blinking blue, red, and green lights.

She couldn't tell how much time passed as Banter and Kiva worked, but she didn't rush them. Lot of data to comb through. And so far, they had the time because no one seemed to be aboard. She looked to Mace to double check that and he confirmed the absence of anyone visible with a shrug.

After some time, Banter said, "Only thing I'm seeing here is some odd code in a storage monitoring system, one of the systems that control and keep the storage units at optimal environmental settings for whatever is being kept there."

Kiva frowned, her attention still on her data bank, as she said, "I'm seeing an odd bit of code in one of the crews' environmental systems. Nothing that would disrupt the function of life support. At least at first pass." Her frown deepened.

"Yeah, this isn't something that alters the storage unit's monitoring system's functionality," Banter said. "That's why it looks weird. It's not...standard Gremoren. But it's not really obvious. And it's in a system that's not vital to the running of the ship."

"The crew cabin environmentals are," Andy said. "Those are very vital."

Banter nodded. "What code are you seeing there, Kiva?"

She flicked her hand and a new data screen rose up in front of Banter.

"Ah," he said. "Look at this." He sent a screen to Kiva's station.

Andy frowned at both of them for a long moment, holding her comments and questions as they studied the code. But she tapped her foot as she waited because the longer they stood in this silent and empty ship, the more her anxiety levels climbed.

"What?" she finally said, when those anxiety levels couldn't take the waiting anymore.

"The code," Banter said, "that tiny bit that looked...weird. Well, it's not Gremoren."

"Yes, you've said that," she pointed out.

"It's Blend," he said, looking at her through the various screen images circling him. "The code is Blend."

Chapter Five

Andy stared at Banter as the news sank in, the flickering glow of various work stations, screens, and the white-light ship's schematic over the central hub casting her crew into strange shadows. The control room was as hot as the rest of the ship, but the news that the Blend had finally learned to hack this supposedly unhackable spaceship gave her a small shiver.

"You're certain?" she asked Banter, to make sure she hadn't heard him wrong.

"Positive. Grew up with it. Hard to miss when you know what you're looking at."

"So... They figured out how to hack a Dragon finally?" Andy asked, moving closer to Banter now.

"I'm not...sure, but..." He glanced at Kiva.

She shrugged and nodded and then shook her

head, a combination of gestures that could mean a lot of things but mostly just looked like confusion to Andy.

Banter said, "It looks like, if the Dragon tries to operate normally, this tiny bit of code will be able to spread. All the ship's systems are *mostly* isolated from each other, right? That's the point. Can't hack it if you can't get at it, and you need to get at a bunch of different systems to get at a Dragon. Well, there are certain things that feed into those isolated sectors from the outside, because they have to."

Andy frowned but waved her hand for Banter to continue as she mentally pulled up what she'd studied about the ship before this. There weren't supposed to be hackable leaks between sectors, but maybe she'd missed something.

"This isn't in the schematics," Banter said, as if reading her thoughts. "They wouldn't want anyone to know about these small breaks in the systems isolation."

"Because the Blend would figure out how to use that to hack the ship," Kiva said. "Which they have, apparently, still managed to do."

"Systems like storage unit monitoring, that has to feed into the general environmental system," Banter said. "But it's also barely barely linked to the weapons system."

"Why the hell would storage units be linked to

weapons systems?" Andy asked. That sounded backward as hell.

"Because what Gremoren usually store in their storage units, at least in part, is more weaponry and ammunition and things for repairing the ship mid-battle. Dragons aren't used for moving people and cargo. They're battleships. So what gets put into storage on a Dragon is for fighting."

Andy pulled in a breath. "Mid-battle, things are getting hot, weapons are taking hits or need repairs or more power. Or they just need more weapons arrays added. Too long to send someone to yet another system to report on what's available? They coordinate all those other systems without linking them, but they need to link storage to weapons? They couldn't just...assign someone to that separate system?"

Banter shrugged. "I didn't build the ships, and I don't think like a battle-hardened Gremoren. All I know is, when I look at the storage units' environmental system, there's this bit of code there that doesn't belong. And that code can migrate to other parts of the storage unit system—it's designed to replicate and move. It's absolutely a virus. And once it infects other parts of the storage unit, it can move through that small link between storage and weapons."

"And infect the weapons." Andy blinked a few

times. "The code in the crew cabin's environmental systems can do the same? Where does it link?"

"It doesn't," Kiva said. "That one is isolated and doesn't seem to link to anything else."

"But you can only fully operate a Dragon with enough crew," Mace said, moving up close to Andy.

"And if enough of that crew dies in a life support glitch..." Kiva said.

"The Dragon is dead in the aether," Andy said with a nod. "So, the Blend found a way to take out a Dragon. Infect its weapons systems through a small leak and kill a bunch of crew through hacked environmental systems."

"That's..." Banter started.

"Diabolical," Kiva finished.

"But effective," Andy said.

"They must expect the Gremoren to come for the ship, then," Mace said. "Are they waiting for them to take it back? Is that why it's just sitting here abandoned?"

"Good questions," Banter said. "You'd have to ask the Blend."

"We just *had* to find the ship," Andy murmured, mostly to herself, shaking her head.

"What now, boss?" Kiva said.

"We can tell the Gremoren where the ship is, and that the Blend have found a way to hack it," Mace said.

"Which will start a war," Banter said.

"We don't tell the Gremoren about the hack and let the Blend have an advantage in that war," Mace said.

"Which'll be good for no one," Kiva said.

"Or we pretend we didn't find the ship and thwart both sides," Andy said.

The others turned to face her.

"The Blend want this ship returned to the Gremoren. They want the code to take over the flagship in battle, to prove to the Gremoren that they're superior, or some shit," Andy said. "And the minute the Gremoren confirm, through us, that the ship was found in Blend space, they'll declare war and fuck the treaties."

"Right," Kiva said.

"They knew from the start the Blend were the ones who took the ship," Mace said.

"If they didn't know for sure, they likely suspected," Andy said. "We turn over the ship here, they'll have proof."

"Which they'll take to the sector tribunal," Mace said. "Use this, and us, to claim that the Blend have declared war."

"The Blend found a way to hack the Destroyer," Kiva said. "They want the Gremoren to get it back. They want this war as much as the Gremoren do."

"Or maybe they just want the Gremoren to know they can hack the ship now," Andy said, as her mind churned through the options. Unlike the

Gremoren, the Blend weren't keen on constant war. But the Gremoren were old enemies. They wouldn't take a threat from them lightly. "Maybe they're hoping the Gremoren will spot the hack and think twice about declaring war."

"Maybe," Banter said. "Or maybe they just want to see the Destroyer fail during an actual battle."

"Either way, the two are about to start something that shatters the treaties and throws the sector into chaos," Mace said.

"Not good for anyone," Kiva said.

"Not good for anyone," Andy agreed.

"If *we* don't find the ship, the two sides will just find another way to start a war," Mace said. "The Blend will just drop the Dragon somewhere someone else can find it, or the Gremoren will come get it since they likely already know where it is, or something else will happen to start the fight."

"But we won't be in the middle of it," Kiva said. "We won't be giving them both the cover they need to start the conflict legally." She frowned a little. "Starting wars legally. What a shite idea."

"We'll lose out on our fee," Banter said quietly.

"Which we were prepared for already," Andy said.

"And we'll lose credibility. We'll take a hit to our reputation."

"That we will," Andy agreed.

"There's another option," Banter said.

"Which is?"

"We remove the code."

Andy stared hard at Banter. "You can do that?"

"With Zander's help, yeah, I can."

"The Gremoren would still have the excuse that the ship was found in Blend space," Kiva said.

"Not if we move it," Banter said.

"Wait." Andy held up a hand. "Your idea is to unhack the Dragon, move it somewhere more neutral, and then turn it over to the Gremoren?"

"Accomplishes your aim of thwarting them both," Banter said. "Without the hit to our reputation. And we get our fee."

"Except we can't move this ship," she said. "Not enough crew."

"We can't fly it in battle," Banter said, "but I think we can figure a way to get it to another system. If the Blend could do it, right out from under the Gremoren guard, we can do it."

"I've been studying the tech," Mace said. "We can do it, with all seven of us working the ship."

Andy looked at each of her fellow crew in turn. They were three people short of the minimum to maneuver this ship gracefully. But she had thought they might be able to at least jump it. They wouldn't need to jump very far. One, two jumps at the most. Just to get the ship somewhere more neutral, outside Blend controlled space.

She settled her gaze on Banter. "Don't think the Blend will try to stop us?"

"Might," he admitted. "But only if they want us to tell the sector tribunal they were trying to start a war."

The idea...had some merit. Andy leaned against a work station, crossing her arms over her chest, her gaze skimming over the schematic.

"If that code spreads in this ship," she said, "it can't spread to others, right?" Double checking something she thought she knew. But then she'd thought hacking this beast was impossible, so she wasn't relying on what she thought she knew anymore.

"The Gremoren keep their systems separate between ships as well as inside ships," Banter said. "This would disable the flagship, but wouldn't infect the others."

"If we move the ship, with the code hack removed, it takes away the Gremoren excuse to start a war," Andy said, "but it also takes away the Blend's warning. Takes away their excuse to spark a war, too. But also their warning."

"We leave the code in, the Gremoren will know the Blend are responsible. They'll still use it as an excuse."

"Would they, though?" Andy frowned. "We leave the hacks in place, move the ship to neutral space, give the ship back to the Gremoren. They see the hacks—I assume they'll find it if we did?"

Banter and Kiva both shrugged and nodded at the same time.

"So, they see the Blend can hack their ships. They get the message. But they can't prove the Blend had the Destroyer, because it wasn't found by a third party in Blend space. Found in neutral space. If they admit to the code being there, that that's how they know the Blend stole the ship, they have to admit to the Dragon being vulnerable." She glanced at the others, holding their gazes. "I'm thinking the Gremoren will not want the sector to know their starship, the pride and joy of their fleet, their flagship, is vulnerable. In any way. That's the point of a Dragon, isn't it?"

"We leave the code in," Mace said, "they get the warning, but they keep their mouths shut and no wars start?"

"We willing to bank on that, boss?" Kiva said. "Leave the Blend code in, the Gremoren know. Might even know we're playing them."

"Can they prove it without revealing they've known from the start?" Andy countered. "Can they prove it without revealing they intended to start a war all along?"

"Lot of guessing going on here," Mace said.

"We've been working with half the data and a lot of guess-work this entire job," Banter said.

"Some complicated shit," Kiva said. "I prefer our usual jobs. Less politics. More find the prize and make the money."

Andy barked out a laugh. She preferred those kinds of jobs, too. But this was the job before them.

"A vote, then," she said. "Get the others on comms."

CHAPTER SIX

After Banter quickly explained what they'd found, the possible implications, and their thinking, Andy said, "So we have decisions to make. First, leave the code in—leave the Blend's warning there—yes or no?"

"Leave the code," Banter said.

"Leave the code," Kiva said.

"Cut the code," Mace said.

"Leave the code," Zander said over the comm.

"Cut the code. Leave nothing to link the ship back to the Blend," Mintha said.

The quiet after Mintha was telling. Andy waited Jenx out.

After that quiet moment, Jenx said, "What about you, Andy? How do you feel?"

"I'm the tie break if we need one. But I want your choice first, Jenx."

"One day," Jenx said, "you'll have to cast a vote that counts."

"When I need to. This one is yours first."

With an audible sigh, Jenx said, "Leave the code. Let the Blend send their warning."

"Leave the code it is," Andy said. "Next, move the ship or just report it? Stay out of the middle of the conflict. Let the higher ups sort out whether there's a war or not. Or move the ship and give them one less excuse to start something?"

"Move the ship," Banter said without hesitating. Zander echoed his choice.

Kiva glanced from the screens circling her, to the ship schematic, to the others in the room. "War sucks for everyone but a few. Move the ship. Make 'em work harder if they want to start a fight."

"Move the ship," Jenx said, this time without hesitation.

"Move the ship," Mace agreed.

"Move the ship," Mintha said. "And make sure we scrub the evidence that we've moved the ship." Always the lawyer.

Andy blinked. "Wow. Consensus on that one." Not even Mintha argued and they always played the devil's advocate if there was a general consensus from everyone else. "Guess we're moving the ship." Andy frowned at Banter. "You sure we can do that?"

"Get Zander down here," he said. "We'll figure it out."

THEY LOCKED THE ABSINEA TO THE SIDE OF the Destroyer because it took all of them to manage the single jump, and they didn't want to mess with the storage units because of the Blend code. There was only a little debate over where to take the ship. In the end, they chose the second place they'd intended to look for it. A neutral system, with a station orbiting an uninhabited but mineral rich planet.

Ngia Station's main industry was mining the planet and using the mined materials to manufacture a lot of the parts and equipment needed for all kinds of starships and starship adjacent tech. Their secondary industry was tech repair and refitting.

It was a logical place for the thieves to take the ship if it needed repairs, more logical than Blend space in some ways. And would have been the first location they checked, if the nearness of the Blend-controlled system hadn't tipped the analysis.

While Andy hadn't thought they'd find the Destroyer, she'd assumed if they actually *did* find it, it would be somewhere more like Ngia Station. So they could leave the ship there, tell the Gremoren where it was, leave the Blend code in so that "shot across the bow" was properly delivered, and get out of this mess with their fee and their reputation intact.

The Gremoren were...not happy about the news.

No one should have been able to track the Destroyer, and yet her team had. And had found it relatively quickly. Normally, that kind of news would be met with enthusiastic praise and joy from a client. Relief. Some show of positive emotion, at any rate.

The Gremoren high commander, who took the news via vid-feed, gave Andy a kind of glare he tried to disguise as a neutral expression. If Andy hadn't already suspected ulterior motives, she'd have been surprised by the response.

"You're...certain the ship was taken to Ngia Station?" Commander Pxin said. His head was large in the vid-feed, making him seem large than he was in real life, and making his bulbous eyes and rounded cheeks look even more exaggerated. Andy had met enough Gremoren over the years not to fall for the trick. The larger their heads in the feed, the smaller they tended to be. Gremoren didn't like to be perceived as small.

"We're certain, commander," Andy said with a straight face. "Sending you visual confirmation now." She flicked the board beneath the vid-feed and sent the track-and-report files to Pxin.

She heard the clear ping when her data arrived. Pxin glanced down, his large eyes moving back and forth as he skimmed the data. Andy waited patiently, her own expression as neutral as she could keep it. Outside of view range, though, she tapped her foot silently against the floor of the Absinea's communication room.

Around her, the various boards and screens they used for communicating across vast swaths of space in something that resembled real time blinked and shimmered. The room's lighting was dim, to make the visual feed clearer. And the airchair Andy reclined in had warmed just enough to keep her comfortable without heating so much it made her sleepy.

At the oval door leading into the room, the rest of her team stood out of sight, clustered together as they listened in on the conversation. Jenx played with one of her braids, rolling one of the beads around. Kiva chewed a nail. Mace kept rubbing a hand over his bald head. Banter and Zander had their heads together and murmured so quietly Andy couldn't hear them even though she was only a few meters away. Mintha had their "lawyer" frown in place, an expression Andy knew meant they were analyzing implications.

While they'd voted to move the Destroyer, Mintha did still have some concerns. Mostly for liability reasons.

Commander Pxin nodded after a moment, leaned to one side as if he was listening to someone just out of view, his mouth compressing into what Andy read as anger, though it could have been mild annoyance for all she knew. Pxin had that kind of pinched face that always looked angry anyway. And reading Gremoren body language really wasn't her specialty.

"Your...data is difficult to argue with," Pxin said.

And why would they want to argue with it, since they were getting their flagship back? But she didn't say that out loud.

"Your reputation is well earned," Pxin said. "We...feared you would be unable to find the ship."

Sure. That's what he was upset about. "We're just glad we could find it for you. Ngia has been alerted that you'll be coming to retrieve the ship. We didn't want them to worry when a second Dragon appeared in their system. One was...enough."

His expression narrowed, giving his bulbous eyes a squashed look and creating folds on his tall brow. A light sheen of the mucus that sometimes coated a Gremoren's skin shimmered in those folds.

"Thank you for your...consideration." He snarled the words.

Wow. Lot of anger there. "You're very welcome. And thank you for dropping the remainder of our fee within the hour standard."

This time his wide, flat nostrils flared. He opened his mouth to say something, which she had a distinct feeling wouldn't be polite, then snapped his mouth closed. Pulled in a deep breath through his nostrils, a gesture clearly visible through the vid. Then said, in a careful tone, "We thank you for all your hard work. Payment will be sent."

And he cut the feed without ceremony or farewell.

"Think we've made an enemy, boss," Kiva said.

"So long as we haven't made an easy war." Andy stood, missing the warm pocket of comfort from the airchair, but happy to have the conversation with Pxin over. "Shall we celebrate? I think we have the makings for a pretty nice dinner."

"To a job well done," Mace said.

"To the averting of a war," Jenx added.

"More like a delay to one," Mintha said.

"But it'll do for now," Andy said. "We got out of this one without making anything worse."

That was an ending she would take. An ending that deserved a drink.

"To the mess," she said. "Let's ensure the Gremoren high command's money is put to good use."

And enjoy the sector peace.

For as long as it lasted.

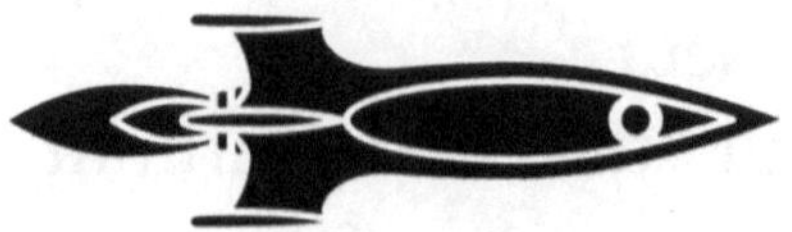

Now Pick a New Genre

Fantasy

CHAPTER ONE

Who steals a dragon?

Jamie stared across the forested landscape, to the mountain beyond. Majestic purple rocks rose high against a deep blue sky. The sun dipped low, casting shadows across the winding valley. The small village behind them, with its active pub and even more active summer festival, had fallen quiet as the afternoon's muggy heat settled wetly over the town and sent most residence to their homes for naps and rest. Leaving only the fading scent of roasted meats and pastries from the lunch feast in their wake.

Once the sun set, the party would resume, turning the little village into a delight of colorful ribbons and streamers, loud songs, lots of drink, more food than Jamie usually saw in a year, and the occasional dragon costume.

None of which she'd be able to enjoy. Because she wasn't here for the festival, mores the pity. She was here because someone had *stolen* a dragon.

The kiss of a pine-scented breeze blew across her cheeks, cutting through some of the muggy heat. She adjusted her stance and hitched her jerkin a little, trying to let some of the cool breeze get between the light armor and her skin. Her leathers were never comfortable in this kind of weather. If she wasn't working, she'd have already ditched the protective gear for a light skirt and homespun shirt. But she was working. And if she was going after someone who'd stolen a *dragon*, she was going to need the armored, bespelled leather pants and jerkin.

She crossed her arms as she stared at the distant mountain and tried to contemplate the audacity of someone *stealing* a dragon. How? How would that even work? The creatures were huge. They breathed fire. They *flew*! Humans, even magical ones, didn't fly. Dragons, even baby ones, flew. In the air. With wings.

How was it even possible to *steal* a dragon?

"I know it sounds impossible," the mage beside her said.

"Impossible. Stupid. Strange." She relaxed her crossed arms, but let her hand fall to her sword hilt at her hip as she turned to face her companion.

Dane Wayton, mage to the Vanshi order and occasional mercenary, was almost as tall as her, but not quite as wide. His dark hair was held back from his face with a series of small braids, which gave his broad features a sharper, more pointed look. The kind of look he said mages liked to cultivate to make them appear mysterious and threatening. While his shirt and trousers were a lighter material than her own leathers, and so not nearly as sticky in this heat, he still plucked at the material of his shirt, waving it in an attempt to capture the breeze. Sweat trickled down his temples, across his pale cheeks. His sharp blue eyes didn't waver from hers as she stared at him, but there were little lines bracketing his mouth. A tell for Dane.

She wasn't the only one who found this whole thing just...weird.

"Why?" she asked. "Why would someone steal a dragon?"

Dane shrugged. "Why not?"

She laughed. "Because they can burn you to a crisp with an errant breath? Slap you into the ground with a flick of their wings so hard your bones crumble. Because they have large teeth and are known to eat any creature stupid enough to irritate them."

"The dragon was a baby."

"Which means less control of their flaming breath and a tendency to chew things as their first-teeth cycle through to adult teeth," she said. "Baby dragons are still dragons."

"Smaller than an adult dragon."

She lowered her chin and gave Dane a look. "Smaller, in the case of dragons, does not mean small. The babies are still the size of that barn." She gestured to the cow barn at the edge of the village. The gray-purple stone and thatched roof building was at least fifteen foot tall and long enough to hold a herd of twenty cows comfortably. It was not a small building. "Not *small.*"

"We're not going to have any idea why someone stole the baby until we find them," Dane said, ignoring her point about the barn. "We complete our mission and you'll have your answers."

"Right. So long as the thief hasn't been chewed on by a teething baby dragon."

Dane's lips twitched with his smile. "I know it's a weird job. But if we fail, Argonia is going to burn down the village." He nodded to the maze of the gray stone, dark pinewood, and thatched-roof buildings and houses lining the cobbled and dirt roads behind them.

Dragon's Let was smallish, but not as tiny as some places Jamie had been. Large enough to have a coaching inn, as it was located along one of the main routes from the Ginian Capital Ramford and the Vanshi order's prime temple at the edge of Linwold. At least four hundred souls called the place home.

The scattering of houses and farms was built along the Agrean River, on lush and fertile land, next to a pine and birch forest full of wild game. Along with a healthy farming industry, they were also known for their delicately designed jewelry created from the local purple stone. And the main street boasted a series of prosperous shops, including a bookstore—which had surprised Jamie when she'd arrived—and a bakery with the best wildberry pastry hand pies she'd ever tasted.

The village had spent many years in peaceful comfort. Living near a dragon's den came with problems and advantages. In the case of Dragon's Let, the last fifty years had mostly been advantages.

Unfortunately, the theft of Argonia's newest dragonling had set the village up to experience more of the problems.

And it was now, officially, her and Dane's mission to get the dragonling back. A mission she was...not as confident of completing as she normally was.

"So, you're sure the thief has taken the little dragon up into the mountains?"

"The High Priestess was certain. I'm just an Undermage, but she does tend to know what she's talking about."

Jamie rolled her eyes. The Vanshi Order were all mages of one kind or another, but the range of skills across the various levels of the order differed greatly.

The High Priestess had the most skills, including farsight—an ability to see things others couldn't. Dane had tried to explain it to Jamie once. Mostly, it just sounded like, "blah blah blah magic something something blah blah" to her, though. Her realm wasn't magic. She was the muscle. Highly trained, extremely talented muscle. But muscle. She left the magic stuff to Dane.

She sighed and glanced back toward the mountain. "We find the dragonling, figure out how the thieves are cloaking it from its mother, retrieve the dragonling from the thieves, make sure it gets back to Argonia unharmed, and hope she doesn't burn down the village out of spite. Have I missed anything?"

"Don't get crisped by the baby—or momma—dragon," Dane said.

"That part does seem pretty imperative to our overall mission success."

Dane chuckled. She liked when she could make him laugh.

Although, for some reason, he laughed the most when she used the occasional big word. She'd taken offense to that the first time they'd worked together, over three years ago now. He'd clarified it wasn't so much the big words as it was her attitude while using them. She still sort of half expected he didn't think the sword-arms and mercenaries were educated. But when she wasn't working, there was a lot of down time. Too much drink gave her headaches. There were only so many pastries a warrior could eat if she didn't want to lose her edge. And there was only so much training she could do, if she wanted to avoid injuries. So, during the down times, she read. A lot. That sort of thing did expand the mind. And the vocabulary.

It didn't provide answers to her current mission, though. Only possible problems. And there were going to be a lot of problems on this mission. Not least because getting a baby dragon to cooperate without it chewing on them was going to be a near miracle.

Which did beg the questions—again—how and why would anyone *steal* a dragon?

Dane adjusted the leather pack across his back, which had their food and water and the bed rolls in it. When they worked together, he carried the gear because she needed hands free to fight if it came to that. He was a good mage, with a wide array of magical skills, but most of them backfired in a fight. So he let her do what she was best at, she let him do what he was best at, and they always accomplished their missions.

Almost always. She was a little worried about this one.

"Ready?" he said.

She sucked in a deep breath. "As I'll ever be." She glanced at his soft pants and shirt. "You sure you don't want some body armor or...something. Something that might get in the way of baby teeth if the baby decides you look like a chew toy?"

He grinned, a charming grin that took away some of the pointy-mage-sharpness he tried to cultivate. She didn't mind.

"I'm not sure any armor will help if the baby really does decide I'd help with teething pains," he said. "I'll be fine."

She raised her brows. "You say so." She let her arms drop to her sides and shook out the anticipation and anxiety thrumming through her blood. "Let's go."

They marched into the forest, leaving the sounds of the sleepy village coming awake, the first few notes of flute music starting up as the villagers recommenced the summer festival activities.

And their attempts to sooth and appease a very angry mother dragon. Giving Jamie and Dane time to complete their mission.

Or die.

But she was kind of hoping they could avoid the dying part. She really wanted another of those wildberry pastries.

Chapter Two

The cave was huge, and dark past the first few feet, and had ominous streams of steam flowing out in little puffs. The scent of sulfur was mild, but there. A scorched section through the trees had left a small, blackened clearing around the cave, and the stronger scent of burnt pine resin overrode the hints of sulfur.

They'd walked all night to get here, resting only a few hours before making the last mile to the cave, following that scent of burnt pine. The rising sun was still tucked behind the mountain, so while it was light enough to see, the forest at their backs was shroud in deep shadows. A cloudy morning ensured it would stay gray and dim even after the sun peaked.

For some reason, Jamie thought the feel of impending rain in the air, that dampness and the hint of a cooling breeze, might be a good sign. Not only would it cut through the daytime humidity, but if baby was in the cave—and the scorched trees were a significant clue that it was—then the rain would put out any errant dragon fires baby set. Hopefully.

"Still love to know how they got the baby away from Argonia," she murmured, keeping her voice low.

She'd been mulling that question all night. No one could just pick up a baby dragon and carry it. An entire army of strong souls would be hard pressed to lift a baby dragon, but the task would be especially impossible if said baby dragon was unwilling to be moved. Teeth. Breathing fire. A rudimentary ability to fly. Babies couldn't cover the distance their parent could, but they could still get up and above any human's head.

Any way she looked at it, the task of taking a baby dragon against its will just seemed impossible. There had to be at trick involved. Magic. A lure. Something. Because baby needed to cooperate on some level to get here.

"Sounds pretty quiet," Dane commented, his voice low.

Whispering seemed a good choice when there was a dragon about. Even the birds and insects in the forest were quiet. Whether that was down to a dragon in residence, a dragon who'd recently torched a section of forest, or to whomever had stolen the dragon, she wasn't sure. But beyond the quiet shooshing sound of a light breeze in the pines, the clearing outside the cave was silent.

"Maybe the baby is asleep," she said.

"Useful."

"Maybe." They wouldn't get chewed on immediately. That was good. But there was still the matter of—

Her eyes widened. Without thinking, she wrapped her arms around Dane and dove to the far side of the cave entrance, taking cover behind a huge boulder...

Just as a superheated whoosh of fire came barreling out of the cave.

She blinked down at Dane. He blinked up at her.

"Thanks," he said after a moment.

"No problem. Are you hurt?"

"Scrapped elbow. Better than being burnt to a crisp."

She couldn't argue with that. Rolling off him, she rose to a crouch, still using the boulder as cover. The flames had caught a tree not yet roasted and set it alight, the heat wafting to her on the breeze along with the smell of a campfire—which she normally loved—and the hint of sulfur—which was less pleasant. If that sky-promised rain didn't happen soon, they might find themselves in the midst of a full-blown forest fire.

Her heart pounding, sweat collecting along her

spine and at her temples, she studied the cave entrance. Waiting for any sign the baby was awake and on its way out. Nothing moved at the cave entrance except one long stream of smoke billowing out. Otherwise, everything was still.

"Anything you can do about the tree?" she asked Dane without looking back at him, gesturing to the still burning pine. She felt him lean against the boulder next to her, glancing around her back to the tree.

"Give me a sec," he said.

His magic was occasionally quirky, so she'd learned over the years not to rush him. If he said he needed a minute, she gave him a minute. But the crackling and pop of the burning tree had her very aware of all the other trees surrounding it.

She kept her gaze on the cave entrance and her shaking hand on her sword pommel, waiting for Dane to do his part. She could still feel the lick of heat from those flames along her spine, a sort of after effect of the close call that left her more shaken than she'd been in the actual moment. Years of training meant she often acted before thinking through the terror of what she was facing. The terror usually hit a few minutes later. In this case, when she realized just how close they'd been to getting cooked before they'd even figured out what was going on.

Concentrating on slowing her heartbeat, and regaining her balance, she lost track of how long it took Dane to come up with a way to put the tree out. Some of the Vanshi mages could control the elements. Some worked spells and potions. Still others had command of the raw energy of magic itself—those were the terrifying mages Jamie tended to avoid whenever they were at the temple.

Dane's skills leaned toward metallurgy. He could infuse weapons with spells—protective spells, poison spells, curse spells, anything he wanted really—and he could work metals and minerals into a wide range of useful objects. He could turn a bit of rock into a crown, and ensure the wearer of the crown received blessings or curses. And if he wanted to, he could break most things made of metal down to their most basic elements.

It was an odd skill, not common among the Vanshi, but one the other sword-arms, like Jamie, really appreciated. One of the reasons she and Dane often worked together on these missions was because he could guarantee her weaponry defeated any enemy.

In this case, though, she kind of thought they got sent on this mission because Dane's boss was punishing him for something. Tracking down and retrieving a baby dragon was...not the sort of mercenary work most mages appreciated. She wasn't crazy about the job either. But since she didn't want Dragon's Let to suffer for the crime of some insane soul, she'd taken the job willingly. If they survived and got a chance to talk over one of those wildberry pastries, she'd asked Dane why he got stuck with this mission.

"Got it," he murmured.

She glanced at the tree, blinking a little as the rocks around it spread out, almost like liquid and began rising up to encase the pine. As the melted rock moved upward, the fire hissed out. After only a few moments, the tree was completely encased in stone. The rock solidified again, leaving a statue of a tree where a burning tree had just been.

"That's interesting," she said.

"You wanted the fire put out."

"Fair enough." She looked back at the cave. "How are we going to get in there without getting roasted?"

"Good question." Dane leaned around her again, one hand on the rock near her head, as he also studied the cave entrance.

"Don't suppose you can create a shield to stop the fire long enough for us to get past it?"

He didn't answer immediately so she turned her head slightly to look at the side of his face. He was frowning at the cave entrance, his brow furrowed.

"Is that a yes or no?" she asked. "Something like you did with the tree?"

"I can, but it'll be too heavy to carry. Even for you." His mouth tightened. "And there's still a chance a sustained stream of heat will melt the shield. I'm good. But dragon fire is...more."

More was a good word for it. "You made my sword capable of standing up to almost anything. It'll deflect the fire a little."

"But not enough to keep us both from getting roasted. A temporary break in the stream. That's it." He glanced at her, his frown dissolving into a rueful expression. "Besides, we're not here to hurt baby dragon. We're here to get baby dragon back to mamma dragon."

"I know that. I wasn't going to use the sword *on* the baby." She shook her head. Her turn to scowl. What did he take her for? "But we do have to get past said baby's flaming breath to be able to help it."

Just as she said that another burst of fire streamed from the mouth of the cave. This one was a shorter burst, and didn't have quite the distance as the last one, so it didn't catch any fresh trees or undergrowth alight.

"What was baby aiming at that time?"

Hardly at them, since they were no longer standing stupidly in front of the cave entrance. There were no other foolhardy souls standing in front of the cave entrance either. Not even a bird setting down on the charred ground. Because birds were smarter than that—they shared the sky with the occasional dragon and knew better than to get into the line of fire. Unlike most humans.

"Good question." Dane shrugged. "Dragon hearing is pretty good. Maybe it hears us and is issuing warnings?"

She supposed that was possible. But... "Why not come out and roar or something?"

"It's a baby," Dane said, with a little glance at her. "It probably feels safer at the back of the cave rather than exposing itself outside the cave. That's got to be instinctive for baby dragons."

"Instinctive like...chewing all available souls like they're chew toys?"

"Yes," he said bluntly.

Okay, that kind of made sense to her.

"And don't forget it's probably scared since its mother isn't around."

If they had a way of getting Argonia here to coax her baby out, that would be helpful. But the reason they'd been sent to find and retrieve the baby, instead of just directing Argonia to the baby's location was that the location was bespelled and blocked the dragon's senses. She literally couldn't *find* this spot, even when circling the mountain repeatedly.

The block didn't work on humans. According to Dane, the High Priestess claimed the magic required to hide the baby from Argonia was too costly and there was no room left for also blocking humans. Since Jamie wasn't the resident expert in magical things, she just had to trust the Hight Priestess and Dane's assessment. But the fact that they'd reached this cave, and obviously the baby, when Argonia was still flying around the perimeter of Dragon's Let, seemed pretty good confirmation.

"Where are the ones who took the baby?" she wondered out loud.

Obviously magic wielders of some level. There as magic involved with hiding baby from Argonia. There had to have been magic involved with luring the baby out and here. No obvious answers to *why* anyone would do this yet, but to do it would have taken magic. And whoever went to all that trouble probably wouldn't want to just leave baby sitting unattended in a cave. Right? Baby could just...fly away.

Unless it couldn't.

"Oh." She straightened. "You don't suppose they've chained the poor thing, do you?" She faced Dane again. "It would be able to fly away otherwise, right?"

"Won't know until we get in there," he said. "And to get in there..."

"We have to get around the fire." She nodded and then winced when another stream of flames shot from the cave entrance. Reminding them just how difficult getting around the fire was going to be.

But something about those bursts...

"There's a pattern, isn't there?" Dane asked.

"There is."

She quietly counted, reaching forty before the

next burst. Another wait, another count, and she reached sixty, but she assumed that was because she started counting as soon as the last burst. After a few more streams of flame, she realized the interval between was pretty consistent. Not exactly the same each time, but roughly the same.

"Reminds me of breathing," she noted.

Dane swung to face her. "Breathing. Like..."

"Is the baby snoring?" That was both adorable and appalling. A baby anything snoring was cute. A snore accompanied by bursts of melting flames...less cute.

"If so, that means baby is asleep."

"Spelled or just a natural sleep?" she asked.

"Have to get closer to see," he said.

"Back to that again." But now they could roughly time the bursts. "All right, we've got an average count of sixty between bursts. Lowest I got was forty."

"So we assume all we have is count forty before another fireball," he said.

Good strategy. "After the next burst, we run inside."

"And hope it only takes us forty to find cover in the cave."

Yeah. And hope baby really was asleep and not just screwing with them.

"Get ready," she said as her mental count neared sixty.

At fifty-seven, another burst of flames shot from the cave entrance.

Before the fire died, Jamie was moving, Dane at her back, as they scurried along the outer cave wall to the entrance. Jamie took a deep breath and turned into the cave opening, her eyes not able to penetrate the darkness beyond a few feet. No cover immediately visible. But there were char marks on the cave floor, a line of black she hadn't noticed earlier.

"Stay out of the char line," she told Dane. Then she spun into the cave and hugged the inner wall, moving deeper into the darkness.

Her internal countdown ticked away as fast as her heartbeat hammered.

CHAPTER THREE

O nce fully inside the cave, Jamie's eyes adjusted to the darkness enough to see a small pile of rocks on the left. The countdown in her head was reaching the zero point and panic made her pulse race. Grabbing Dane's hand, she hurried them to the pile, ducking behind the cover of solid stone, just as another burst of flames, following the char line in the middle of the floor, swept past them.

She blew out a breath that ruffled some of the fine hairs on her forehead up. "Close," she whispered.

Dane's response was a murmured grunt.

The scent of sulfur was stronger inside the cave, mixed with a sort of damp earthiness she might have liked if there weren't a baby dragon in here breathing fire at regular intervals. Without conscious effort, she'd started the countdown in her head again the minute the line of flames died down. Risking a look around the rocks, she found the deep shadows still too dark to penetrate. But she'd swear she saw a slight iridescent glimmer from inside that darkness.

The parts of the cave she could see were thick purple rock and near the entrance a few errant ferns —those that hadn't been burnt by dragon breath. There was a dampness in the air, and it was cooler than she'd expected with a dragon in residence. Which, given how hot it was outside, was a nice change.

The next burst of fire barreled out of the cave as they watched. The flash of light and heat washed over her face, sucking away the cooling effects of the cave interior. But with the added light, she glimpsed a little deeper back into the cave. Just enough to see a large pair of purple-red nostrils raised above a closed snout.

The fire died abruptly, plunging them back into darkness, the damp chill enveloping them as the heat from the fire faded.

She tapped Dane on the shoulder and pointed in the direction of the dragon.

"See anyone else?" he whispered against her ear.

She shook her head. Whoever had managed to get the dragon here, they didn't seem to be around. Or if they were, they were hiding somewhere behind the baby, where the dragon's fire bursts weren't illuminating them. They hadn't left any evidence of themselves near the front of the cave, where she and Dane crouched.

So they were inside. And she had a good idea where the baby was. But still no idea who was behind this.

She edged to the side of their cover closer to the baby, hoping to get a better view into the cave's deeper shadows. The rock piles rose a little here, so she had to scramble up on top of it to see. She climbed carefully, watching her footing. The last thing she needed was to dislodge a vital rock that upended their only cover from dragon flames. Also, it might draw the baby's attention and she wasn't sure that was a good idea. Even if they were here to rescue it.

When the next burst of flames roared past, she was above it and able to see a little farther back into the cave. Still no signs of those responsible for this, but she got a better view of baby dragon's long snout. Long enough the baby would be able to chomp her in half before eating her. The purple-red scales around its raised nostrils shimmered but outside of the fire burst, the baby didn't seem to move. There was a little puff of smoke that rose from its closed mouth just as the fire burst ended. And a little snuffling sound.

Then the back of the cave was plunged into blackness again.

The back and forth between dragon fire heat and cave coolness made her shiver. She stared into the dark for another few seconds, but without the fire to illuminate things, she couldn't see. There was only so much her eyes could do.

She backed down the rock pile just as another flame burst down the tunnel. And leaned in to Dane to speak in his ear. "Good idea where the baby is. I think its asleep. Its not moving. And the flame bursts seem to be associated with an outbreath."

"It is snoring," he said, sounding bemused.

"Scary kind of snore."

"We're inside. Now what?"

"We need to get closer to the baby and see what's holding it in place, or keeping it asleep. If it's spelled... We'll have to find a way to break the spell. The only way to reunite baby and momma dragon is to get it to fly out of here and return home. We can't carry it."

Dane's huff of sardonic agreement was almost silent.

"So we need to get it moving," she whispered, "get it out of this cave."

"Probably making a lot of noise and waking it up will be bad for us."

"Was thinking the same thing. But I'm pretty sure baby isn't still here just because it took a nap in a random cave where momma can't find it. Even if we wake it, if its not spelled asleep, it might not be able to leave the cave."

"I didn't pick up any warding on the outside of the entrance as we came in." He set his hands against the damp, stone wall and closed his eyes.

Another line of fire roared past their pile of rocks, lighting up the cave wall for a moment. The purple stone glittered prettily.

"No warding that I can find," Dane said with his eyes half closed as he studied the stone with whatever inner workings mages used on these things.

Jamie had witnessed mages at work a lot over the years. Came with being a sword-arm for the Vanshi order. But the actual mechanics of *how* they did these things? No matter how often Dane tried to explain, she just didn't *get* it in her bones. Which was why she carried the sword and let him worry about the magic stuff.

"There is magic here," he said after another few minutes. "Not in the cave structure, but...inside here. Something." His frown deepened, his voice so quiet now he was barely making sound. She had to lean in very close to hear him.

"Dragons are magic?" she said and asked at the same time.

She wasn't actually clear on that point. The adults had something that got called magic, but it was such a very specific kind of dragon magic, unlike anything humans could wield, she wasn't even sure whether to call it magic or not. It wasn't like spells. It wasn't a manipulation of elements and energies. It was...well, dragon magic. A part of them. So maybe it was just biology.

"This isn't the baby," Dane murmured. "Something else. Something...elemental. Something...confining."

That made sense at least. And confirmed the baby was being kept here involuntarily. "We need to get closer," she whispered, half to Dane, half to herself.

Getting close to the baby was dangerous, but necessary if they were going to see how a dragon could be kept in a cave against its will while there weren't any magic wards on the cave entrance. Actually, as far as she knew, there were no wards that could contain a dragon in a cave. If there had been, humans would have used them over the years.

Dane gave himself a little shake and nodded. "We do. I need to see what's been done. The sense of it is too vague through the rocks."

Another blast of fire arrowed through the cave. Jamie used the temporary light to see back into the blackness again. Another view of the dragon's snout. A glimmer of scales higher on its face. Its eyes weren't open, as far as she could tell in that brief moment of light. But the break in darkness didn't last long enough for her to confirm that.

"This way." She went the long way over the pile of rocks, carefully climbing to the top again and then easing down the other side on her butt, placing her hands and feet on the looser rubble gently until she was sure nothing would shift and move. A rockslide would be bad.

Dane followed, just as carefully and slowly. They froze each time the baby breathed out another stream of fire. From this side of the rock pile, the heat was intense. Washing over her like a sunburst. Leaving behind cool air and tingling awareness that they were entirely too close to those deadly flames.

She edged along the cave wall, using it to find her way in the dark, one hand against the rough stone. She stepped carefully here too, ensuring she wasn't stepping on anything that might make noise before putting her full weight down on her foot. The process was agonizingly slow. Moving this way, silently in an unfamiliar environment. She took advantage of each wash of light from baby's snores, but those glimpses didn't last long. And the deeper they moved into the cave, the less they helped.

The wall of the cave started to angle away from the baby. Jamie paused and whispered in Dane's ear, "At the next flash of light, we have to move out into the open. Stick close. Hold my belt so we don't get separated."

She felt his nod at the same time as she felt his fingers wrap around the leather belt that kept her scabbard at her hip. She was tempted to draw her sword but resisted. She might need both hands to navigate the darkness. And she didn't want to accidentally stab anything that didn't need stabbing. Like her own foot.

Or the dragon.

Another burst of fire, and she could see across the huge open space between her and the baby now, see a little more of its body. Its head rested on the rocky ground, snout angled toward the front of the cave, eyes definitely closed. The little row of sharp scales down the length of its long neck. Its front feet curled up next to its neck. Purple-red scales and some deeper burgundy scales twined along its neck in a pattern she suspected spoke volumes to pray animals. The pattern made her a little nervous for instinctive rather than logical reasons.

The baby was so large, she couldn't see the back of its body. If it was like its mother, it would have some spikes at the end of its long tail. But she wasn't sure how long that tail, or those spikes, would be at this age. It should also have wings folded along its back. She'd been told the baby could fly. All dragons in their part of the world flew. But there were a few species that used things other than wings, a kind of mist-force that carried them through the air. Argonia had wings. Everyone assumed the baby did too.

But since no one outside of the thieves had seen

the baby in person, the details were still up for debate.

Blackness surrounded them again, the light from the front of the cave a faint glow that did little to illuminate anything. Cold air back here now, and the dampness on her skin made her feel clammy and chilled every time the fire cut off. If not for the mission, she might have loved the respite from the muggy heat outside.

They started forward, her taking careful steps, Dane holding tight to her belt. The progress so painfully slow, her muscles shook. Another fire burst, another useful visual assessment of their path. She moved a little farther left, hoping to bring them in close to the baby's side, near the base of its neck. Hard for it to swing around and blow fire at them there, and she'd be able to judge where its feet were. At least for long enough to hopefully run for cover if they needed to.

Not that there was much cover out here in the open part of the cave. No convenient stalagmites to hide behind. Just wide open space and a few scattered pebbles between them and the dragon.

A faint sound, like a chinking noise, had her freezing in place. Dane froze instantly too, not even bumping into her. She held her breath as she listened. A faint rustling, that chink of metal moving, a little puff of air.

Her heartbeat hammered hard as she strained to

hear every whispered sound around her. A soft animal huffing noise. Was there a cow in here? Something for the baby to eat when it woke up? Or was that the baby?

She'd never heard baby dragon noises before. If that was the baby, it sounded a bit like a dog whining in its sleep.

The metallic clinking was the more significant sound, though. That reminded her very distinctly of...chains.

She wanted to tell Dane to look out for the source of that noise, but they were too close to the baby now. She didn't dare speak. She had to hope he'd heard the same thing she'd heard, and was thinking along similar lines. They'd worked together enough, she thought he just might be because his hand tightened briefly on her belt. Enough to let her know he was aware of the noises that had stopped them both.

She waited for another burst of light before moving again, waited for the brief flash to illuminate their surroundings.

This time she looked specifically at the baby's front legs and the base of its neck. She hadn't spotted anything like a chain or metal cuff before. But she'd gotten such brief glances—because most of her attention had been on baby's face and, most specifically, baby's mouth and eyes—that she hadn't looked long at its neck and front feet. The focus proved useful.

She reached back and grabbed Dane's hand on her belt, hoping he'd see what she'd seen. The darker black metal hoop at the very base of the baby's neck, near its shoulders. The black metal was so dark it almost looked like shadow against the purple-red scales. But now that she knew what she was looking for, the thick cuff was obvious.

Dane leaned into her back and breathed, "Saw it." His voice was so low it was barely sound.

She nodded and they started forward again. That metal cuff around the neck had to be the thing keeping the baby here. Maybe even the thing that controlled it. She'd need Dane to figure out what sort of magic was in it, but she was certain there was some. Having some clue what they needed to do next had her pulse racing with both excitement and anticipation. Her gaze narrowed in the darkness and her nostrils flared, the scent of damp rock and sulfur strong.

They were within a few yards of the baby by the time the light flared again. Eyes definitely still closed. Definitely sleeping. Snoring. A little movement to adjust its position—a sign the dragon was a baby.

Most dragons, once asleep, barely moved. They could sleep for months, go into a kind of hibernation for years if circumstances called for it, and once in those deep sleep states, they were motionless, almost like a part of the earth. Moving so slowly and so infrequently as to be unnoticeable to a human.

Babies, on the other hand, shifted and adjusted themselves in sleep like more ordinary animals. But thanks to that baby adjustment, she got a good look at the cuff around the dragon's neck before they reached it.

As they were plunged back into darkness, she could feel the dragon near this time, a sort of animal instinct for the large, scale-covered creature so very very close. Her skin tingled with the sensation, the awareness. Her more primitive brain urged her to run away and fast because she was standing too close to something that could eat her. Her primitive brain was smarter than her logical brain.

She stopped when she was certain she could feel the dragon only a foot in front of her and waited for the next burst of fire.

When it happened, she realized she was standing only inches away from the baby's front leg. Another step and she would have bumped into it. She wanted to close her eyes against that view, but didn't dare. Not and waste the precious seconds of light.

Those seconds gave her a closer view of the black metal collar around the baby's neck. She couldn't see a chain, but she assumed there was one since she'd heard the chinking sounds of one. The collar would have a chain that attached to something to keep the baby from leaving. But in that limited window of light, all she saw was the ring itself, made of some dark metal, black as shadow, and she thought she saw some sort of pattern etched into the metal, but the light cut out before she could be sure.

She reached back with one hand and tapped Dane's arm, then she adjusted their stance so she stood between him and the general direction of the baby's head, but he was closer to the metal ring. Once in position, they both waited for the next baby snore and release of fire. Thanks to all those flashes, her eyes weren't adjusting to the darkness in between. She relied on her other senses, listening intently, feeling the brush of air over her skin. The fine hairs on her arms raised as the cave's chill set in around her, but she didn't dare shiver. Any sort of sharp movement might draw the dragon's attention. They weren't sure if it was sleeping normally or bespelled, and until they were, she didn't want to risk waking it before they were ready.

She glanced briefly toward the cloudy morning sunlight at the cave entrance. The charred and stone-encased tree beyond was just visible. Nothing else attempted to come into the cave. Good, but likely because of the regular streams of fire pouring out.

At the next flash of firelight, Dane moved away from her back and as close to the ring as he could get. She divided the few seconds of light glancing between him and the baby. She bit back a warning when he reached out to touch the metal ring.

And then they were plunged into darkness again.

Dane hissed in a breath. She reached back for him, instinctively, to pull him away from the collar. But he whispered a harsh, very quiet, "Don't." And she let her hand drop.

How he'd known she was reaching for him, she'd have to ask later.

She felt something large shift beside her. A stirring of the air. Then a little clink noise, that metal on metal sound she'd thought was a chain moving. Another brush of air. Something moved in front of the light from the cave mouth, cutting off even that faint glow.

And then she felt a puff of hot, sulfur-scented air.

Right in her face.

Chapter Four

Jamie froze. She didn't even blink. She wanted to reach for Dane again, but that would involve moving and she couldn't move. If she moved, the dragon might...react.

Another light puff of air against her face. A very distinct sulfur scent. And that carnivore musk that came from a creature whose diet included animal consumption. No additional burst of light by which to see. Probably good because she was quite certain that light would be coming right at her if she did see it, so better to stand here in the solid dark with a baby dragon breathing in her face without the help of its regular bursts of fire to see by.

Her throat was dry. Her hands shook. And despite her inability to move in that moment, she still found herself panting to breath. Panic was setting in.

Even in the blackness, she swore she saw darker spots dancing at the periphery of her vision.

The thought of passing out, leaving herself open to getting eaten, and worse, leaving Dane vulnerable to getting eaten, appalled her. This was her job, her *duty*. She protected the mage she was sent out to protect while they completed their part of the mission.

She tightened her fist around her pommel, both a reflex and a reassurance the sword was still there. Not that she assumed she could do much against a dragon with her sword. But since Dane had infused the thing with some magical attributes, she hoped one of those attributes would be useful against a baby dragon.

Except they weren't here to hurt the baby. They were here to ensure it was returned to its mother so momma dragon didn't burn down Dragon's Let.

How did she convey that to the baby? How did she let it know they were here to help and not hurt it?

Behind her, Dane whispered, "Stay still just a few more moments. Almost got this."

"Explanation later, right?" She spoke so quietly she wasn't sure he'd hear her, but he grunted a response she assumed was yes.

Another puff of dragon-scented warm air brushed against her face. And then a little bump. A brush of scaled skin against her cheek.

She pressed her lips together so she wouldn't scream, and braced herself against the less than delicate bump that was enough to push her backward a step or two.

A little sound, something halfway between a coo and a hiss. Such a strange combination she couldn't make much sense of the sound. Only that the dragon was making it. And she hoped it was a good sound and not an "I'm about to chew on you because my teeth are sore" sound.

Seconds ticked by in the darkness.

Because she'd been counting between fire bursts, in the background of all her other thoughts, she found herself counting again. She wasn't sure what she was counting for. Counting the seconds she had left to live maybe?

Behind her, another sharp intake of breath. And then a quiet, "Yes!" from Dane.

"Hope that means good things," she whispered. Her throat was so dry, she forced herself to swallow a few times. But since the air around her tasted a little too much like sulfur, she gave up.

Dane moved up behind her, and set on hand to her shoulder. She was proud of herself for not jumping. But she'd been as aware of his movements behind her as she was of the dragon in front of her blocking their exit and breathing on her.

A moment after she felt his hand on her shoulder, a small blue light grew in the cave. Giving her her first view of the baby dragon, whose nostrils were only an inch from her face.

Underneath those raised nostrils were a lot of teeth. This was not a reassuring view.

But since the light wasn't coming from a burst of fire from the baby's mouth, she'd take what she could get.

The very large black eyes a few feet past the raised nostrils blinked in the blue light, a little whorl of movement as the irises shrank. Jamie didn't want to look away from the dragon, in case it decided *she* looked edible, but she did glance up long enough to see the mage light overhead. The small ball of blue energy casting the dim glow, letting her poor human eyes see in the blackness.

She appreciated being able to see what was going on around her—imagining what was happening had been difficult on her nerves. But her entire body remained very aware of each dragon breath, and each dragon shifting movement, and every brush of colder air, and the faintest sounds. She was almost overwhelmed by her own wide-open senses. Because what she was standing face-to-face with was more than a little overwhelming.

"Okay," she murmured, not wanting to startle the dragon. "So, baby, we're here to get you back to your mother. She's a little worried about you. We are not chew toys, for the record. And neither of us will hurt you."

The dragon made a little gurgling sort of noise. A sort of grunt with a faint hiss at the end. She took that as understanding, though she didn't think baby dragon's spoke human languages. Adult dragons could. But babies...

Well, she wasn't actually sure.

"Do you understand me?" she asked.

The baby snuffled and then tapped her gently with its snout. Its mouth was very obviously closed when it did this.

Right. So. Not attempting to eat her or Dane. Yet.

To Dane, she said, "What did you do with the metal collar? What was it?" She didn't take her gaze off the dragon.

"Containment collar. Basically, a way to keep Alomere here from flying or reaching out to contact his mother."

"Alomere?"

"His name had to be etched into the spell on the containment collar for the spell to work."

"Someone found out a baby dragon's name?"

That was...difficult. The dragons usually didn't reveal their names until they were adults. Because names had power in magic and in dragons, so she'd been told. Baby names were never revealed. And if the dragon had a distinct gender, that was usually not revealed either until they were adults and their names were made known.

"Not sure how they found out," Dane said. "But

it was there in the spell. Prevented him from calling his mother telepathically."

Well, that made sense. That was how the thieves could hide the baby—hide Alomere—from his mother. They'd known there had to be some kind of masking spell, and something to prevent the baby from just flying away. Collar, chains, and magic.

"You broke the spell, right?" she asked, just to be sure.

"I did. I hope that means Alomere has reached out to his mother. She will probably be on her way."

"Wish we could ask him who actually did this. And why. I'm not sure leaving someone who can kidnap a dragon running around the countryside is a good idea."

"I can say whoever they are, they're a powerful mage. Couldn't tell from the working on the metal what their intentions were with Alomere, but I could tell it took a great deal of skill and magic to make the containment collar. And knowledge of the dragon, which should have been impossible."

"Any idea where your kidnapper or kidnappers have gone?" she asked the baby, without expecting a response.

He snuffled and turned his huge head away, which brought the cave entrance back into view—escape, though she felt less compelled to run away now, when she was pretty sure baby didn't intend on eating them.

Her relief evaporated as the baby adjusted itself and stood. She and Dane scrambled away from him, since a baby dragon, even one not inclined to eat them, was still a giant creature, and she didn't want to get stepped on by accident.

They hurried to the far side of the cave to give the baby room to move, Dane's little ball of blue mage light following them as it stayed just over Dane's head. When she was pretty sure they were out of the way of large limbs, she faced Alomere again. Baby gave his wings a little flex and wave, not fully expanding them, but bringing them out to his sides a little like a stretch. The pink membranes looked so delicate, pulled tight between the thicker purple-red scaled joints.

Once he'd finished stretching his wings, Alomere turned and faced them, made another snuffling, gurgling hiss of a noise and turned to move deeper into the cave, rather than out of it.

That...was not what she'd been expecting.

As he moved, the sounds of metal clanking across the ground drew her attention to the containment collar. It had dropped to the purple stone ground and the chain it had been attached to was now clearly visible. Not a long chain, but long enough the baby might have been able to at least stand. The end of the chain attached to a thick loop of metal bolted into the cave wall. It looked like a sturdy piece, both chain and loop were made of thick black metal, the links easily the size of her head, and the metal as thick as her thigh. But even with all that weight, she wasn't sure the chain itself would have held baby without the addition of the spelled collar.

"Do we follow?" she asked Dane, hesitating to go deeper into the cave's impenetrably dark interior.

"You asked him where his kidnappers were," Dane said. She glanced back in time to see him shrug. "Better to find whoever did this than let them roam free to do it again. I'm not sure Argonia will be as patient the next time her baby goes missing."

Fair point.

Keeping her hand on her sword pommel, she followed the dragon farther into the cave, grateful Dane's mage light cut through the blackness as they went. She couldn't see all that far ahead of her—baby dragon's immense bulk was in the way even if the darkness hadn't been so thick—but being able to see where she was stepping and avoid tripping at an inopportune moment was helpful.

The cave stretched back farther than she'd realized. Made sense in some ways since a dragon— even a baby one—needed a lot of space. But the depth of the cave, and the length of the tunnel Alomere led them down took them much deeper into the mountain, down a slight angle. Jamie wasn't afraid of enclosed spaces, at least she never had been before, but the closing in of the tunnel around them was not a comfortable sensation.

Baby fit, though. And if Alomere fit, then there was more than enough room for two small humans. She almost laughed. This would be one of the very few times in her adult life as a sword-arm that anyone would possibly consider her small.

The deeper they got into the tunnel, the stronger the smell of damp, musky mold. And something else underneath. A sort of mineraly scent she couldn't quite place. Not blood. Not that kind of flavor. But something like...dirt? Soil? Something that spoke of earth to her even as it coated her tongue. The temperature dropped significantly, too. From the muggy heat outside to this cold chill that made her wish for a cloak. And again, she realized that if it hadn't been for the dragon situation, she might have liked being inside this cave. Her leather armor felt a lot more comfortable here.

In Dane's mage light, the blue glow against the purple walls created bouncing shadows that arched up high overhead. She couldn't see the ceiling. And despite the dampness, still no rocky fingers from above or rising up from the cave floor. Though, with a dragon passing through, maybe all such structures had been swept smooth. Alomere seemed to know where he was going. She assumed he'd been this way before.

A dripping sound joined the sound of their quiet footsteps. Just drips, though. No gush of an internal waterfall. No horrifying sounds of water rushing through the tunnel at speed. Just *drip drip drip*. And the moisture on the walls condensed into visible drops. A low-ground fog coalesced around them, covering the tops of her feet and hiding the smooth stone ground.

She frowned back at Dane and nodded to the fog. It felt, in this case...foreboding. Dane's mouth flattened but he didn't comment.

Beyond Alomere, deeper in the tunnel where she couldn't see, Jamie heard another sound. A clinking sound. Not the water drip. Not a roll of rock against rock. This sounded like...metal banging against metal.

"Hammering," Dane murmured.

That was it. Hammering. A metal hammer against a metal anvil. Rhythmic and steady. She could count her heartbeats to the steady beat.

Alomere stopped at that moment, suddenly enough, Jamie had walked within a few inches of his tail before realizing he wasn't moving forward anymore. The tunnel around them had widened again, giving Alomere enough room to curve his long neck so that he could look back at them. Snuffling a little, a puff of steam rising from his nostrils, he stared at them with his large black eyes.

She assumed he was trying to let them know something, but not being able to speak baby dragon was a little inconvenient in this moment.

Since speaking at all seemed like a bad idea, given

the steady sound of that hammering ahead of them, she eased up next to Alomere. The dragon turned to face forward again as she and Dane reached his head.

Where Alomere had stopped was still in a dark tunnel, but ahead was very clear light. Flickering yellow-orange light, like firelight. Throwing wobbly, dancing shadows into the tunnel. The sounds of metal striking metal were a lot more distinct here, and now she heard the quiet murmur of a voice.

One voice. Chanting.

She frowned back at Dane. "A spell?" she mouthed.

He nodded, his gaze mostly on the flickering firelight ahead.

But only one voice? Did that mean only one soul ahead? Because if that were the case...

How had only one individual kidnapped a whole baby dragon?

Alomere brought his huge head down near her so that he was looking at her with one big eye. The fact that his one eye was as large as her upper body was more disconcerting at this angle. An inner lid flickered across the eye followed by the outer lid, like a blink or a wink, she wasn't sure. And then, very gently, Alomere bumped her with the side of his head. Not enough to even throw her off balance. Just a little tap, a faint touch. And then he rose up a little and stared forward.

She took all that to be encouragement for her to follow him.

A baby dragon at her back. An unknown threat before her. Her sword. And Dane's magic.

This was proving to be quite an interesting day.

CHAPTER FIVE

With Alomere settled on his haunches in the tunnel, Jamie and Dane crept forward, toward the jumping firelight and the sounds of a hammer striking metal. That sound was much more distinct without the bulk of a dragon in the way to absorb and mute some of the noise. The tunnel's moisture felt thicker here, the fog along the ground making each step forward risky. And water beaded and dripped down the rock walls.

Dane extinguished his mage light, leaving the baby dragon in darkness as they used the light ahead as a guide. Jamie assumed the dragon wasn't afraid of the darkness, but since Alomere could breathe fire and provide his own light if he needed it, she didn't worry too much.

The firelight came from a larger cavern that

opened up high overhead and angled a little farther downward. The sense of having an entire mountain above them got stronger here, making Jamie acutely aware of just how deep under the mountain they'd come.

This cavern was decorated with the hanging fingers of stalactites and the upthrust points of stalagmites that Jamie would have expecting in a cave with this much moisture. The irregular rocky spikes littered the cavern floor, rising through the fog, and dropped down from a ceiling too high for her to see. The scent of that minerally mix that was almost like soil got stronger here too.

And in the center of the cavern, a forge. But not like the usual blacksmiths forge, not like the stone cottage in Dragon's Let overseen by the husband and wife who made both sturdy shoes for horse and oxen, repaired plows and carriages, and forged delicate hinges and metal details for the cabinet makers. Not the flames in a brick stove and the bucket of water and the anvil.

No, this forge was something...else.

The fire wasn't set into a brick or stone stove that could intensify the heat and contain it, but was out in the open in a large pit circled by stalagmites. Inside the pit, lava rolled and boiled, but above the lava was actual flame. Not the usual red and yellow flames either, even though the lava was an intensely bright red. The flames were so hot they were nearly white.

Which should probably have been melting the surrounding stalagmites.

Also this wasn't a volcanic mountain, at least according to everyone who'd lived in these lands for the last ten centuries. Lava was not...expected here.

Next to the lava and flames pit, a giant pool of water, also set into a pit in the cavern floor. This looked a little more natural, like something she'd have expected to find in this cave. Water dripped down from the overhanging stalactites and dripped into the pool. The waters were a strange color, not clear and not blue or green. A sort of iridescent purple, shimmering like there might be oil in it.

In between the lava pool and the water pool, a giant block of metal. She supposed that was the anvil, but it was larger than any she'd seen before, and it wasn't shaped like any anvil she'd seen. A big, uneven rock, with dips and curves and irregularities over most of it. Only one section on the top flat and smooth. And next to the giant anvil, another stalagmite thrust up from the cave floor, but this one wasn't made of the surrounding purple rock and didn't have that slight white sheen of condensation. This one was black as the anvil and smooth and as thick at its base as the dragon's neck and as small at its tip as Jamie's little finger.

The whole place smelled faintly of the lava sulfur and cavern mold but also...that weird smell she hadn't been able to identify. A sort of metallic, minerally smell that coated the back of her tongue. Not blood. Still not that. It was...

Whatever was being hammered on the anvil.

The person working at the anvil hadn't spotted Jamie, Dane, or the dragon where they hovered at the mouth of the cavern. A man, with thick muscles, his pale skin slicked with sweat. He was bald, but he had a tattoo on his head that she couldn't see clearly. He wore a pair of leather trousers and an armless leather jerkin over his chest.

The length of metal he held on the anvil with thick metal pliers glowed red-yellow as he hammered it, turning it this way and that to shape it. She watched him plunge the glowing stick of metal back into the flames above the lava pool, watched the metal go white, then the man returned the piece to the anvil and hammered some more, folding the length in half, flattening it, then folding it in half again. He continued that process. Into the flames. Hammer, fold, flatten, fold, flatten. Into the flames.

And as he did this, he chanted. There was a rhythm to the sound, almost like a song, but she didn't recognize the words. Something about the cadence, though, reminded her of the spells Dane worked. Specifically Dane's spells as opposed to some of the other spells she heard regularly at the Vanshi temple.

She motioned Dane farther back into the safety

of darkness in the tunnel and then against his ear said, "He's working magic like yours?"

Dane nodded. "Similar. A...variation on what I can do."

"The lava pool?"

"Fired by dragon flames."

"You're sure?"

"Has to be the reason Alomere is here. There's no lava in these mountains." At her raised brow, he touched the purple rock at his back and then whispered, "I would feel it."

She nodded. "What's he forging?"

"Not certain. But it looks like a sword."

"A sword made of dragon flame and magic sounds..."

"Dangerous."

"Do we stop him, or do we just get the baby out of here?"

Their mission was to find and rescue the dragon from his captors. Which they'd mostly done. Returning Alomere to his mother was the point.

Jamie had wanted to stop whoever had kidnapped him, so they wouldn't try this again. And what was happening inside that cavern... The flames. The forge. That was the real purpose. So while it wasn't their mission, Jamie couldn't help but feel that stopping the production of a sword forged from dragon flame and magic probably *should* be their mission.

"Alomere can leave now," Dane said. "He can return to his mother and that should end the trouble for Dragon's Let." He glanced toward the cavern mouth. "This is not something the order would allow if they knew it was possible."

Just then a hiss from inside the cavern.

She and Dane crept back to the entrance. The blacksmith, whoever he was, had plunged the long length of glowing white metal into the shimmering pool. Steam from that contact rolled across the ground and filled the tunnel like fog. The fog they'd been walking through as they approached the cavern.

As the smith brought the length of metal out of the pool, she finally got a look at it without the heat masking its overall shape. It was a black metal, similar to the metal that had been wrapped around Alomere's neck, and appeared to be coated in oil that glistened in the firelight, the same sort of glistening that covered the water pool.

"Is that oil?" she asked against Dane's ear.

He tilted his head to one side and shrugged. She assumed that meant he didn't know.

Whatever the substance was, it gave the long length of black metal a strange iridescence. Within that iridescence, she swore she saw purple symbols flicker down the length, winking in and out of visibility as the smith turned the metal a little, examining it.

The black length didn't quite look like a sword

yet. It was the right length for a good long sword, and generally the right width. But it was still thicker than the sword in her scabbard, and the edges hadn't been hammered sharp yet.

How many times had he folded the metal so far? How much more work went into the object before it was a completed weapon?

Dane probably knew, but she figured the explanation would take too long and require more than a shrug and a head shake to answer.

She nudged Dane and motioned him to follow. They returned to Alomere, who'd hunkered down in the darkness, his nostrils puffing smoke, his head resting between his forefeet. Despite his size, he looked like a baby in that moment. Black eyes wide and both inner and outer lids flickering in a series of blinks. She wasn't even sure what it was about his position. Sort of gathered in on itself. Like he was scared.

Something that scared a dragon was...

Well, if she were being honest, a bit terrifying.

Though she was less worried about Alomere eating her just then and that was good.

She crept as close as she dared, right alongside his snout. That put her in shockingly easy chewing distance, but she needed to say something to him, and she didn't want her voice to carry.

As quietly as she could manage, hoping dragon hearing was better than the blacksmith's, she said,

"You need to leave the cave and return to your momma. Can you do that?"

A little huff that resulted in more steam from Alomere's raised nostrils.

"She's waiting for you. You won't have to do much to find her. You can fly." At least she thought he could. He had wings that seemed to function. "Just get high enough and move way from the mountain. Without the containment collar, she'll see you and come for you." Jamie glanced back at the cavern. The flickering glow of light from inside just touching the inside of the tunnel mouth. "We'll take care of the blacksmith. You need to go home now."

She got a very gentle nudge from Alomere, a tap of his snout which still sent her a single step sideways. She gave his snout an absent pat, a gesture that would later surprise her. He wasn't a horse for Holy Mal's sake. But fortunately for her, baby didn't take offense.

He rose up above her, standing, though his head remained hovering just beside her. Alomere looked behind him, then at the cavern entrance, then back behind him.

Jamie gave his snout another little pat and gestured him back the way they'd come. "Go settle your mum's worry," she murmured. "She's missed you."

With another snuffling snorting hiss noise, Alomere turned and headed back down the long tunnel. His purple-red scales blended so seamlessly with the darkness, he vanished from her sight before the quiet sounds of his movements faded.

Dane gave her a look. "Good idea?"

"For Dragon's Let? Yes. For us..." She sighed. "We could follow Alomere, or we can stop the blacksmith."

"I need to stop the blacksmith. You can follow Alomere."

She lowered her chin and gave him a look. "A sword-arm leave behind her mage just because there's magic involved? How insulting that you'd suggest it."

"No insult meant." He looked back at the fire light flickering inside the cavern mouth. "Worry. I'm worried about what he's doing."

"Me too."

They edged back to the cavern side-by-side, their steps slow and quiet.

"Ideas?" she murmured as they hovered in the shadows, watching the smith work.

"I'll put out the fire," he said. "If I can. That'll put an end to the process. And with Alomere gone, he won't be able to restart the...furnace."

She could see why he hesitated over the word. An unnatural pool of lava and dragon's flames wasn't exactly an ordinary forge's furnace. "He'll just go after Alomere again," she pointed out.

"Argonia won't let him now. She'll take Alomere somewhere inaccessible."

Jamie gave him that. Argonia wouldn't allow another human, even a mage, to get near her baby after all this.

"I'm going to need you to distract the smith while I work." Dane held her gaze.

"I can do that part." She very quietly pulled out her sword, though there was still a slight metal-on-metal snick sound when the blade cleared the metal ringed top of the leather scabbard.

"Stay out of the water pool," he warned. "I'm not sure what that glistening stuff is."

"And obviously stay out of the lava pool since we do know what that is."

He gave her a look. She grinned. She was scared, because she didn't know what was happening in that room and the unknown was as terrifying as the known when the known was a dragon. But having her sword in hand now filled her with a sense of... rightness. The weight and heft of the familiar blade was settling. Her body and brain readied for a fight.

She did like a good fight.

"How long do you need?" she whispered.

"Not sure. I have to fold the surrounding rock around the pool without letting the lava leak out and ensuring the rock can withstand the lava so it doesn't just melt through."

"Sounds complicated." And outside her skillset. But that was why they worked together. He did the magic stuff. She did the physical stuff. She thought her part of the job was a lot less complex. "I'll give you as much time as you need. Don't get distracted."

She gave him a look this time. He sometimes got their rolls backward and tried to help her. That almost always just got in her way.

His mouth flattened, as if he really wanted to protest, but then he nodded.

"Remember, even if it looks like I'm losing the fight, do *not* stop doing your part." She wanted no misunderstandings here.

They'd been through this before. Still. She had to ensure he concentrated because his part of this was going to be so difficult. And being the distraction often meant...not calling on her full skillset to beat an enemy. But in the heat of battle, Dane had been known to forget that.

He jerked his head in a nod this time, his expression exasperated. She grinned, waggled her eyebrows.

And swung into the cavern.

Walking directly toward the smith.

Chapter Six

Jamie swung her sword to get the smith's attention. He looked up from hammering the long piece of metal and his thick brows snapped down. Sweat dripped across his temples. The glow from the lava pit illuminated the cavern in dancing shadows, but she still had to give her eyes a moment to adjust to the brighter light.

"Who are you?" the blacksmith snarled. He glanced past her, then glared at her again. "Where is my dragon?"

"On his way home to his momma," she said. "And it was very rude of you to kidnap him. His momma was going to burn down an entire town because of it."

He hefted the still red-yellow glowing piece of metal off the giant block anvil with the pincers. "I don't care about some insignificant town," the smith said with narrowed eyes.

"Figured as much," Jamie said. "But I do. So dragon is gone. And you need to turn yourself over to the Vanshi order for judgment."

She didn't expect him to set down his length of metal and turn himself over to her. She probably should have expected his laughter.

"The Vanshi have no power over me. They can't stop my work."

"Sure they can," she said, swinging her sword again. "That's why they sent me."

"A sword-arm is no match for me."

"We'll see," she murmured. "But before we do, I really want to ask why. Why kidnap a dragon and risk all this? What could possibly be worth it?"

"You have no idea the power I will wield. The strength. I will have dominion over these lands. All will fear and bow before me."

She sighed. "That's it? That's all you want? Power. Strength. No noble cause? No righteous endgame?" She shook her head. "Who even are you?"

"My name is Balsin the Destroyer. And you will bow before me."

He swung the still hot metal around and pointed it at her like a sword.

She readied her own sword in a two-handed grip and waited for him to approach. A power-hungry man determined to rule over others. It was almost too predictable. Too...irritatingly ordinary. If they hadn't sent baby away, she'd be tempted to just let Alomere chew on this person. He deserved to be a dragon chew toy.

She waited on him to approach, gaging his movements and strength, watching the way he used the pliers to hold the long chunk of metal in one hand. So. Strong. Which seemed obvious given he was a blacksmith—or at least capable of the work. And he swung the metal back and forth in front of him with some ease. He was agile in his movements, too. Not a large-but-easy-to-push-over sort of man who depended on his strength but had no real fighting skills.

Good to know.

He swung the long piece of metal at her like a sword, though it was still firmly held in the pliers. Somehow, he made it work, though. The heat of it sliced past her closer than she was comfortable with.

The sword was still glowing hot. Should it still be doing that? She wasn't sure. Smithing wasn't her specialty. It was Dane's.

She hoped everything he'd put into her sword would hold out against that length of glowing metal.

Another swing and she countered this one, bringing her own blade up to catch the downward slice. Her sword held. Though there was a sizzling sound when the two weapons connected. She glanced up. The glowing metal sparked and brightened but it wasn't melting her sword. That was good.

As the smith tried to bare down on her, she slipped sideways, rolling away from him and letting his weapon slide down hers. Her physical strength seemed to be well matched for his, but he had more muscle. She had a better weapon. Or at least one designed for this kind of fight.

She risked a glance toward the lava pool. From her perspective, nothing was happening. But she'd learned with Dane that sometimes magic took time to be visible. She faced the blacksmith again just as he swung at her, bringing the length of metal around in a sideways arc. She jumped out of range, then did a quick assessment of her surroundings.

Not too close to the lava or water pools. Good. Getting backed against the giant block of metal he'd been using for an anvil. Bad.

She rushed farther away from the main part of the forge—if it could be called that—drawing Balsin into a more open area.

The ground beneath her felt like it was vibrating, but she wasn't sure if that was Dane, the blacksmith, or something else. An earthquake while they were down here would be a very unpleasant irony. She hoped Alomere got out.

The smith came after her suddenly, at speed, spearing the thick length of metal at her. She dodged to one side, felt the hiss of the hot metal brush her skin, and bit her lip on her hiss of pain.

She couldn't risk looking down at the wound but she didn't feel blood on her arm so she hoped it wasn't too bad. A burn rather than a slice. She could deal with a burn later.

Balsin swung at her again, and again. She drew him back from the lava and water pools, deeper into the cavern. Which was probably a bad idea, but she needed to give Dane time and space. The floor rumbled more. But not consistently. She'd feel tremors and then they'd die down.

Lunging under Balsin's next swing, she risked a glance toward the pools. There were more stalagmites around the lava pool now. At least she thought there were. The lava and fire beyond were almost entirely blocked now. And she thought the stalactites overhead were lower, just about touching the stalagmites to make a solid wall. That hadn't been the arrangement earlier. Dane was definitely doing something.

The light was lower in the cavern now, too. Less firelight from the lava pool. The shadows had deepened. She was sure of it.

She caught sight of one stalagmite starting to grow, from the ground up, which struck her as a strange sight since that wasn't how they were usually formed, and then the blacksmith was swinging at her, and she had to pay attention to the fight.

She caught a few blows on her sword, but mostly she dodged and ducked and avoided contact. Using her sword only when she needed to to push Balsin's away. Another rumbling underfoot.

Balsin turned away from her to look at his lava pool. The hanging stalactites and upthrust stalagmites were knitting together, blocking the pool completely, a wall of solid rock between them and the fire. A flare of blue light overhead replaced the glowing lava and lit the cavern, creating its own set of strange shadows and weird illusions. But she welcomed the change.

The blacksmith did not.

He shouted and charged toward the pool. Jamie let out a curse of her own and raced after him. He slammed against the still forming wall of rock with his shoulder, then took a swing at it with the length of glowing metal he'd been using as a sword, all before she could reach him. When nothing happened, when the wall held, she paused.

From behind the column of rock, Dane stepped into view. "Sealed off now," he said, to both her and Balsin. "Great choice of location," he added to Balsin. "The rocks around here are...interesting."

She wanted an explanation for that later.

"What have you done?" Balsin shouted and started toward Dane.

Jamie moved then, fast, putting herself between the blacksmith and her mage. Balsin snarled at them both, raised his proto-sword like he intended on charging them with it, and then the ground shook. Hard.

Jamie frowned back at Dane. "You doing that?"

"That's...not me."

"What...?" Balsin looked at the ground, then at the cavern entrance.

They all looked toward the cavern entrance.

As Argonia moved into view, announcing herself with an earsplitting screech.

Chapter Seven

Jamie and Dane fell back, moving quickly behind the cover of one of the stalagmites. The blue light from Dane's mage light still lit the cavern, giving them a decent view of the dragon. She looked really, really pissed. And with a fully grown, adult dragon standing in the cavern entrance, blocking their one escape, they were stuck.

"This isn't good," she said.

"Not if we get caught in the crossfire," Dane said.

"Hope Alomere is okay."

"You have a good heart."

"I'm about to have a dead and burnt heart if we're not careful."

An adult dragon was not something Jamie had ever aspired to see up close. Argonia did not disappoint. She was magnificent and massive and terrifying.

In the blue mage light, Argonia's colors were hard to see. From a distance, she'd always looked red, so Jamie assumed up close she was mostly red scales. In the blue light, they looked black. Her eyes glowed, almost white in the dimness. The spikes circling her tail were twice the size of Jamie's sword. And Argonia was at least three times the size of Alomere, who had already been terrifyingly huge.

Argonia let loose a stream of fire, straight toward the blacksmith. The interior of the cavern lit up like a momentary sunburst.

Balsin dove behind the rocky column Dane had created around the lava pool.

"Will her fire destroy your wall?" Jamie asked just before Argonia issued another earsplitting screech.

Dane winced. Then said, "No. The minerals in here are...unique. That's why he could use this cavern. There's a particular mineral, one that's able to withstand dragon flames. At one time, the Vanshi sold shields made of the stuff, a century ago, but it's hard to find and mine, so the shields were expensive. And only idiots draw the attention of a dragon, so mostly no one wanted the shields."

"Interesting. I'll hear more about that if we survive." She hadn't studied the history of the Vanshi order the way Dane had. She hadn't needed to. She just needed to be good with a sword. But she did like these little insights into their history. Dane didn't hold back the criticisms in favor of blindly holding up the order as infallible, either.

"So we're safe behind these stalagmites?" she asked as another roar of fire lit up the cavern. That burst was longer, and hotter, and thicker than Alomere's baby flames had been. Which was just terrifying.

"Safe enough. For now. But..." Dane nodded as Argonia moved deeper into the cavern, her spiked tail swinging. The spikes pierced a random stalagmite, shattering it into rocky rubble.

"Ah. So. Safe from the fire. Not from the spikes."

"Or the teeth," Dane confirmed.

"Good to know."

In a move so fast it was shocking, Argonia dove around the edge of the rock column Dane had created and sent another blast of flame at the blacksmith.

He dove, but not in time to fully avoid the fire and it caught on his leather jerkin. Flames rose around him.

He rolled on the ground, coming up behind the barrier of another rocky tower, in a position where Jamie could see his back. The leather was gone. And his skin was blistered and blackened.

Argonia's fire had just blasted through leather designed to keep a blacksmith safe while working with very hot things.

Jamie hissed in a breath of sympathetic pain. Not that she felt sympathy for Balsin. He'd brought this on himself being stupid enough to kidnap a baby dragon. But that just had to hurt and it was hard for her not to imagine the pain.

"No!" Balsin screamed at the dragon. "I will not be stopped now!" He held up the length of metal he gripped in the pliers. The proto-sword still glowed red-hot. "This will have to do," he said, quieter but loud enough his voice carried to Jamie and Dane.

Balsin raised the metal like a sword, in two hands overhead. But where Jamie thought he'd charge the dragon with it, instead...

He drove the sword right through his chest.

Jamie gasped and almost moved out from the cover of the stalagmite except that Dane stopped her with a hand on her arm. She wasn't even sure why she'd leapt forward or what she thought she'd do.

The length of metal hadn't gone all the way through Balsin, and the way he'd folded forward over it, a part of her wondered if he had actually stabbed himself with it.

He jerked and pulled the metal free, holding it out to one side, angled toward the ground. Liquid dripped along the still very red length onto the floor. She assumed the black, thick ooze was blood.

"What the...?" Dane murmured.

Balsin dropped the proto-sword, letting it sizzle

against the stone floor as he dropped to his knees. Clenching in around himself.

Argonia let loose another screech and stomped toward the blacksmith, her movements making the ground shake.

Jamie wasn't sure what to do. She couldn't stop a dragon from eating him. She didn't want to watch the dragon eat him. And he had brought this on himself by kidnapping the dragon's baby. But still...

"Argonia!" she called and stepped just far enough from behind the rocky pillar to be seen, but not so far she couldn't dive back behind its cover.

"What are you doing?" Dane hissed.

She kept her gaze on the dragon when she said, "He's already killed himself. She doesn't need to eat him or burn him. Alomere is safe. He's no longer a threat." She spoke loud enough for Argonia to hear, hoping she understood the way Alomere had seemed to understand.

The dragon screeched, so loud a stalactite dropped from the ceiling and shattered on the ground. Jamie winced. Okay. Maybe she shouldn't have tried. She just...couldn't not.

Argonia nudged Balsin with her snout, hard enough he fell over to one side.

Jamie blinked when his collapsing body made a chinking sound. Like...like rock against rock. "What in the name of the four holies?" she muttered.

"What?" Dane leaned around the pillar now.

Then abruptly pushed away from it to stand at her side. They all stared at the blacksmith.

As his body was encased in stone.

Not unlike the way Dane had encased the flaming tree outside in stone. Even in the blue mage light, with its weird shadows, it was obvious.

"He turned himself to stone? That's what the sword could do?" She glanced at Dane while keeping Argonia in sight. "Why?"

"I have no idea."

"The sword is still glowing," she said because she wasn't sure what else to say about the fact that Balsin had turned himself to stone.

"Magic. I have an answer for that at least."

Even though *magic* didn't explain anything. She supposed it was a kind of answer.

Argonia nudged the stone blacksmith again, a little harder, hard enough to make the body slide across the stone floor a few feet. Well away from the sword. Then the dragon looked directly at Jamie and Dane.

Fear kept Jamie in place. She wanted to dive back behind the pillar. But she didn't want to make any sudden moves.

Argonia made a snorting hiss of a noise, not too different from some of the noises Alomere had made, and she tapped the air above the glowing proto-sword with one long talon, careful not to touch the metal.

Jamie waited, not sure what the dragon was getting at.

A stream of smoke wafted from her raised nostrils. She turned toward Dane's column of rock around the lava pool, and very precisely, broke a hole in the rock with one of the long spikes on her tail. She didn't shatter the column. Just punched a hole in it.

"Wh..." Jamie wasn't sure whether to ask what or why so she settled for the *wh* sound and hoped Argonia understood.

The dragon gestured with a claw at the sword again, then gestured at the hole in the rock column.

"I think she wants us to put the sword back into the fire," Jamie said and asked at once.

Dane nodded. "Seems like."

"That...proto-sword or whatever it is turned Balsin the Destroyer to rock."

"Don't stab yourself with it, you'll be fine."

"If that was supposed to be funny, it wasn't."

"I know."

In other circumstances, that last might have actually made her smile. They both edged forward, Jamie keeping a wary eye on Argonia. The dragon actually moved backward so she was a few yards away from them, keeping the distance between them constant. Not that the distance meant much, but Jamie appreciated the show, and understood Argonia was attempting to reassure them.

She stared down at the glowing metal. The pliers still held it firmly. She wondered how it hadn't slipped from them when Balsin lost his grip. She reached down and picked the metal up with the pliers, holding it away from her to avoid both the heat and the blood still coating it. The whole mass of metal felt awkward and heavy. She had no idea how Balsin had been using this like a sword. There was no balance at all.

She glanced at the blacksmith's now fully stone body.

Maybe it hadn't been meant for fighting.

Shaking off the sense of discomfort at what Balsin had done to himself, she carefully brought the proto-sword to the hole in the rock column, and without any hesitance or ceremony, pushed the whole thing, pliers and all, through the hole.

The hiss and leap of flames from within had her jumping backward, closer to Dane, who'd followed her.

After a glance at Argonia, Dane closed his eyes, and did his magic thing, closing the hole in the column, once again sealing up the lava pool.

They turned in unison, even Argonia, toward the water pool with the unknown oily substance floating on top.

Without waiting for conversation, Dane closed his eyes again and started working his magic. After several moments, the stalactites from overhead grew until they encircled the pool and joined with the stalagmites growing taller around the pool, forming another column of hard rock. The rock knitted together to create a solid barrier. If she hadn't known the pool was there, Jamie wouldn't have guessed one existed.

Once the column was in place, Argonia nudged it with her snout. Then nudged the newly repaired column around the lava pool. And then, she turned her enormous body carefully, and with remarkable agility—she didn't break off a single rocky stalagmite —and left the cavern.

Leaving Jamie and Dane blinking after her.

Chapter Eight

"Huh," Jamie said, staring at the cavern entrance where Argonia had just disappeared. The mage light flickered blue shadows around them. Silence but for the dripping of water and the retreating sounds of an enormous dragon leaving.

"She didn't kill us," Dane said. "That has to count for something."

"Well, we did free her baby."

"Fair point." He glanced at Balsin. Or rather the stone statue that was now Balsin. "Should we just leave him?"

"What would we do with his stone corpse?"

He shrugged. Then frowned. That frown that made Jamie nervous.

"What?" she asked, putting her hand to her

sword pommel for reasons she couldn't have explained if asked.

"Why?" Dane murmured quietly. "Why go to all this trouble and then just..." He gestured at the stone form. "Just destroy himself? A man so driven for power, he risked kidnapping a *dragon*? Doesn't seem like the kind of person to just give up."

"He didn't give us much time to dig into his personality and motivations. Maybe he was just bone deep terrified of being eaten by a dragon."

"Then he wouldn't have stolen her baby."

That was hard logic to argue with.

"Maybe we should seal off this cave," she said, also glancing at the body. "From outside. Seal up the entrance all together. You can do that, right?"

"I can do that." He nodded. "And it's an excellent idea."

Even as Dane said those words, the statue of the blacksmith seemed to...twitch. It was just a faint movement. Could have been explained by a tremor running through the ground and making the stone body slide a little across the rocky floor. But...

The ground hadn't shaken. And Jamie was certain her luck wasn't that good.

"Gotta go," she said, grabbing Dane's arm. "Now. Light the tunnel ahead of us."

She took the rear, watching behind them as they raced back to the cave's entrance, toward the fresh, hot air and pines and the potential for a wildberry pie if they survived. Noises, things she couldn't quite explain, echoed up the tunnel toward them. Sounds like stone scrapping against stone, a moaning sound. The sound of bones crunching. A scream that didn't come from a human mouth.

Whatever was happening behind them was bad. And the faster they sealed up this cave, the better.

"Cave complexes have other exits," Dane muttered as they skidded through the section where Alomere had been chained.

"But that exit won't be right on top of us and Dragon's Let. Time to prepare if...whatever is back there gets out."

He didn't argue further. They burst from the cave entrance, the hot muggy air hitting Jamie in the face after the cold tunnels. Sweat immediately gathered beneath her leathers and at her temples. But the fresh, pine-scented air felt like they'd reached a safe spot.

So long as they could block the cave.

Dane started working immediate. Rocks and stone knitted together over the entrance, moving inward.

Slowly. Too slowly.

Jamie glanced around. No sign of Argonia or Alomere anymore. She wasn't sure if that was a good sign or a bad one, but she hoped Alomere was safe and Argonia was satisfied with the outcome enough to leave Dragon's Let alone.

Sounds echoed up from the depths of the cave. Moaning. A screech that reminded Jamie of Argonia's but more...ragged? A strange sound. The echo of rocky movements and rumbling. A crash.

And the ground beneath them tremored.

"Hurry, Dane," Jamie muttered, despite knowing he couldn't go any faster than he was going. But she really didn't want to see what was coming up that tunnel.

He didn't bother to respond, which was good. She wanted him to concentrate, not waste time berating her for rushing him.

A glow of light from deep inside the cave lit the dark walls. Jamie pulled her sword from her scabbard and settled herself in front of the still slowly closing cave entrance. She had no idea what was coming. But Dane needed time. She'd give him time.

She bounced on the balls of her feet, waiting. The strange moaning sounds had turned into something like a ragged hiss. The release of steam from a boiling kettle. Rising in pitch so that it almost hurt her ears.

She winced, but held steady, sweat dripping down her back. The surrounding mugginess feeling like a blanket made heavy with water. Rolling her neck, her heartbeat hammering, she watched the distant glow in the tunnel grow brighter. A white light rising up from the depths, moving along the tunnel walls.

Getting closer.

Rock covered half the entrance now. Still not enough. Still too much room for...whatever was coming to get out.

Jamie kept her attention on the approaching light, watching it grow, watching it brighten.

"Something's coming," she murmured.

Dane didn't answer.

She swung her sword, loosening her tense shoulders. Pulled in a long, slow breath.

She could see something inside the light now. A sort of shadowy shape without a clear outline. The ground trembled beneath her. The light lurched.

The rock covering the cave entrance closed a little more.

Not fast enough. Not fast enough.

The lurching light and that kettle-pitched scream of releasing steam that made her ears hurt. Closing in on the entrance. Sound getting louder. Light brighter. Shadows rushing away ahead of the brightness.

Another heavy ground tremor.

And something lurched into view.

Jamie's mouth fell open. "Cursed Mother of Light and Dark," she muttered. "What is that?"

White flames encircled something that was...not like any creature she'd seen before. Long, bulky. Six limbs ending in sharp claws. Maybe scales, though it was hard to tell as the creature was enmeshed in flames. A long neck. Things that looked like stubby, vestigial wings on its enormous barrel-shaped body. A head that looked half-formed. Part of it a snout with one raised nostril. One large eye above the snout on the side of the head. Another part pulled back from the snout into an oval shape. A smaller eye on that side, and a mass of flesh that could have been a nostril.

But there were teeth in the malformed mouth. Lots of teeth. Long teeth. On full display as the creature opened its crooked mouth and let out that kettle-screaming hiss.

Jamie wanted to cover her ears to block the sound, going right into her skull and piercing her brain. She didn't dare take her hands off her sword.

The rock covering the entrance knitted closer together, leaving a smaller and smaller escape route.

Jamie sincerely wanted to hurry Dane again, because that creature, that monster, looked right at her in that moment.

And lurched forward. Fast.

"Dane..." She raised her sword, prepared to fight.

The rock circle revealing the interior of the cave got smaller. Closing in. Closing down.

Only a human-sized opening remained when the creature hit the rock with the force of a battering ram.

The collision made some of the rock crack.

Jamie swallowed, hard. But held her place, sword at the ready.

The creature hit the knitting rock again. More cracks.

She kept most of her attention on the creature, but could see the rock mending, sealing over those cracks. But the inward progression to close off the entrance stopped as that mending took place.

Dane couldn't do both at once.

The creature hit the rock barrier again.

Dane needed a few more minutes. A little more time.

Better give him that time.

She rushed forward just as the creature's head connected with the rocky covering again and without a solid plan but to distract and wound, she stabbed her sword into the center of the giant monster's head.

Her sword sank into something that felt both squishy and also hard. Like she's slipped the sword through rock and into a pot of jelly. The sensation was disturbing and not like anything she'd felt during a sword fight, and it took her a full beat before she roused herself to try and pull the sword free.

The creature reared back, nearly pulling her off her feet, almost dragging her through the remaining opening in the rock.

She jerked her sword free and stumbled backward, her heartbeat hammering against her ribs.

A smell like rot and sewage washed over her. Making her gag. Then a sound so piercing and loud echoed out of the cave, Jamie did cover her ears with her hands, one side awkwardly because she refused to release her sword. But the noise was pitched so painfully, she thought it might burst her eardrums. Her eyes watered, from the noise and with the putrid stench coming from the cave.

She realized some of that stench was closer to hand and turned to see a black, oily substance dripping along her sword. It sizzled and burned the ground at her feet. Though there was no scrub or burnable plant life left outside the cave thanks to Alomere's snores, the oily substance still managed to melt the rock.

She jerked the sword away from her body, wincing as she lost a small barrier between that awful sound and her ears. She hurriedly checked herself. None of the oily substance had dripped onto her. And it didn't seem to be eating into her sword. Whatever magic Dane had worked into the sword's metal was holding against whatever noxious substance was melting the ground beneath it. But she doubted her own frail flesh would hold up as well as her sword if she came into contact with that... whatever it was. Blood?

Though she felt like she might throw up from the smell, and the noise hurt her brain, she realized the rock continued to knit inward, continued to close the cave entrance. Dane was still working. The remaining hole was less than human-sized now. The creature beyond couldn't get through that space.

Without breaking the rock.

She waited, her brain on fire, her body shaking, waited for the creature to show itself again. Sword held away from her body, but ready to swing. She kept the tip pointed downward, so the burning goop dripped to the ground. Wished she could remove the stuff from her sword. Didn't dare look around for a suitable place to wipe it off. Not even sure how to clean the stuff off.

The creature's head appeared at the ever-shrinking hole. This time, just the snout and large eye. That black oily stuff dripped through the white flames, across the creature's face.

Jamie started forward, intent on that single eye, that potential vulnerability.

Heat washed out of the hole, so intense it took her breath. The normal outside heat and mugginess at her back seemed cold in comparison. She continued forward, watching the eye watch her.

The circle of rock shrank.

She didn't roar or charge or raise her sword as she approached, didn't do anything that might make the eye move away.

Until she was a foot from it, and the heat was so intense, she thought it might melt her. She felt like she was melting, burning. But she still raised her sword, suddenly, and plunged it forward, aiming for the eye through the narrowing hole.

The white flames encircling the creature flashed

around her sword. The creature moved. She never connected. But the overwhelming heat pushing through that shrinking circle eased. The creature no longer right up against the rock.

And in the moments she'd gained him, Dane closed the rest of the hole. Rock knitting together faster and faster.

Sealing off the entrance.

CHAPTER NINE

Jamie dragged in a long, deep breath, ignoring the putrid smell and taste of the creature's blood still tainting the air outside the now sealed cave. She kept her sword out to the side, the black goopy blood dripping from it, but her shoulders relaxed.

When Dane finished knitting and thickening the barrier, he moved close enough to set a hand on her shoulder. "You injured."

She looked at herself. "Oh, guess I did get a few burns." She nodded to her other arm and shoulder, her sword arm. Her hand was smoking and bright red, starting to blister. Her forearm hadn't fared much better, and her bicep only slightly less red, but at least no blisters were forming there.

"Yuck," she said. "I'm gonna need a healer."

"Hurts?"

"Not until you mentioned it."

Which was only a little exaggerated. The pain had started to seep into her consciousness when she'd looked down and seen the burns. It was the kind of pain that zinged along nerves and made her nauseous. Though deep sword cuts, gouges, or stabs left her feeling a lot worse, so she supposed she'd take the burn. Nothing was black. She wanted to assume that was a good sign. And she could still hold her sword with the damaged hand. An even better sign.

"I would like to get that oil off, though," she said, lifting her sword just a little. The motion pulled at her skin and made her painfully aware of the burns, so she very gently set the sword on the ground. "Anything you can do to help?"

Dane frowned. "Give me a moment."

She waited him out, pulling her wounded arm close and nestling it against her stomach because that took some of the strain out of the muscles. She'd have to wait for her wildberry pie until she got the injury tended. She wasn't looking forward to the hike back through the forest to Dragon's Let, though. But since neither she nor Dane had been killed, she'd take the wound.

From behind the rocky barrier to the cave, Jamie thought she heard that screeching sound, but the buffer of rock kept it from piercing her ears and head. Whatever that creature was, they'd pissed it off by trapping it. She was a little worried about it finding another way out. Something like that, made of flame and acid blood... That was the kind of monster that could wreak havoc on the countryside.

She remembered the vestigial wings, half formed and looking useless. If it couldn't fly, did that make things better or worse? Then she thought of the way the head seemed half formed, part dragon part... something else. And then she thought of the blacksmith. The way he'd stabbed himself with a piece of metal forged in dragon fire and water covered by oil they'd never identified but which had been dangerous enough Argonia had encouraged them to seal it up.

Oil. Fire.

She glanced back at her sword. The black oil covering it was slowly creeping off the sides of the blade and into the rocky ground. It burned into the ground, melting and dissolving most, but not all, of the rock and sinking deeper until she could no longer see it. When her sword was cleaned, she picked it up with her uninjured hand, and watched the holes in the earth created by the oil heal under Dane's magic.

"You're very good," she commented as she awkwardly tried to reinsert her sword into the scabbard using the wrong arm.

"Thank you." He flashed a charming smile.

Which reassured her that he wasn't hurt either. "That was the blacksmith," she said, nodding toward the sealed cave and the monster beyond, it's weirdly piercing screeches still audible. "Balsin the Destroyer indeed."

Dane nodded, frowning as he looked back toward the covered cave entrance. "I think you're right."

"He was trying to turn himself into a monster. That was the point of the sword…or whatever it was he was actually forging."

"A dragon," Dane corrected. "He was attempting to turn himself into a dragon."

"But only got the process halfway."

Dane nodded.

"So now he's a flaming monster who drips burning oil from his wounds."

Dane nodded again.

"Which is…bad."

"It's bad."

"Not trapped indefinitely."

"Caves are too extensive. There will be another exit. Once the creature stops to consider it, he'll go looking for that exit."

"You think… You think he's in there? Balsin. That that creature can think and is conscious of… what's happened?"

"No idea. The spell wasn't ready. He hadn't finished the process. Hard to say what the result was, using an incomplete process for this kind of metamorphosis."

The ground shook suddenly, a trembling that had Jamie reaching for her sword again with her uninjured hand.

They both stared at the rock-covered cave entrance. But then a fast beat of wind swept across Jamie's back, blowing dust and tree detritus into the air. The push of air at her back was so strong, she took an involuntary step forward.

Jamie and Dane exchanged a look. Then slowly turned.

Argonia sat a few yards away, her wings now folded against her sides. She was so huge, Jamie had to crane her neck to see all the way up to the dragon's head. A head hovering over them in a way that would make it very easy for Argonia to drop her mouth and eat them.

Jamie didn't take her hand off her sword, even though pulling it with her uninjured hand and using it against a dragon were...unlikely.

A ripple traveled through Argonia's scales. Out in the sunshine, her full magnificent glory took Jamie's breath. Her scales were a dark maroon color that held an iridescent red glitter. Her body was thick and muscled. The spiles along her back were raised now—they'd been flattened in the cave and Jamie hadn't noticed them. The rims around her huge eyes were layered with brass-colored scales. And the spikes on her tail were also a bright brass color.

The sheer size of Argonia was more obvious

outside the cave, too. A massive creature that made Jamie feel decidedly...bite-sized.

Argonia, on all fours, kept her head high above them and stared down. Her spiked tail swished once.

"Kind of wish I spoke dragon," Jamie murmured to Dane.

"Me too," he said.

A voice pierced her head. "Do not worry. I speak human."

Jamie raised her brows, glanced at Dane from the corner of her eye.

"Heard it too," he said without looking away from the dragon.

"I am here to reassure you," Argonia said.

Reassure them? About...?

"I will ensure the monster does not leave the caverns. If he finds an exit, we will destroy him."

"We?" Jamie asked.

"Dragons."

Ah. No one knew how many there were. They were territorial and wide spread and sometimes slept for centuries so that the locals living next to them forgot they were there. Even the Vanshi order had no accurate count for the number of dragons currently alive. They just assumed there weren't very many.

"There are enough," Argonia said.

And Jamie would swear there was humor in the booming voice echoing through her skull.

"You freed my offspring," Argonia said. "You

prevented that human mage from completing his planned metamorphosis."

"Not entirely," Jamie said, wincing.

"But he is not...complete. Not a full dragon. He would be harder to contain if he'd achieved his goal."

Probably have been a bad thing, too. The monster was bad enough.

"Did you know? Before this. That the person who'd kidnapped Alomere was attempting..." Jamie gestured back to the cave.

"I suspected. That's why I came here after I had Alomere safe. To stop the..." She paused as if looking for a word. Then, "The blacksmith. To stop Balsin."

"Is Alomere safe?" Jamie asked, just to verify. "He's okay? No injuries? No long-term dangers from what he's just been through?"

There was a beat of silence before Argonia said, "He is well."

"Good. Good." Jamie let out a breath. "So Dragon's Let is safe?"

"Dragon's Let is safe."

Jamie relaxed a little more. Job accomplished.

"The...creature," Dane said. "It's made of fire and bleeds a very dangerous oily substance. But its wings aren't fully formed. It won't be able to fly."

"Thank you for the information," Argonia said. "It is good he cannot fly."

Jamie agreed.

Argonia suddenly lowered her head, the move so

swift Jamie jumped despite herself. She was only a little mollified by the fact that Dane had jumped too.

Argonia put her snout directly in front of them. Jamie couldn't even see the dragon's eyes like this. Only raised nostrils. And a currently closed mouth. Behind which were a lot of teeth. And flaming breath.

"You are wounded," Argonia's voice came into Jamie's head.

She glanced down at her burned arm. "I'll see a healer. I'll be fine."

"The wound is from the creature's flames?"

Jamie nodded.

"Stand very still," Argonia said.

Jamie opened her mouth to ask why. Then Argonia opened her mouth and Jamie did as commanded and froze. She was tempted to dive away, but disobeying a dragon who'd so far not eaten her seemed the wrong sort of impulse.

Dane did take a step closer to her.

So if she got eaten, they'd get eaten together? Jamie wondered in perverse amusement. That was actually kind of sweet, if deranged.

Argonia's long, forked tongue flicked out from her partially opened mouth, tasting the air. Her tongue, all on its own, was as thick as Jamie, though the forked tips were smaller, more delicate.

And it was with those delicate tips that Argonia gently licked Jamie's wounded arm and hand.

Jamie hissed at the first contact, the sensation of anything touching her burnt skin excruciating. But the pain numbed quickly. So completely, Jamie nearly staggered under the relief. And once she was no longer seeing spots from the pain, she realized just how...precisely Argonia was licking her arm. Her tongue was large enough to have swept Jamie up off her feet. But those delicate forked tips moved over Jamie's skin like a cooling cloth. And only over her arm and hand. No accidentally licking her anywhere else.

Without the pain to distract her, Jamie watched the process, fascinated. A little shocked. A lot awed. And maybe just a little disgusted. But as she watched the redness in her skin fade, the blisters heal, her arm lose the swollen puffiness, all those various emotions settled into a single awed sense of...amazement.

And gratitude.

By the time Argonia lifted her head again, Jamie's arm was a little pink, like she'd just risen from a particularly hot bath, but all other signs of the injury were gone.

Jamie blinked up at the dragon. "Thank you." She hadn't even known dragons could do that. Nonetheless thought one might heal her.

"You released Alomere from his captor," Argonia's voice in Jamie's head again. "I thank you."

And without another word, she rose up on her hind legs, her wings beat the air hard enough to drive

Jamie and Dane back a few steps. Jamie covered her face against the stinging brush of dust and pine needles in the wind churned up by the dragon's wings.

A moment later, Argonia was airborne, her wings wide, tilting as she caught a thermal current and rose higher.

Jamie and Dane stood watching her disappear into the sky. The muggy heat settled around them as the breeze from her departure died. Pine scent overpowered the lingering stench from the creature's blood that had coated Jamie's nostrils and the back of her throat. Sweat trickled down her temple. And suddenly the cool interior of a pub and the delicious promise of sweet pastry sounded like heaven.

"I don't have to forgo a wildberry pie for a healer now," she murmured, her gaze still on the tiny red dot that was Argonia.

"I could eat some pie," Dane said.

"Job accomplished?"

They both glanced back at the rocky wall where the cave entrance had been. The sounds of screeching from inside had died down the moment Argonia landed. No doubt the creature was looking for another way out.

"The dragons will stop him," Dane said.

"You're sure?"

He glanced at her. "I'm sure. And the Vanshi order will monitor the situation, as they do."

"So until we have another mission..."

"We eat pie."

They started back into the forest, heading downhill on the return trek to Dragon's Let.

"And the bookstore," she said. "I'd like to stop in at the bookstore. I have a few coin to spend." She winked.

Dane smiled. "Fair. Pie first. And a cool pint. Then some books. The festival will still be underway. We should take a few days and enjoy the celebration."

"Perfect." More celebrations meant more pastries.

The cool shadows of the forest closed in around them. As the sun eventually dipped low in the sky, the afternoon turning to twilight, the worst of the heat finally eased. They walked in companionable silence back to the now safe village.

And Jamie enjoyed the momentary peace.

And the promise of wildberry pie.

Now Pick a New Genre

Thank You

Thank you for trying this experiment of mine! I hope you enjoyed all the various ways a dragon could get stolen. If you've enjoyed this type of storytelling and had fun jumping around the different genres, look out for more Pick Your Genre collections from me.

For more on my books, please visit my website at www.katsimons.com, or my store, Kat Simons Books. You might also consider joining my newsletter to stay up to date on releases and news. New subscribers get two exclusive stories in two of my series, and all subscribers get the occasional discount coupon to my store, as well as excerpts, cover reveals, and more.

If you prefer, you can also follow my author page at your favorite vendor or at Book Bub.

Thanks again for reading!

Books By Kat Simons

Pick Your Genre

Who Steals a Dragon

Paranormal Romance

Tiger Shifters Series

Romancing the Leopard: A Tiger Shifters-Cary Redmond Crossover Novel

Seven Families: Wolf Series

Urban Fantasy

The Cary Redmond Series

Cary Redmond Short Stories and Collections

Demon Witch Series

Joan of Kerry Series

Contemporary Fantasy

Haunts and Howls Collections

Tombstone Wizard

The Unshattered Sword

Destiny Through the Cats Eyes

Going Out of Business: Everything's for Sale

Contemporary Romances

Designed for You

Poinsettias and Possibilities

Mystery and Thriller

Ross and O'Neill Adventures

Galileo's Pendulum

Percy James Mysteries

Movies May Murder

Cookies Can't Crime

Coming 2023

About the Author

Bestselling, award-winning author Kat Simons earned her Ph.D. in animal behavior, working with animals as diverse as dolphins and deer. She brought her experience and knowledge of biology to her paranormal romance and urban fantasy fiction, where she delights in taking nature and turning it on its ear. She writes urban fantasy, contemporary fantasy, and paranormal romance in series which combine action adventure, the otherworldly, and a frequent dose of sexy romance.

The latest book in her bestselling romantic urban fantasy series about Protector Cary Redmond, *The Trouble with Death and Demon Gods*, is out now. As are the newest stories in the romantic urban fantasy Demon Witch series, including the first "meet cute" for Angie and her demon hunter boyfriend Sebastian in the novella *Howling Dreadful*. Kat also launched a new Paranormal Romance series in 2023 that combines romance heat and fated mates with a touch of horror. The first three books in her *Seven Families: Wolf* series are out now.

After spending many years writing primarily paranormal and urban fantasy romances, in 2022, Kat also debuted in contemporary romance with the release of her first contemporary romance novel, *Designed for You*. First, but not the last, because Kat loves writing trope-tastic romance fun with heartwarming Happily Ever Afters.

And if that's not enough, Kat also released her first action-adventure thriller, *Galileo's Pendulum*, which brings a mix of science history and fast-paced adventure to a little light forgery as her heroes race around the world to save an ancient relic. Her upcoming action-adventure mystery stories combine similar elements of adventure, world travel, and science—some of Kat's favorite topics.

For a little more in the mystery genre, Kat also writes a soft-boiled, amateur sleuth series set in New York City. The Percy James series, about the adventures and exploits of a front desk receptionist working in a boutique hotel on the Upper East Side of Manhattan, launched in 2023 with *Movies May Murder*.

Kat also publishes fantasy, science fiction, and the occasional hockey romance under the name Isabo Kelly (https://www.isabokelly.com), because of course she does.

After traveling the world, living in places like Hawaii, Germany, and Ireland, Kat now lives in New

York City with her family and a library's worth of books.

For more on Kat and her future books

Website: https://www.katsimons.com/
Newsletter: https://bit.ly/KatSimonsNewsletter

Kat Simons Bookstore
https://tanddpublishingbookstore.com/

Social Media
Facebook Page: https://www.facebook.com/
KatSimonsAuthor
BookBub: https://www.bookbub.com/authors/kat-
simons
Instagram: https://www.instagram.com/isabokelly/
Twitter: https://twitter.com/IsaboKelly

KAT SIMONS NEWSLETTER

Don't miss the latest Kat Simons news, updates, excerpts, cover reveals, and more. All new subscribers get two free stories.

Mate Run

A Tiger Shifters Paranormal Romance short story

and

When Cary Met Ariel

A Cary Redmond Urban Fantasy novella

Join Now!

https://bit.ly/KatSimonsNewsletter